THE VALLEY OF DEATH

John Rourke ran forward, across the makeshift bridge toward the roughhewn rock fortress.

An energy weapon was fired toward him, blue-white bolts of plasma flickering through the maelstrom of molten rock below. Another energy bolt, then another.

John Rourke kept on running.

One of the Nazis rose up from behind the wall and fired almost point-blank. Rourke was already moving, throwing himself flush against the rocky surface. As his hands caught an outcrop, the bridge beneath him fell away as the volcanic eruption shook the earth below. Rourke clung there, his rifle swinging wildly from its sling.

The Nazi brought his weapon to bear in line with John's head. Rourke released his grip with his right hand and desperately grasped for his HK-91. He punched his weapon upward, firing on automatic, the rifle's recoil tearing at his wrist.

Suddenly, the head of the Nazi killer exploded, and his body fell back, out of sight.

The earth shook again. John Rourke was losing his hold . . .

#23

CALL TO BATTLE
BY JERRY AHERN

ZEBRA BOOKS
KENSINGTON PUBLISHING CORP.

To our good friend Richard Gilliam, a guardian angel for the Ahern family on occasion, and much appreciated—all the best . . .

ZEBRA BOOKS

are published by

Kensington Publishing Corp.
475 Park Avenue South
New York, NY 10016

First printing: March, 1992

Printed in the United States of America

1

John Rourke stared down at his son, Michael. Rourke's right hand held Michael's right hand. "You'll be okay, son. You did well."

Michael was pale from loss of blood, almost fragile-looking, like the little boy he had ceased to be. He forced a smile, nodded, said, "Thanks, Dad."

John Rourke glanced at the two stretcher-bearers, signaled them to move out; they continued on their way, Michael between them, carrying him toward the medevac helicopter. The helicopter, one of several on the ground here, waited just beyond the patio, in the grassy yard between the house and still-burning garage, its rotor blades swishing lazily through the warm air.

The garage was very near the stables, but the stables were unoccupied, used only for storage. So far, crates of weapons and containers of explosives were all that had been found within the structure. A fire truck was parked between the stables and the garage. Its crew worked to extinguish the garage fire but, more importantly, strove to prevent the fire's spreading to the stables and touching off the saboteurs' explosives. The plastique itself would not detonate, of course, from flame alone; but other items stored within the stables might explode and then in turn cause the plastique to blow.

Natalia sat on one of the patio chairs. A medic was kneeling beside her, tending to the deep graze wound across her upper arm, just below the joint. Rourke himself had cursorily examined the injury, satisfying himself that it was minor.

When her wound was patched, she would follow Michael to the hospital at Pearl Harbor, Rourke knew. He would have preferred to see her stay behind to assist in the preliminary evaluation of the captured intelligence data. Without her noticing him, Rourke studied her face. She looked battle worn and tired, but it was always beautiful. Michael was a lucky man to have her.

The two men and one woman whom Rourke had captured in the structure's basement—he'd shot a fourth person—were seated on the far side of the patio. They had been about to burn computer printouts and degauss magnetic computer disks, thus destroying the information that was the very purpose of this raid to secure. The three were surrounded by several of the SEAL Team personnel under Lieutenant Commander Washington. Other prisoners, including the man who surrendered to Rourke, were martialed together near two of the Honolulu Tac Team vans. These vans, Rourke had been told, would be "loaned" to the Navy, in order to transport the captured personnel to Pearl for interrogation.

Paul and Annie, neither of them injured during the assault against the estate, disappeared into the basement record center moments after Rourke emerged from it in the wake of securing the house.

And now, John Rourke had absolutely nothing which required immediate doing. The cigar he'd lit in the basement was long since burned down and discarded. The magazines for his rifle were reloaded, as were the magazines for his pistols. The men and women about him—personnel from the Honolulu Tac Team and Washington's SEAL Team—seemed flush with victory and each moved about as though he or she was on the most important mission imaginable.

Indeed, the battle was done. But their rest would be brief. The war with Eden still remained to be won or lost.

Perhaps what was gained here would retard that war's start, an attack on the Hawaiian Islands centering on the new Pearl Harbor naval base, the attack's intent much the same as a similar attack made on December seventh of 1941 by the Japanese: cripple the U.S. Fleet. But the attackers this time would not be flying Japanese Zeros. The attackers would be SS personnel, exiled from New Germany in Argentina, spearheading the forces of Eden, with a host of technologically advanced weapons at their disposal.

Eden was the new nation occupying the Eastern half of what, Before The Night of The War, had been the United States of America.

The United States of America, these days, more than six centuries after the Japanese attack on Pearl Harbor and a postwar period which led inexorably to thermonuclear destruction, consisted of two states only. One of these states was composed of the Hawaiian Islands; the second was Mid-Wake. Mid-Wake was a domed community beneath the Pacific Ocean, almost equidistant between the islands of Midway and Wake, hence the name.

Hawaii, like virtually everything on the Earth's surface, was swept clean of things manmade, scoured during the Great Conflagration, when the ionized atmosphere caught fire at dawn and burned away cities and governments and the men who had made them. Mid-Wake, a scientific base originally designed for undersea research and involved in experimental studies concerning the planned building of a permanent United States space station, was not destroyed.

The ancestors of the current residents of Eden survived as well, but by totally different means, making what transpired at Mid-Wake seem almost ordinary by comparison. The core of Eden's population grew from the survivors of a group of one hundred and thirty-two persons who, preserved in cryogenic sleep, were launched into space on the very Night of The War. The shuttle fleet which carried them was a lifeboat for humanity, an Ark to return and begin civilization anew when the storm of warfare and its even more destructive aftermath abated.

Unfortunately, the Eden Project returnees brought back with them many of the same ills which had precipitated mankind's near-total destruction before; principal among these faults were the lust for power at any price and the willingness to hate. These negative qualities were shared among only a few of the returning personnel, but as in the old adage about the rotten apple, so it was with Eden.

Today, Eden was controlled by a puppet dictator, a Nazi. Eden's war machine was the most powerful and potentially deadly on Earth. Nuclear weapons were once again being built at a frantic pace, chemical and biological weapons were rumored to exist in Eden's vast arsenals as well.

Six persons on the face of the Earth survived from the days Before The Night of The War: John Rourke's son and daughter, Michael and Annie; the man who became Annie's husband, Paul Rubenstein; Natalia Tiemerovna; Rourke himself; and his wife, Sarah. But Sarah was in cryogenic sleep, the only means of keeping her

7

alive.

On the night that their third child, a boy, was born, Sarah was shot, the bullet entering her brain, lodging in so sensitive and remote an area that the projectile was accessible, perhaps, to only one man. That man was Doctor Deitrich Zimmer, the same man who shot her, the same man who kidnapped the infant to whom Sarah had just given birth.

That child was, these days, known as Martin Zimmer, the Nazi dictator of Eden. Because of sophisticated genetic surgery and the lies of Deitrich Zimmer, Martin—although he was all but physically identical to John Rourke and Michael Rourke—was no longer a Rourke, no longer the child Sarah had nurtured in her body for nine months.

Deitrich Zimmer twisted the boy, made him into someone to whom good and evil were not moral considerations, only useless abstractions for the weak.

Then, both Deitrich Zimmer and the boy utilized cryogenic sleep until the time was right to awaken—awaken to conquest.

But, before they slept, Deitrich Zimmer ordered his neo-Nazi followers to strike the supposed repository of the cryogenic chambers in which John Rourke and his family slept. Those cryogenic chambers, held at Mid-Wake, were destroyed. And, in Deitrich Zimmer's supposition of victory, there was safety for Rourke and his family.

The night Martin was born and Sarah was shot, John Rourke himself was critically injured. Slipping more deeply into coma by the hour, the one hope of saving him and preserving Sarah—her condition was inoperable—was a gamble, a slim chance that the coincidentally restorative benefits of cryogenic sleep might somehow keep her alive and sustain his life so that his body might naturally be able to rise above the comatose state.

Unbeknownst to him then, of course, his son, his daughter, his daughter's husband and his best friend, Paul, and Natalia all volunteered to take The Sleep, in order that The Family might be preserved, somehow, someway in some future, whenever that would be.

And this was now, one hundred and twenty-five years after the night Sarah was shot, a world once again on the brink of self-destruction. John Rourke was one of six human beings to survive The

Night of The War and live into this present age, one of only six human beings who remembered what once was and its destruction.

And John Rourke had promised himself that, while he lived, he would fight to keep the destruction and the death from recurring.

"John?"

He realized he was staring off into the sky, and he turned to the sound of the voice, Natalia's voice. "How are you feeling?" Rourke asked her, standing up.

She looked up into his face, saying, "I've been better, but I've been a great deal worse, too. I want to go to the hospital, just in case—"

"Michael needs you," he finished for her.

"Yes."

"We'll be fine here. Make sure your arm gets looked at, too. Won't hurt."

"No," she nodded, smiling, and then she leaned up to him, standing on her toes, and kissed his cheek. "It's starting again, isn't it," Natalia almost whispered, "everything like before? Are people crazy?"

"We won't let them be crazy this time," John Rourke promised her.

Natalia gave him a brief smile, then started across the patio, toward the grassy area beyond and the choppers waiting there. Rourke followed her with his eyes. He still loved her, and she loved him, he realized. The only thing that was changed was that she realized she loved Michael more, what he—John Rourke—had always wanted for her and for Michael. But now that it had happened, he felt the loneliness of his life more acutely than he had ever experienced.

If—once—Sarah had the operation she needed, which still only Deitrich Zimmer could perform, all would not be happiness. Because Rourke would have to stop Martin Zimmer and Deitrich Zimmer from taking the world beyond the brink once again. And that would most likely mean killing Martin, their son, Sarah's child.

Years ago, in order to ensure survival, he had tampered with the cryogenic chambers, allowed the children, Michael and Annie, to grow to adulthood while he and Sarah and Paul and Natalia slept on. And in the process, he denied Sarah her children, seeing them grow up. When Sarah awoke, she all but cursed him for what he had done, depriving her so. And now, once she was restored, he would do worse, kill the child for whom she had nearly died when she brought him into the world.

Sarah would never forgive him.

9

John Rourke was used to loneliness, self-inflicted, and it would not end, perhaps it would never end for him. And however inured he was to loneliness, he did not like it.

"John!"

Again, he realized he was staring off into the sky. The voice he turned to was Paul's. "Yes, Paul?"

"We've got problems, John. Annie and I've been going through the printouts that were all piled up there in the middle of the basement for them to burn. There's a reference to an SS commando unit. It's coming ashore on Molokai—" and Paul rolled back the cuff of his windbreaker. "In less than a half hour, if they're on schedule. They couldn't have been alerted to what was going on here, so they should still be coming."

John Rourke started walking toward the younger man, asking, "Any indication this is the first prong of the invasion?"

"No. From what we could pick up, it looks like they're coming here to soften up things, terrorism."

John Rourke looked at the black-faced Rolex on his left wrist. It was almost as old as he felt. "Get Ed Shaw and Lieutenant Commander Washington. Tell them. Have them get some people together. I'll arrange transportation."

It was starting again.

2

Aboard the helicopter gunship, John Rourke changed to what he considered more suitable – and less flashy – clothing. He removed the garish Aloha shirt he'd worn when he disguised himself as a German tourist in order to get one of the estate guards down to the front gates. Less than two hours ago; all that seemed an eternity away.

His hair was still dyed blond to go along with the disguise, but the dye would shampoo out. Yet, there was no time to do that. He changed into black jeans, a long-sleeved black knit shirt – he pushed the sleeves up almost to his elbows – then started to pull on his boots.

Paul was reloading magazines for his German MP-40 submachinegun. The others aboard the helicopter – thirty men, in all, from the Honolulu Tac Team and Washington's SEAL Team based out of Pearl Harbor – saw to their weapons as well. Like SEAL Teams from the Twentieth Century, these SEALs seemed to have rather eclectic tastes in weaponry. The issue military pistol these days was an energy weapon, but these men did not carry the issue weapon. Instead, their sidearms were cartridge arms.

And he found the particular type most curious.

During the latter portion of the Twentieth Century, considerable controversy raged between those who were afficionados of the Colt/ Browning-style .45 ACP and everyone else. John Rourke had periodically found himself on both sides of the issue, and occasionally in the middle. His own personal sidearms of preference were Colt/ Browning-style .45s, reduced drastically in size and manufactured by the original Detonics firm. Yet, he often carried a revolver as well, and sometimes the 9mm Parabellum cartridge suited a particular tactical need and he used it.

Cartridge arms of the Nineteenth and Twentieth Centuries were only from two sources, these days: original pieces of enormous collector value (like the guns Rourke himself wore) and reproductions made by Lancer.

John Thomas Rourke assumed none of the SEALs carried original antiques, but to a man they carried Colt/Browning-style .45 ACPs.

What made him smile was the thought that if, somehow, those staunchest of the staunch supporters of old Slabsides could have known that, nearly seven centuries after the first .45 Auto rolled off the line as the original 1911, the same basic gun was the choice of an elite unit such as this, they would have smiled, too.

There were knives of every description, most of these based on familiar designs as well, Bowies, tantos, Big Ugly Ones, double-edged commando daggers of the Fairbairn-Sykes or stouter Randall patterns.

The pilot's voice came over the intercom. "We are approaching the L.Z. Touchdown in five."

John Rourke slung the double Alessi rig which carried the twin stainless Detonics CombatMasters across his shoulders, then looked to the rest of his weapons . . .

They'd exited the chopper in admirable time, the Tac Team and SEAL Team personnel—they trained together often—functioning smoothly as a single unit, setting up perimeter security the instant after the chopper was on the ground, maintaining that security as Rourke, Rubenstein and the others, Ed Shaw and Lieutenant Commander Washington among them, reached the treeline, then covered the security element's withdrawal.

The grass here was high, untrammelled, whipping wildly back and forth in the cool downdraft of the rotor blades, the palm fronds moving as well.

Once they linked up, they split again, but into two operational teams, Rourke and Rubenstein staying with Shaw and his Tac Team personnel, moving northwesterly toward the beach, which was more than a mile distant . . .

* * *

Over the intervening centuries since John Rourke had first visited Hawaii, the coastlines of the islands had changed radically, on account of natural volcanic growth and on account of the generally lowered sea levels – a result of glaciation in the northern hemisphere – which had significantly increased the collective Hawaiian land mass. Now, there were high-ranging cliffs, more like the English coast near Dover than anything John Rourke had seen here centuries ago.

They stopped to rest and reconnoiter at the height of these cliffs, where the coastline lay more than a hundred feet below them, rugged in the extreme, with black rocks like a fortress wall against the attacking breakers, the waves advancing, retreating, assaulting the land again. This was not the sort of coastline John Rourke would have chosen for a clandestine landing.

The potential for arriving unseen was significant, but even more significant was the potential for arriving dead unless every man jack of the SS commando unit was a superb swimmer and reckless in the extreme.

Rourke said as much to Paul Rubenstein and Ed Shaw. Shaw responded, saying, "They couldn't have picked a more remote spot. No one comes here. The occasional fishing vessel or pleasure craft might lie well off the coast, there," and Shaw gestured to the west. "But they won't have the risk of bumping into military personnel, civilians, anyone. We've trained on cliffs like these, but the surf down there is too wild to risk a man's life in a training exercise."

John Rourke looked at his watch.

Washington's team should be in position.

And, in ten minutes, it would be within the window for the arrival of the commando unit.

"We'd better move out," Rourke advised.

"Agreed," Shaw nodded, then began signaling his men.

There were niches within the cliff faces, perhaps once volcanic pipes, now the haunts of the occasional seabird – wildlife was returning, in some cases in significant numbers – or merely empty holes in the bleached rock. In one such hole, John Rourke, Paul Rubenstein, Shaw and two of the Tac Team men stopped, the other ten men moving on, to find similar positions here midway along the cliff faces over the rockstrewn beach below.

13

Shaw and the two other Tac Team men began unlimbering their powered hang gliders.

John Rourke watched Paul's face. The expression there was one of skepticism, but Rourke said nothing. After a moment, Paul asked Shaw, "Why do you guys use those things? They're like a kite with a lawn mower motor!"

"A lot of the terrain was given a beating since The Night of The War, and in some places – a lot of places in these islands – the terrain was pretty rugged to begin with. Electronic sensing gear is so high-tech these days, if we had a helicopter waiting to come in anywhere within a mile or more, the bad guys'd know it. This way, we can move in fast, silently, and we have such a low sensing profile, we don't usually get spotted. Once the bad guys are on the beach, we can get down there in seconds."

"They can shoot at you," Paul noted.

"Hard to hit a fast-moving aerial target. Anyway, we can shoot back. You wanna fly one?" Ed Shaw grinned.

Paul grinned back, "Only if I have to, Ed."

John Rourke racked the action of his HK-91, chambering one of the 7.62mm Boatails. He moved into a kneeling position. The safety on, he settled the rifle to his shoulder, surveying the beach over the rifle's iron sights. Theirs was a waiting game now, waiting until the commando team started up onto the beach. When the enemy fought its way past the rocks, through the surf, their equipment suddenly feeling as though it weighed twice as much as it had, their breathing hard and rapid, their attention focused only on making it through, getting onto the beach, then it would be time to strike.

War wasn't a sporting proposition.

3

Nearly an hour passed. Rourke's head was starting to ache slightly from the eyestrain caused by constantly peering out over the ocean, both with unaided eyes and through the borrowed pair of German field glasses he was using.

Nothing relieved the sea's surface except the occasional bird. Many species of wildlife, birds included, were preserved over the centuries at Mid-Wake, Lydveldid Island, New Germany and at the Chinese First City, the creatures subsequently released to the wild. This was, at first, done under controlled conditions. Such controls had long since vanished. Although the diversity of species was vastly reduced, the numbers among those species extant were growing steadily. Rourke found that wonderfully encouraging.

Far in the distance, the normal naval traffic could be observed, but veering off from the coast of Molokai here and toward Oahu. Much of this was military, the majority originating in an American port, but there were some Chinese and Australian vessels as well; and, of course, Russian freighters. The Russians, although they had only paramilitary police units for domestic security, and a Coast Guard, were very active in merchant shipping. Eden vessels rarely came nearer to the Hawaiian Islands than just close enough to engage in electronic espionage, a role the Soviet Union had always played with much gusto in the days Before The Night of The War.

The Tac Team personnel worked so much with the SEALs that they were able to identify each vessel by profile. The Tac Team personnel were, as was usually the case with such units, on the

15

young side. The oldest among them was Ed Shaw, somewhere in his middle thirties, Rourke guessed, and Shaw was their commander in field operations such as this.

There were other personnel that belonged to the Honolulu Tac Team, Tim Shaw, who was Ed's father and Emma Shaw's father, too, among them. Many of these men, as Rourke was able to ascertain, were older, but not all of them. The Tac Team worked as a street unit and for SWAT and HRU applications. Depending on the gravity of a particular situation, both elements functioned together or separately. These younger men, in snatches of conversation Rourke overheard, would joke about the older guys (their most polite way of referring to them), but Rourke noted a distinct hint of respect, as well.

There were periodic low-frequency radio checks with Lieutenant Commander Washington's SEAL Team personnel. The same story came from their observation post: Nothing.

To relieve the monotony, Rourke took one of the spare bootlaces from his musette bag and showed the Tac Team personnel how to make one of the old OSS string holsters, a trick he'd learned years ago, Before The Night of The War, from one of his best friends. One merely tied the ends of the shoelace together—a bootlace was a little long for the thing but he wasn't about to cut it—and formed a circle, this made into a double loop. Then, one slipped the pistol—Rourke used a .45 volunteered by one of the Tac Team men—within the loops, inside the trouser band. Loosen the knot, then tighten it to fit and trim away the excess. That was all there was to it. The loops kept the pistol from sliding down inside the pants when the string holster was cinched up properly. In an emergency, the holster could be discarded and no one would give it a second look.

This demonstrated, they returned to the boredom of waiting. Rourke lit a cigarette, in the confined space of the rock niche preferring it over a cigar because so many of the Tac Team personnel were nonsmokers, a self-discipline Rourke commended.

An hour and a half was gone, still nothing in sight on the ocean's surface. A squall line was forming to the north, blue-black thunderheads rolling in rather quickly, low over the water.

Ed Shaw suddenly said, "Maybe we got it wrong, or somehow

the SS found out we hit the estate and they cancelled the insertion or—"

"Think again, Ed," Paul almost whispered. Paul was looking through the electronic imaging telescopic sight of a counter-sniper rifle one of the Tac Team personnel carried. "Try about two o'clock on the surface, maybe two hundred yards out."

John Rourke dropped into a prone position beside Paul, his elbows set on the rock, the German field glasses to his eyes. Around them were the sounds of field glasses being uncased, gravel crunching as men repositioned themselves with equal haste. At first, Rourke saw nothing, so he put the glasses down, focused his eyes on the approximate spot, then raised the glasses and tried again.

This time he saw something on the surface of the water, only an irregularity, unidentifiable, but somehow out of place. Paul was saying, "It's a snorkel. Someone near the surface, maybe reconning the beach."

The optics were treated, of course, but Rourke ordered, "Glasses down, everybody. Pull back. Ed, tell Washington, and tell him to have his men do the same."

"All right," Shaw said. "We got 'em."

Just because the SS commando unit was coming toward the shore, there wasn't proof positive of victory. Rourke decided not to burst any bubbles, however, so he didn't mention that at the moment . . .

Dark shapes moved near the surface of the water, breaking the foam-flecked crests of the waves with their bodies. Rourke's eyes squinted against the light as he watched them over his iron-sighted rifle. "Be patient," John Rourke counseled the men around him. The storm clouds were rolling in more rapidly now Rourke gave the weather system between five and ten minutes before it crashed over the beach.

There were telltale clicks, scrapes and ripping sounds within the cavelike niche of rock here in the cliffs, too soft to be heard more than a few feet away, the sounds those of safeties being checked, equipment snaps and buckles double checked, hook and loop fasteners being resecured, a knife blade given a few last-minute honing strokes.

The radio frequency shared by the Tac Team and Washington's SEAL Team was continually open now, because if the SS commando unit moving out of the water and onto the beach had not picked up a transmission by now, they would not pick it up at all. The danger, of course, had been that they scanned. Rourke would have done so, moving such a large body of men. These SS personnel apparently had not. A tactical error, and everyone made one from time to time; only occasionally were they critical. Similarly, Rourke would not have brought such a group in without cover of darkness, even in so remote and little-frequented a spot as this.

But, this latter would not be a tactical error, rather circumstances imposed by the inescapable exigency of some rendezvous that could not be set for a more advantageous time.

Fortunately, those problems he mentally enumerated were those of the SS unit's commander, not John Rourke's. But John Rourke's problems were sufficient without borrowing those of someone else. The size of the SS unit was impressive, vastly larger than Rourke had anticipated. All told, he estimated there were some sixty men in diving gear reminiscent of the underwater equipment he had first used with the heroic men of Mid-Wake more than a century ago, but obviously further advanced.

To his credit, Ed Shaw did not ask, "What the hell do we do now?" But the question was implicit in his tone when he murmured, "More than we thought, huh?"

Their numbers—the Tac and SEAL Teams combined—amounted to a rough half of those of the enemy.

John Rourke glanced at Paul Rubenstein, saw the worried look in his friend's eyes as Rourke advised Ed Shaw, "Get the rest of your people and Washington's people ready to move out. All the men with these powered hang gliders? How safe are they?"

"Pretty safe, if the operator does his part."

"Controls pretty simple?"

"Just a joystick. Push it forward and you nose down, pull back—"

"I get the idea. How about lateral orientation? Side to side?"

18

"Yeah."

"And speed?"

"Twenty-five miles per hour, tops, but you've gotta ride the thermals or you crash like a stone. You're not thinking—"

"Yes I am," John Rourke nodded . . .

Fully five minutes had passed, Rourke strapped into the harness for the powered glider. He thought, sometimes, when he encountered technology so radical as this, that he had to be dreaming, that this was all a nightmare and, when he awoke, he would still be aboard the jet passenger liner on The Night of The War on his way to Atlanta, Georgia, and none of this was happening at all, but rather all of this was a figment of his imagination, engendered merely by something which disagreed with him in the airplane food.

It would have been a nice thought, in most ways, except for Paul and Natalia, and the wonderful friends his now adult children, Annie and Michael, had become for him. And so many other fine people he had met, such as Jason Darkwood, Sebastian, General Varakov, and some of the other Russians, too.

And, oddly, he thought of Emma Shaw.

She was a marvelous girl.

John Rourke readied himself near the cave entrance, ready to soar like an eagle over the beach or fall flat on his face and die like a turkey with clipped wings.

But life itself, as he'd learned the hard way, was nothing short of a gamble.

4

John Rourke jumped into the void beyond the ledge. As he glided outward, he pushed his body upward with his hands and arms, securing his feet into the break-away stirrups. In the next instant, he pulled the throttle two thirds back, the bank of miniaturized ramjets which were set in the wedge-shaped wing above him firing. Rourke started to climb after one sickening instant of dropping like a stone. In that instant, he could not help being reminded of the Greek legend of Daedalus and Icarus, and wondering if fate had cast him in the juvenile lead?

But the powered hang glider rose and there was not an ounce of wax in the contraption, to melt as he soared upward and toward the sun. And the sun was obscured by the gathering storm clouds.

He banked slowly, instead, testing, coming to port and out over the beach. The ramjets were silenced and, except for the natural whooshing sound made by his wings as they cut the air, there was no other noise except for a continuous, low-intensity hiss.

His headset rang in his ears, "We're moving in!" It was Washington's voice, and Rourke certainly hoped the SEAL Team commander and his men were moving in. It could become very lonely very quickly for four men flying over this beach, set against fully sixty heavily armed enemy personnel. And, he was confident that all of the commandos would be men. Nazis, as well as being racist, were generally by philosophy sexist as well.

There were Tac Team personnel on both sides of John Rourke now and they started a gradual power dive toward the beach. "Fire at will," Rourke ordered. "Fire at will!" He'd known a man, years ago, who'd always made a joke of that, perennially quipping, "What's everybody got against Will, anyway?"

Rourke had traded weapons with Paul Rubenstein, swapping the long-range capable HK-91 for the more maneuverable German MP-40 submachinegun and its faster cyclic rate.

Rourke fired as he and three other of the Tac Team personnel soared over the beach. The men below them started to return fire, but Rourke was through the first pass and over the water before any enemy fire could come close to him or to the three other men from the Tac Team. Shooting accurately from the powered hang glider was, he discovered, even more difficult than shooting accurately from a moving horse, and that was next to impossible. But the horse analogy stood him in good stead as he suddenly realized what his tactics should be.

He banked the powered hang glider in a gentle arc to starboard, less than thirty feet over the crests of the waves, more than half a magazineful remaining in Paul's submachinegun.

Shaw's men and Paul Rubenstein were roping their way down the cliff face on power descenders, but the swarm of SS commandos on the beach were concentrating their fire toward the men in the powered hang gliders, John Rourke at their center.

Rourke and the three men with him made another pass, and this time Rourke adopted the technique so well perfected by the Confederate cavalrymen of The War Between The States. He waited until he was at almost point-blank range—in this case, perhaps thirty feet—and stabbed his weapon toward the target. This same method—using the handgun at saber range during the Civil War and at close pistol range now—worked. Rourke brought down three of the SS commandos as he throttled back and banked to starboard, just avoiding the rock face of the cliffs.

He began another pass, the submachinegun nearly empty, again waiting until he was close. The enemy on the beach was trying to hit a moving target, and when holding his fire until he was close, minimizing the inherent difficulties of his firing position, he at least had a stationary target.

The Schmiesser, as Paul called it, was empty at last as John Rourke flew over the waves, banking again, turning on the thermal toward the beach.

From his right, coming in low over the sand, John Rourke saw another group of men flying powered hang gliders, six more, SEAL Team personnel, Lieutenant Commander Washington leading them. The SEALs, despite their demonstrated preference for cartridge arms as handguns, were carrying submachinegun-sized energy weapons, of a type Rourke had never seen before in action.

These guns were in action now.

Their cyclic rate, if that were the proper terminology for an action containing no moving parts in the conventional sense, was slow. But as Rourke witnessed while the wedge of SEAL Team personnel fanned out across the beach, their firepower was devastating. And these men, well-practiced it seemed in firing from their moving platforms, used a similar technique to his own.

Rourke changed to a spare magazine, then throttled forward and left, swooping down nearer the beach.

As he started to pick a target, the volume of fire heavy now from the commandos, at the far left edge of his peripheral vision, he saw Ed Shaw himself take a series of energy bursts to the hang glider wings, the wings catching fire, their ram jets immediately flaming out, Shaw spiraled downward toward the sand.

In the next instant, as Ed Shaw lay sprawled there stunned, unconscious or dead, a half-dozen of the SS men swarmed over him. Firing into them, if Shaw were somehow still alive, would ensure the Tac Team leader's death.

Rourke banked the powered hang glider steeply to port, throttling back, then radically forward on the joy stick, climbing, then descending, swooping over the beach, low, with the butt of Paul's German MP-40 racking one of the SS commandos across the jaw, shooting another with a short burst in the chest and neck.

He was nearly over the six commandos who fell upon Ed Shaw, Rourke's left hand poised over the emergency release for the glider harness, the submachinegun hanging at his side on its sling.

It was imperative to gauge the distance as accurately as possible, so the momentum of his body would carry him into the knot of men, but he would be clear of the powered glider.

He hit the release lever, his shoulders wrenching, the sensation like that of the sudden deployment of a parachute after uncontrolled free fall. His body twisted, his arms reaching out.

His body slammed into and over three of the men, the SS men stumbling, falling, Rourke rolling onto one, kicking another in the face.

The powered hang glider was soaring upward as Rourke caught sight of it for an instant; then, it veered sharply downward, crashing against the cliff face, the synth-fuel exploding, a fireball belching upward.

Rourke was up, to his feet, his right hand on the pistol grip of the submachinegun, arcing the weapon upward on its sling. Rourke rammed the Schmiesser's muzzle into the throat of a third one of the commandos.

Rourke wheeled toward the remaining three.

Shaw was alive, his clothing partially consumed with flames, his hands on the arm of one of the commandos, the commando's wetsuit aflame as well. Shaw and the SS man—both of them were on fire—grappled over a knife.

John Rourke wheeled half left, and with his right foot snapped a double Tae-Kwon-Do kick to the SS commando's left rib cage. The force of Rourke's kicks sent the man hurtling over Shaw and into the sand. As the man rolled, the flames consuming his wetsuit extinguished. John Rourke moved toward Ed Shaw, but Shaw was to his feet, starting to run, panicked, Rourke realized.

John Rourke had seen other good and brave men lose it when their clothing was aflame, and Shaw had lost it. John

23

Rourke dodged past the two remaining SS commandos, throwing a body block against Ed Shaw, knocking the Tac Team leader into the sand, rolling him over onto the flames, then rolling him over again. Rourke scooped up handfuls of sand, hurtling them over the still burning portions of Shaw's clothing.

There was a blur of movement, Rourke dodging right as the buttstock of an Eden assault rifle smashed downward, glancing off Rourke's left shoulder.

Rourke turned half around, punching Paul's submachinegun forward, jerking back the trigger, spraying out half the magazine, killing the man, then emptying the Schmiesser into the sixth man.

Rourke stepped back, letting the submachinegun fall to his side on its sling as he drew both full-sized Scoremasters from his waistband, thumbing back the hammers. From near the cliff face, he heard Paul Rubenstein shouting to him, "Trigger control!"

Rourke called back to his friend, "Touché!"

When he'd taught Paul how to use firearms in the immediate aftermath of the aircrash which united them on The Night of The War, he taught the phrase—trigger control—to Paul as a mantralike watchword against spraying an automatic weapon empty, as Rourke himself had just done.

Shaw was to his knees, grumbling, "I'm all right."

Rourke took Ed Shaw at his word, then started forward, joining the Tac Team and SEAL Team personnel who battled the SS commandos here on the beach amid the foaming surf.

Rourke's eyes squinted against the light, but rolling in fast over the water were the dark thunderheads. Rourke advanced along the beach, the Detonics Servicemaster in his right fist bucking once, a shot into the throat of one of the SS men who stood over the body of one of the SEALs. The Nazi was about to finish the Navy man with a diving knife.

Rourke turned to his left, firing point-blank into the chest of another of the SS men, this one charging toward Rourke, assault rifle spraying into the sand. Original eight-round Detonics extension magazines were up the well of each Scoremaster, giving Rourke nine rounds per gun with the chambers loaded, one round now spent from each.

Rourke kept moving.

Rain began, not falling, but driving in icy wind-driven sheets which rolled savagely over the beach. Rourke was immediately drenched, his clothes plastered to his body. He fired both pistols at two of the SS men running for the cover of one of the black volcanic rocks – most were of enormous proportions – strewn about the higher ground of the beach. Rourke dropped one of the men. The second man hurled a grenade, Rourke shouting the alert, "Grenade!" Then Rourke threw himself down to the sand.

The explosion came and went, Rourke's ears ringing with it, a shower of sand assaulting his body amid the torrent of rain.

Rourke looked up, wiping his left forearm across his face to clear his eyes. He fired both pistols simultaneously, killing the man who'd thrown the grenade.

Within the explosion's kill radius, several men lay dead or dying, at least half of them from among the SS commando party.

Rourke was to his feet, thumbing up the safeties on both Scoremasters, grabbing up a weapon from the sand, one of the German assault rifles.

Rourke stabbed it toward a knot of the SS men, firing a controlled burst, then another and another, then another still, putting five of the SS commandos down dead. A man charged toward Rourke from his left and Rourke wheeled toward him, fired, killing him, the assault rifle empty.

Two men came at Rourke now from the rocks.

Rourke spun toward them, stabbing one of the men in the face with the assault rifle's flash hider. Simultaneously, Rourke's left hand freed the Crain Life Support System X knife from its sheath. Rourke raked twelve inches of steel across the chest and throat of the second man.

John Rourke was all but surrounded now.

He hammered the buttstock of the rifle into the face of one man, rammed the LS-X knife into the chest of another. Rourke hurled the empty assault rifle at still a third. Rourke's right hand reached out, catching a fourth man at the side of the head, by the left ear, then slamming the man's head downward as Rourke's right knee smashed upward. Rourke wrenched the knife clear of the man he'd just stabbed, hacked it across the shoulder of the man he'd kneed in the face and severed the sling of the assault rifle the man carried. Rourke had it now, scooping it up from the sand, firing it as he rose to his full height, killing three more of the commandos.

Two of the powered hang gliders swept through the rain, skimmed the surf, their pilots firing into a group of fifteen SS commandos trying to escape the beach. From the far left edge of Rourke's peripheral vision, he could see Paul, rallying some of the Tac Team men, cutting off the rest of the commando force.

Rourke discarded the emptied Eden assault rifle, slicing the sling of another free from the dead man to whose body it was still attached. Clamping the rifle's buttstock against his side to steady it, Rourke advanced, closing in from the rear of the commandos who were in flight.

There was nothing left but killing.

In more than six centuries, John Rourke was inured to it; but he prayed he would never come to like it, no matter how long he lived.

5

Emma Shaw, changed into a man's sized extra-large pink T-shirt which came down to her knees and nothing but her panties on underneath, sat cross-legged on the old-fashioned overstuffed sectional sofa. These days, so much furniture was air filled, but she'd grown up with furniture like this and liked it still. Her eyes were focused on the video panel set into the wall of her little house in the mountains. She was rarely off duty enough these days to use the place, but she had a lot of leave time coming and decided to use a few days and get away, to take advantage of what would probably be the short lull before a long war. She needed to think.

Snow lay soft and white on the giant pear-shaped leaves of the magnolias outside her front windows, beyond the small porch. In the days Before The Night of The War, some actual cold weather training exercises were run in the Hawaiian Islands by the Marine Corps, but the weather was nothing like this. Of course, it was rarely cold enough in the Islands for snow to stick to roadways (it did not now), but often cold enough in the higher elevations for the snow to form a beautiful icing on the magnolias, the pines, the palms and the rest of the lush vegetation here. The pineapple growers always groused about it, but there was never a hard enough freeze to cause them more than some anxiety.

On the other side of the island, everything grew better, of course, denser and greener because of the vulcanism which over the centuries periodically renewed the soil. She had chosen this spot because, if she lived to be a hundred (which

27

lots of people did these days) no volcano (unless a new one emerged) could touch her here.

Emma Shaw's eyes drifted back to the early evening news broadcasts. It was footage from a remotely piloted SkyVid that she watched now, flying over the beach where only a comparatively short while before John Rourke and her brother and a lot of other good people—some of them dead—had repelled an amphibious assault by troops "as yet unidentified, but rumored by official sources to be Nazi commandos in the employ of Eden. Eden's ambassador to the United States, Doctor Ernst Wiley, was unavailable for comment. Those same officials, speaking on condition of anonymity, indicate that Doctor John Thomas Rourke played an important role in foiling the attack.

"Doctor Rourke, the almost legendary survivor from more than six centuries ago through the use of experimental cryogenic technology, holds the rank of Brigadier General in the United States Armed Forces from the period more than one hundred years ago when Mid-Wake, our progenitor state, fought against the forces of the then-Communist-dominated Russia. Due in large part to Doctor Rourke's heroic efforts, the United States and its allies defeated the Soviet Union as the culmination of a war which lasted for more than five centuries and all but wiped out human life on the surface of the planet.

"Channel Three's Jaquie Warren caught up with Doctor Rourke as he exited a Naval helicopter after the successful mission involving Navy SEAL Team personnel and the Honolulu Tac Team."

The video flickered. There was toothy, big lipped, platinum blonde surfer girl Jaquie Warren buttonholing John as he exited a chopper, assault rifle in hand, hair odd-looking and wet, his face a mask of exhaustion and exasperation. "Doctor Rourke. I'm Jaquie Warren from Channel Three Up Close News."

"How nice for you," John told her, smiling.

28

Emma laughed. Jaquie Warren didn't.

"Doctor, I understand that you spearheaded the counterattack against the commando force sent against the Islands this afternoon and—"

"The men of Commander Washington's SEAL Team and Ed Shaw's Honolulu Tac Team were a pleasure to watch. It's a rare treat to see such shining professionalism."

"But, I understand Doctor Rourke that you—"

"Yes, I was right there watching the whole thing. They were magnificent. You'll have to excuse me."

Emma Shaw flicked channels to MTV.

She knew the real story, because her brother, Ed, had called her to assure her that he wasn't seriously injured, thinking she might have heard that his glider was shot down and his flame retardant suit had caught on fire. She hadn't heard, but breathed a sigh of relief. "That John Rourke, and Rubenstein, too. Talk about two terrific guys to have on your side, Emma! Whoa! I was on fire—the synth fuel was all over me and burning—and the damn heat was getting at me through my suit, see. Doctor Rourke gets all these guys off me, then decks me with a tackle—coulda used him when we used to play football, Sis—and puts the fire out, then—so help me!—he takes out better than a half-dozen guys single-handedly! One tough guy, lemme tell ya. But I'm fine, Sis."

When Emma Shaw closed her eyes, she could see John Rourke. She even dreamed about him when she slept. Football. She laughed. She used to play football with Ed and her dad, and they used to let her win just because she was a girl. One time, she almost broke Ed's arm and then they stopped letting her win and she enjoyed it more. When she'd make a play and do it right, she could really feel good about it.

Emma Shaw stood up, got up off the couch and walked across the large single room which was her "Great Room." The A-Frame, a combination of synth-stone and synth-wood prefab units, had a fourteen-foot vault at the height of the

29

ceiling where the joists met. It looked like a mountain cabin should look, a real fireplace that could burn real wood as well as synth-logs, the whole nine yards. Barefoot, she walked up the three steps to the level of the little hall and turned left toward the kitchen. Her phone was resting on the counter and she picked it up, started walking back toward the couch, touching the numerals for the Pearl Harbor Base Locater.

She got John's number and had herself connected. To her surprise, no answering unit cut in. It was John himself. "Hello?"

"John, uhh. It's Emma Shaw."

"Yes?"

"I'm sure you probably don't want to, but would you like to come up into the mountains to my place for dinner? I'm not half bad cooking."

"Sure."

Emma Shaw dropped the telephone. "John!" She was on her knees on the steps. "You still there?"

"Yeah. Sure it won't be too much trouble?"

"No! No, nothing I like better than cooking!" There were several things she liked better than cooking, including flying and some things she wasn't about to mention to John Rourke over the telephone. "Easy to find my place. Just come up Highway 1 to the turnoff for Darkwood Way. Follow Darkwood Way until you're up into the mountains. You'll see a sign for Theodore Roosevelt Drive. Take that up, north. You'll see my box." Why did she say that? "My delivery box, I mean. Just come on up the drive. Shouldn't take you more than thirty minutes."

"What time?" John asked her.

She looked at the clock on the vidscreen. It was nearly seven and she'd have to take a shower, fix her hair, dress, make dinner. "Eight-thirty? That's too late, isn't it?"

"No, that's fine."

"Just dress comfortable, huh?"

30

"Sure. Should I bring anything?"

She thought for a minute. She'd grocery shopped and had plenty of booze. "What do you like to drink?" It'd probably be the one thing she didn't have.

"Well, I used to be partial to Seagram's Seven."

What the hell was that? "Uhh, John?"

"Yes?"

"What is that?" She should have watched more old movies when she was a kid, not the westerns but the spy and detective flicks. But she'd always liked the westerns.

"Blended whiskey."

She sighed her relief audibly. "I've got plenty of that! See you, then."

"Looking forward to it."

She hung up. What if he'd wanted to say something else? Had she cut him off?

Emma Shaw spun on the balls of her bare feet and looked toward the kitchen. "It's microwave time!" She went into action . . .

John Rourke had just walked in from debriefing when Emma Shaw caught him on the telephone. As soon as she rang off, he called Commander Washington for a recommendation on getting a car. Washington said it would be all right to check out an FOUO electric car from Pearl's motor pool. Then Rourke called the hospital, checking again on Michael. Natalia, who'd been looked at, was fine; she was with Michael, who was sleeping and doing well, too. Then he called Paul, telling him, "Remember Emma Shaw? She asked me up to her place for dinner. Tell Annie, huh? See you tomorrow."

Emma Shaw was a pretty girl, but more important than that she was intelligent and gutsy; he enjoyed talking to her and could use some relaxation.

After making his phone calls, he changed to a new flint in the battered old Zippo windlighter he always carried and refilled with synth-fuel. These days, lighters were either the disposable kind, but synth-fueled, or more commonly electric. He preferred what he was used to. The Germans were working on self-renewing metals, something about which he hadn't read sufficiently to understand fully. But, if he had it right and could get them to make flints for him, he'd never have to change flints again.

But, that would be too perfect; without work, what was life?

He cleaned his guns, too, reasoning that after he got out of the shower there would be no sense getting his hands all covered with lubricant. Emma Shaw implied she was a good cook; a homecooked meal and some good conversation would be a treat . . .

The robot vacuum, thank God, was back from the shop and working. While it sucked its way over the floors, she'd gone about the house in its wake, trying to keep up, grabbing up everything small enough to be conveniently moved, giving a lick and a prayer with the ultrasound duster, then moving on . . .

John Rourke scrubbed at his hair to get out the blonde dye he'd washed in to accompany what he considered his less than inspirational performance as a German tourist. He hadn't had the time to wash it out before going off with the SEAL and Tac Teams. He smudged off the steam on the crystal of his Rolex. A couple of minutes to dress, then a quick walk down to the motor pool and off . . .

Emma Shaw was running out of time even before she got out of her T-shirt and panties and stepped into the shower. Once the water was on, she scrubbed shampoo through her hair with one hand while she lathered her body with the other, sort of like whistling, jumping up and down on one foot, and rubbing her tummy at the same time. She told herself to calm down. Regardless of the time (she refused to look at her wristwatch, at the same time reminding herself to get it off her wrist when she dressed because the timepiece was too clunky and mannish looking), she stood under the warm water, the conditioner rinsed out of her hair, no other purpose for standing there naked and wet than that it felt good.

But her mind was not idle.

She was about to entertain a living legend, a twentieth-century adventurer who was, in a technical manner of speaking, still married and despite the fact that she tried to ignore it, who outranked her considerably. And he was terrific looking, with just the right sprinkling of grey in his dark brown hair, those gorgeous brown eyes so full of soul and meaning and—"You're losing it, Emma," she told herself. If she kept thinking about John Rourke, she'd need another shower . . .

John Rourke, hair combed, stood naked in front of his two black ballistic nylon bags. There'd been no opportunity to organize his lodgings and, at any event, clothes these days didn't wrinkle so there wasn't much concern over keeping them in his bags. He took out a grey tweed sportcoat, black short-sleeved knit shirt, black slacks, black socks, a pair of underpants, a handkerchief and one of the two dress belts he owned. The belt, lined, was made for him Before The Night of The War by Milt Sparks. He'd treated the leather each time before taking The Sleep and each time after Awakening. A little Brasso (he had the Germans reproduce the venerable old product for him) and the brass buckle looked as good as it had the first day he'd gotten it. But now, the buckle polished, he didn't even need the Brasso . . .

* * *

Emma Shaw, her terrycloth bathrobe cinched at her waist and her hair wrapped in a bath towel stood, feet planted firmly in pink scuffs, staring into her closet. At her BOQ, she had a couple of civvie dresses, blouses and skirts, some jeans and whole bunches of uniform-related items, everything from dress whites with A-line skirts and funny hats to battle dress utilities and flightsuits. In this closet, however, reposed the bulk of her wardrobe. There were four bridesmaid's dresses—one pink, one purple, one yellow and one baby blue—each of which she had worn exactly once, discounting fittings. From there, ritziness went downhill quickly.

Twentieth Century women dressed in a style anywhere from Donna Reed's to Madonna the singer's. Emma Shaw's closet contained neither demure-looking full-skirted shirtwaist dresses nor erotic-looking corsets and garter belts. What would a six-hundred-year-old Twentieth-Century man of the world (God, how many women would he have, have, whatevered with?) expect her to wear? Her watch—the one that was waterproof, shockproof, antimagnetic and just about everything else she needed for combat—was still on her left wrist. She looked at it now. It was eight o'clock and her hair was still wet and dinner was only started, not done.

There was a system she could use if she had to: close her eyes and reach into the closet and wear whatever she touched. With her luck, it'd be one of the awful looking bridesmaid's dresses. And, boy, would that be subtle, she thought . . .

John Rourke slipped his feet into the pair of black leather loafers and picked up his double Alessi shoulder rig. He slung it on, the twin stainless Detonics miniguns already secured. Inside the waistband of his trousers, clipped to his belt, was the A.G. Russell Sting IA Black Chrome. He put on his tweed sportcoat, a spare magazine in each side pocket. He got his wallet, his money (the necessity for money again after all these years was an odd experience), the battered old Zippo, his cigars. The entry card key to his quarters was inside his wallet. He grabbed three items which he clipped into the left inside breast pocket of his jacket: the smaller of the mini Mag-Lites, a brass Heckler & Koch ballpoint pen and a B&D Grande pen-shaped folding knife.

On impulse, John Rourke picked up a pack of German cigarettes. They were filterless (to his liking), tasted as good as any American brand he'd ever tried Before the Night of The War and were entirely noncarcinogenic — plus they were more acceptable indoors than a cigar . . .

In bra, panties and slip, Emma Shaw picked up her dress from the bed where she'd laid it.

Earrings. Bracelet instead of wristwatch. A slender gold chain for around her neck. She had it all planned out as she started pulling the garment on over her head. It was navy blue, a sundress with wide straps, a full skirt and two big patch pockets. Still on the bed was the crocheted shawl she could put across her shoulders if the evening turned chilly. The shawl was the one thing she'd ever crocheted in her life which had turned out all right. Another advantage to it was that she could casually drop the fact that she, herself, had made it. Men loved that sort of thing.

She reached her hands behind her and started doing the buttons. What if John Rourke came early? Emma shook her head, telling herself that he'd probably be late, unfamiliar with the roads as he was. Just because he was the great survivalist didn't mean he'd be able to find her house that easily. And he'd just be leaving about now, anyway.

Her buttons buttoned, she tied the little sash belt in a bow at the back, then turned around so she could see the bow in the mirror. It looked a little wilted, but okay.

The gold chain went on around her neck, then the simple gold bracelet on her left wrist. A ring? No. She'd probably knock the stone out while she was making dinner and they'd wind up spending the rest of the night going through the food with a sieve looking for it.

She sat down at her vanity mirror and brushed her hair.

Up? Down? Down.

She tossed her hair back and started stabbing the spike from the first gold earring toward the hole in her lobe . . .

Totally electric, with cruise control to govern speed and headsup map display in the windshield, the For Official Use Only car he'd borrowed from the Navy was like driving no car at all. All John Rourke did was keep his left hand on the steering wheel and occasionally make the steering wheel move slightly. The steering was self-compensating to the road contour and, on a straightaway, the car even steered itself. Should, the vehicle for some reason veer more than a preset acceptable margin to either right or left, beepers sounded and the onboard computer's voice alerted the driver.

The sailor at the motor pool had shown Rourke how to program Emma Shaw's address into the onboard computer. Now, on the headsup, he could see the position of this car relative to destination, the car a little blip moving inexorably toward the X which, indeed, marked the spot.

If he stayed here in civilization, he'd have to get a real car, with a manual transmission, no computer gimmicks, an internal combustion engine. Such cars were made, principally in New Germany, but were quite expensive. He wondered if that vehicle of vehicles could be recreated, with 454 V-8 and the pulling power of one of Hannibal's elephants, the Chevrolet Suburban? John Rourke smiled; there would be some practical application for the wealth he had acquired through his general's salary for being comatose for the last one hundred and twenty-five years.

But that world of Suburbans and Zippos and all the rest was gone, and to all but a very few like him such things were curiosities from a past known only in history books and old films. At times, John Rourke felt like Rip Van Winkle, as if he had fallen asleep in one world and awakened in another. But in Washington Irving's day, the pace of the world was far slower, technology moving at a snail's pace.

In the Twentieth Century, it was not uncommon to know a man who had been born at the very end of the previous century and grown up trimming the wicks of oil lamps and hitching horses to a wagon only to live to see man riding on a pillar of flame, hitching his fate to the stars with the Mercury and Apollo Programs and into the age of the Shuttle, humanity's first reuseable spacecraft.

Then came humankind's self-destruction.

Young and old perished; death never discriminated.

There was talk of a space program, again, reaching off the planet into the unknown.

One thing he had never seen—and he reminded himself now that he should seek out—were the log videos from the Eden Project. While the crew of the Eden Shuttles slept, their onboard cameras did not, but kept on feeding data on a constant basis into the computers. What secrets lay there?

He'd find out, if he lived that long . . .

Emma Shaw had everything ready. It was eight twenty-five according to the kitchen clock. Dinner was on hold. If John Rourke arrived on time, they would eat at nine, just fashionable without being late.

She'd even dusted off the bottles of liquor as she'd taken them out of the kitchen cupboard and set them at the side of the counter separating the kitchen from the steps leading down into the Great Room.

The finishing touch.

Perfume.

Or would he prefer the subtle scent of kitchen smells about her? It wasn't as if she'd been peeling onions or cooking cabbage.

Emma Shaw abandoned her kitchen for the bathroom, taking care of nature, then brushing out her hair again.

He'd probably be late.

What if something came up? More Nazis from Eden? Would he have called her? Would there be time?

She heard the video monitor chime and she flicked the switch to activate the display screen set into the vanity mirror.

It was John Rourke.

Emma Shaw swallowed hard. He looked so . . . She turned off the screen, touched the light switch panel, throwing the bathroom into darkness, then dashed down into the Great Room and across it toward the front door. "Just a sec!" She stopped at the door. She smoothed her dress, straightened her straps so her bra straps didn't show, patted at her hair.

She should have used the perfume . . .

When Emma Shaw opened the door, John Rourke took a step back. It was involuntary. Backlit, she reminded him of Sarah. Her hair, her figure, her height, the set of her shoulders with classic feminine slope, yet lowered, not raised as if in fear or apology. And what would Sarah think? Would she understand that they were just comrades-in-arms getting together for a friendly meal and conversation? Of course she would. He had never been unfaithful to his wife, no matter how close he'd come to it with Natalia. And, even though Sarah lay comatose and near real death in cryogenic sleep, a bullet lodged inoperably deep within her brain, John Rourke would not be unfaithful to her now.

"Hi."

"Hi," John Rourke almost whispered.

"Come on in, John."

"I was unintentionally rude; I should have brought something, like a bottle of wine or—"

38

"No. That's all right." John Rourke crossed the threshold and Emma closed the door. "Take your coat?"

"Sure." Definitely cigarettes and not cigars. He took the pack of German cigarettes from one of the jacket pockets, then John Rourke shrugged out of the jacket. He caught her grey-green eyes as they caught his guns in the double shoulder holsters. She turned away, slid open the closet door and his coat disappeared.

As she turned around toward him, her left wrist brushed back a lock of auburn hair from her forehead. "Have any trouble finding it?"

"The house? No. Took an FOUO out of the Pearl motor pool. The car drove me up here by itself," Rourke added, smiling. He began removing the shoulder rig. There was a small table opposite from the closet where he could set the guns. His little knife wouldn't really matter.

"Kind of take the fun out of it, don't they? Driving, I mean. Must have been terrific to really drive. Like flying still can be when you turn off the right things," Emma enthused.

But she looked a little nervous. He wondered if he should make some comment about her hair or her dress or something? But, that would be unprofessional. He told her instead, "Nice house."

"Want the nickel tour?"

"Smallest I've got's a twenty," Rourke responded.

"How about a drink?"

"Sure."

"Why don't you fix, okay? I've got something in the microwave I need to check."

"Fine."

"This way," she told him.

Rourke watched her walking across the room for a beat; she reminded him of Sarah in some physical ways. He shook his head and followed her, past a comfortable-looking couch that seemed more like something from his era than hers, up

39

three steps to the kitchen. The counter had several bottles of liquor set on it and some glasses. He picked up a bottle of vodka. The brand name was unrecognizable. He set it down and picked up the bottle of blended whiskey. It was the same story. He remembered the expression about any port in a storm as he cracked the seal. "Ice?"

"No."

"You don't have any ice?"

"Ohh, no!" Emma laughed. "I mean, I don't use ice. I've got ice, though." She went to what Rourke assumed was a refrigerator, opening a large panel which didn't look like a refrigerator door at all and was set between part of the counter spaces. She touched a lighted rectangle within the door and what seemed to be an icebucket emerged and ice fell into it with a comfortingly familiar clattering sound. The ice stopped falling and she took the bucket away and closed the door. "Here you go, John."

"What do you drink?"

"Scotch."

"How many fingers?"

"Fingers?" There was a look of puzzlement in her eyes as she looked at him over her shoulder. He realized she was beautiful. "I don't understand. Fingers?"

"A primitive measuring system. A lot of scotch or a little?"

"A little."

Rourke set down the blended whiskey and picked up the unrecognizable brand of scotch. He poured two fingers into an appropriately sized glass. She set the icebucket down on the counter, then gently pressed the rim and the lid which had evidently sealed over it opened. He handed her the scotch. "Put your own water in it. I could never get it right."

"Fine. I like a lot of water, anyway."

Rourke took three ice cubes—they were perfectly formed—and put them in his glass. He touched at the rim of the icebucket and the lid fanfolded out toward the center, closing.

40

He poured whiskey over the ice until the ice was submerged and set down the bottle, closing it. The tap in the sink shut off.

When Rourke looked up, she was standing on the other side of the counter, holding her glass as if raised for a toast.

John Rourke smiled, clinked glasses with her. "To good friends and comrades-in-arms."

Emma Shaw smiled a little oddly, but touched her glass to his.

6

Wilhelm Doring looked magnificently handsome. His short blond hair was caught up in the wind and the fine mist of spray blowing over the prow of the hired Russian vessel. His chest swelled beneath the black turtleneck, his strong chin jutting defiantly forward, the set of his brow in profile more than human.

And she was drawn to him like a moth to the proverbial flame.

He was all that was German and strong and pure, a hero of the race.

As if he'd read her thoughts, he turned away from the sea and looked at her. By the yellow light of the lamp swaying in rhythm with the swells, attached to a bracket a meter or so away and just above his considerable height, she could just make out his expression. Wilhelm Doring seemed at peace. And he smiled at her. "What is it, Marie?"

"I was getting a little nervous, Willy," Marie Dreissling said with total candor. She had never been able to hide anything from him since the moment she met him, almost nine weeks ago. But it seemed to her that her life had not begun until that moment, that she was reborn.

"Soon we will be moving, and then there will be no time for nervousness." He rolled back the knit cuff of his sweater and his eyes turned down to look at his watch. "In one hour." His voice was resonant, a deep, rich baritone, musical, but in no way anything but totally masculine. "So, that is very soon. In another fifteen minutes, we will have the final briefing, and after that the equipment checks, then move into the prelaunch sequence."

"Can we trust these Russian pirates, do you think, Willy?"

"We require an insertion platform; the Russians will provide that. Afterward, we will require the Russians no longer. Do not worry about it." He walked toward her. She stood, arms limp at her sides. His hand touched at her cheek and she shivered. "You had best prepare yourself, Marie."

"Yes, Willy."

He walked away and Marie stood there, the wind whipping her hair, molding her clothing against her, making her aware of every square centimeter of her body. Willy.

Marie forced herself to breathe . . .

"You're a very good cook, Emma," John Rourke announced between forkfuls of potroast. And she looked very beautiful in the light of the candles which burned between them on the smallish table. It would have been presumptuous to mention that, so he didn't. The music playing seemed to surround them. "Great stereo system."

"Stereo?"

"Your sound system."

"Ohh, thanks." He even liked the music. It was soft jazz of some kind, with a subtle Latin flavor. "More wine?" Emma asked.

"No, never been much of a wine drinker," Rourke told her. "Your brother's a good man."

"Thanks for saving his life," Emma said, smiling. Rourke felt slightly embarrassed. He hadn't mentioned her brother in order to solicit a reaction like that. He'd just been making conversation. "Was the fight on the beach as tough as it looked on the news, John?"

"I didn't see the news."

"Looked like one hell of a fight."

"We encountered a more substantially sized force than we'd

43

anticipated," Rourke said. He set down his fork and knife and leaned back. "That was a wonderful meal."

"I made dessert."

"I'll try," he smiled.

"Apple pie."

"I'll force myself," he smiled again.

"Want vanilla ice cream on it?"

"A la mode? Sure."

"A la mode?"

Rourke laughed. "It means 'of the fashion' in French."

"Ohh. Do you speak a lot of foreign languages?"

"Pretty good Russian, okay German, good Spanish. I've got a little Icelandic I picked up and I know Sign."

"Sign?"

"Deaf-speak." He moved his hands rapidly. "See?"

"What did you say? I mean, nobody's deaf these days with implants and everything."

"I was just illustrating what I meant," Rourke said, taking his lighter and the package of German cigarettes from the table beside him. "Mind if I smoke?"

"What did you say, John? With your hands, I mean?"

Rourke asked, "Cigarette?"

"Not just now. What did you say to me with your hands?"

He inhaled smoke, exhaled. He focused his eyes on the cig-arette's glowing tip. "I said 'You are pretty,' but I was just giv-ing you an example of Sign. I mean, you are pretty, but I—"

"John Rourke. You're quite a man." She started to get up. She was standing before he was able to get her chair, but he stood.

"What do you mean?"

She walked around the table, leaned up and very quickly kissed him on the cheek. "I'll get your apple pie," Emma Shaw almost whispered . . .

Doring watched the faces in the semicircle all but surrounding him. The eyes set in those faces—bright, alert, eager and intelligent—watched him back. The air in the Russian vessel's salon smelled stale and slightly sour, as if food had been left too long and allowed to spoil. From the cuisine they'd experienced since joining the freighter at Port Reno, that seemed indeed like the logical explanation. The group consisted of ten men besides himself and only one woman, Marie Dreissling.

"Gunther, stand at the door."

"Yes, Willy."

Gunther—tall, blond, muscular and possessed of a ready smile—drew his pistol from beneath his sweater and went to stand beside the already closed door between the salon and the main companionway.

Wilhelm Doring looked at the others. They were so young to risk their lives; but their names would be immortal. "A review before we get started, hmm? So. Our purpose must be foremost in our minds! While the other units infiltrate Hawaii for open military action against the Americans, our purpose is at once more subtle and more important. Remember, in order for our work to achieve its necessary effect, the nature of our group cannot be discovered."

"Willy?" Reinhardt Kleist was possessed of a voice that was high for a man, and the fellow was painfully aware of it. So he spoke in a whisper, and was sometimes hard to hear because of that.

"Yes, Reinhardt?"

"Willy, I was wondering. Has the, the device been tried?"

Wilhelm Doring smiled. "I have been waiting for someone to ask that question since we began training for this mission. And, I will assure you, the answer is yes. Suitable subjects were fitted with the identical device and death was instantaneous." The "suitable subjects" were Icelandic sailors found shipwrecked off the coast of Eden, then flown inland to the training site. "So there is nothing to worry over in that regard."

Reinhardt's face lit in a smile of relief.

45

"Any other questions, then?" Doring asked, expecting none. And, there were none. "Good! Then we rendezvous as arranged for the equipment check." He looked toward the doorway. "Gunther!"

"Yes, Willy," Gunther nodded, making his pistol disappear beneath his sweater as he opened the door.

Wilhelm Doring looked at his wristwatch. In less than an hour, if these Russian pirates had any suspicions, it would no longer matter . . .

He sat at the far end of the couch, his legs crossed, a cigarette burning between his fingers. Emma Shaw carried his drink in her right hand, her own in her left. She was wearing the shawl now and she threw out the line as she handed John Rourke his drink. "I was a little cold."

"Live in a home centered around a natural granite cavern like we did and you become used to a little chill in the air," he smiled.

Emma set her drink on the coffee table, then dropped to her knees beside it, a few feet away from him. She arranged her clothes, drawing the shawl closer around her shoulders. She tried again. "My mother taught me how to crochet."

"My daughter sews and things, a lot. Crocheting's like sewing, I guess."

"I don't sew; I mean, I do buttons and hems and things, but I don't make clothing." She fired her best shot. "I enjoyed making this shawl, though." Folding the shawl closer around her, she lowered her eyes.

"It's pretty."

"Ohh! Well, it's pretty basic really," Emma said, tugging at a length of fringe.

"You know, I have to tell you something, Emma."

Still on her knees, practically at his feet, she leaned forward. "Yes, John?"

John smiled, inhaled on his cigarette. As he began to speak, he exhaled smoke through his nostrils. They flared a little when he did that and it looked wonderfully sexy. "Well, the old mountain men had all that fringe on their buckskins and a lot of people thought it was for decoration. But, it really wasn't. Know what it was for?"

Emma Shaw sat back on her heels. "No, John. What was it for?"

He laughed. "Well, when something needed repairing — like a ditty bag or a piece of harness — well, they'd just tear off a piece of fringe and use it."

She looked at him, looked at her shawl. She tugged at a piece of its fringe. "Can't do much harness repair with dazzle yarn," Emma said at last. "How did a Doctor of Medicine become a weapons expert and everything?"

"My dad was in the OSS —" He hesitated.

She smiled. "I know that one: Office of Strategic Services during World War Two, predecessor of the CIA. That's what you were in, right?"

"Right."

"John?"

"Yes?"

"You made the last toast," she said, raising her glass. John Rourke extinguished his cigarette, raised his glass, touched it to hers. "Here's to getting to know each other better." Someone should have yelled "Hussy!" at her, but Emma Shaw didn't care.

7

Wilhelm Doring, Marie Dreissling beside him, Reinhardt Kleist, Gunther Brach and the eight others of the special unit—they were not even given a name, this for security purposes, only a radio call designation—moved aft along the portside of the *Vladivostok Queen.* When the wind which blew so strongly over the Russian pirate ship's bow would momentarily abate, the smells of onions and sausage, unprocessed tobacco and cheap vodka wafted toward them from below decks.

The vessel's captain, who called himself only "Dimitri" and a half-dozen of his crewmen stood all the way aft of the superstructure near the opening in the rail with the ladder leading downward toward the small dock rigged there. From that dock, the inflatables would be activated and rigged with their silent running outboards.

Dimitri and his men were visibly armed, as they always were, and if Dimitri had it in mind to kill his passengers and steal their belongings—weapons, explosives, the inflatables themselves, all useful in his pirate trade—now would be the man's moment.

In the last fifty years, then accelerating in the decade just past, piracy on the high seas had flourished. As shipping grew, so did the pirate fleet. As the pressures of potential world warfare mounted, the powers which could have quelled the pirate trade were too involved in their own matters to look to it seriously. The majority of the pirates were, of course, Russian, many of them the descendants of the people of the Soviet Underwater City, conquered by the Americans of Mid-

Wake more than a century ago. But many were disaffected men and some women, these latter known for their brutality, from among the populations of other world groups, including even some leathery-skinned descendants of the Wild Tribes of Europe.

Wilhelm Doring stopped a few feet forward of Captain Dimitri. "Greetings, Captain. Soon, you will be rid of us."

"Yes, but I shall miss having such intriguing passengers as yourselves, and not to mention well-paying. We've come to see you off." Within the scope of Wilhelm Doring's experience, Dimitri's voice was only comparable to the sound made when a file was rasped over coarse metal, only it was deeper. "As I offered, we can always lay off the islands and wait for your return."

"As before, Captain, the offer is well-intended, I know, but unnecessary. If we leave the islands, we will be using different transport." Doring sensed that there were more of Dimitri's men nearby. And, logic dictated it. Dimitri and his men were armed with cutlasses and knives and at least two handguns each, but only two of them carried energy rifles, these slung almost casually. If Dimitri was intent on killing his departing passengers and stealing their belongings, he would have more men ready to step in.

The Wild Tribesman, Rene, who was Dimitri's first mate, was nowhere to be seen. And Rene had been eyeing Marie Dreissling ever since they first joined the vessel. Odds were that Rene and a dozen more of these seaborne brigands were lurking somewhere above, in the rigging which shadowed the superstructure, guns charged, knives and cutlasses keen.

Doring kept Marie well back from him, between him and Reinhardt. And he started forward toward the opening in the rail. The butt of the energy pistol carried in the tactical thigh holster on his right leg almost touched Doring's fingertips.

Dimitri took a step forward. "Esteemed passengers, I must say a proper farewell."

"I am sure," Doring said, nodding.

Dimitri extended his hand to Doring. Doring's right arm arced slowly upward. They clasped hands, as if in friendship. "My young friend. I wish you fair seas to the islands and that, whatever your secret mission is about, it goes well and you live to tell of your exploits to your great-grandsons."

"And I wish to you, Captain Dimitri, all that within your heart you wish to me."

Dimitri, who was left-handed, had probably done this a dozen, or a hundred times before.

Wilhelm Doring, on the other hand, although right-handed by birth, had trained himself to be ambidextrous in all things except writing (which he could manage with his left hand but did poorly). Doring sensed the body movement, the resetting of the shoulders, the tightening of Dimitri's grip. Doring's left hand grasped the hilt of one of the several knives he carried. This one was patterned after the Fairbairn-Sykes commando knives of more than six and one-half centuries ago. The blade was slender and double-edged, designed for close-range killing.

Doring freed the knife from the inverted sheath sewn into the lining of his open battle vest.

Doring's left fist tightened against the double quillon guard of the knife. He punched the blade forward and upward, coming in below the level of Dimitri's belt and the body armor vest which the pirate captain habitually wore. As the steel penetrated, Doring jerked back, still grasping Dimitri's right hand, throwing the big Russian off balance. Dimitri's own blade missed Doring's abdomen by inches, skating off Doring's armored battle vest as Doring twisted right.

Doring shouted to his band, "Now!"

At the far right edge of Doring's peripheral vision, he could see Reinhardt shoving Marie back and out of immediate danger, then swinging up his energy rifle to fire.

Doring let go of his knife as he twisted his right hand free of Dimitri's grasp. The big Russian was down to his knees, doubling forward to the deck, screaming, "Kill them!"

Doring's left hand was already moving his energy rifle into position, his right flexing to recover circulation as he grasped his pistol. There was a blur of motion to his left. Some of Rene's men, he surmised. Doring fired his pistol indiscriminately toward the knot of Russian pirates which had surrounded Dimitri as he wheeled half left and fired the energy rifle toward the blur. Indeed, it was a man, then another and another, cutlasses and energy pistols in their hands. In the light of the swaying lamps here near the rail, their faces looked yellow and tightly drawn into masks of hatred.

Two of the pirates fell. Then, as Doring stepped back, something struck the energy rifle from his grasp, the weapon swung on its sling and crashed against his left thigh.

Doring wheeled left. There was a whooshing sound as steel sliced air and Doring ducked.

It was Rene, the leathery-faced Wild Tribesman, first mate to Dimitri. In Rene's right hand was a cutlass, in his left a pistol. The pistol fired now. Doring flinched, his pistol off line; there was no chance to fire in his own defense. But in the same instant, the body of one of the pirates fell between Doring and Rene, the pirate—already dead—taking the shot.

There were bursts from energy weapons all around him now, and the ringing of steel as cutlasses and knives did their work.

Marie screamed, "Willy! Look out!"

Doring had his pistol up, to fire. As Doring leveled the weapon, Rene's cutlass swiped toward him. Doring dodged, but the cutlass caught the pistol less than an inch forward of the trigger guard. It was a backstroke of the cutlass, so instead of breaking Doring's wrist, it tore the gun from Doring's hand. Doring stumbled over a body.

As he fell to his knees, his right hand found the hilt of a cutlass, the weapon fallen to the deckplates. Rene's cutlass swept down toward Doring's head and Doring arced the cutlass up. The massive curved blades locked for less than a second. Doring dodged back, to his feet now, his left hand groping for

51

the pistol grip of his energy rifle. But Rene charged, hacking with the cutlass and Doring had no choice but to use the only weapon to hand. Their blades locked, parted, locked again.

Rene's cutlass moved with the alacrity and unpredictable agility of a snake, feinting toward Doring, withdrawing, flicking forward again. But Doring blocked each thrust; and he did it, however effectively, less than gracefully, while Dimitri's Wild Tribesman first mate was an obviously accomplished swordsman.

The rate of energy weapon blasts was so rapid that it was impossible for Doring to tell one shot from the next. Everyone around him was in motion, a confusion of hands and arms and legs and falling bodies.

Doring's left hand found the pistol grip of his energy rifle and he stabbed the weapon forward now, blocking Rene's downwardly hacking cutlass with his own blade as he fired the rifle point blank. Rene's center of mass seemed to collapse into itself and there was the smell of burning flesh . . .

The smell was overpowering. This current epoch so much replicated the 1960s that it sometimes felt uncanny. Although the shape of the vessel was a little odd—rather like the barrel of a smallish deck cannon—within it, over a dancing candleflame, chocolate melted. Emma was making fondue.

Fresh strawberries and thick slices of banana were set out on two smallish plates, one to either side of the vessel itself at the center of the coffee table.

Rourke sat on the couch. Emma Shaw knelt on the opposite side of the table. She stabbed a piece of banana with one of the small-tined, long-handled forks. Rourke speared a strawberry. "What will you do when this war with Eden has come and gone, John?"

"Wait for the next war," Rourke said honestly.

"That's a terrible thing to say," she almost whispered, her eyes focused on her now chocolate-dripping banana slice.

Rourke immersed his strawberry. "I'm speaking from experience, Emma, not from preference. After we ended things with the Soviet Union, I started up my clinic, my hospital. My wife and I were living together, our baby was due. Aside from Commander Dodd and the political strife which he was attempting to generate within Eden, things looked positive. It's almost as if mankind can't live without strife, though. Perhaps it's some fault in our genetic makeup. There are some people who will risk everything—of theirs and everyone else's—in order to try for power over mankind. Nazi, Communist, doesn't matter really. "A rose by any other name . . ." The result's the same."

"You're a pessimist," she told him.

Rourke smiled as he ate his strawberry. And through a mouthful of chocolate and strawberry he told her, "You're almost right; I'm a realist. The intent is different, but the result's the same, I'm afraid."

"Fine. Then say by some miracle it becomes an ideal world. What then?"

"I'd like to explore it, see what's out there. And if we ever got a space program going—which we won't in my lifetime because we're too busy trying to survive—see what's out there as well. But I'd probably try to bring my medical education up to the level of the present century, then go back in the doctor business," Rourke concluded.

Emma said nothing, just impaled a strawberry.

As Rourke drowned a banana slice in the chocolate, he said, "A lot depends—everything, really—depends on whether or not Sarah can be saved now. And Deitrich Zimmer's the only man who can do it, it appears, if indeed he can."

"What would you do if the bullet in her brain can't be removed, if she can't be awakened, John?"

"Once that's certain," Rourke told her, "that no process currently known could save her, I'd take The Sleep again, stay with her until the day that she can be brought back."

Emma put down her fork. She said, "Even considering everything, your wife's a lucky woman."

53

John Rourke smiled. "I know you meant that as a compliment, but I don't know how lucky she is to have me for a husband; sometimes, I think I'm a curse to her. But she'd do the same for me, I know." Rourke exhaled, took a sip from his drink. "But there'll be a way of making Deitrich Zimmer do what has to be done."

"Then?" Emma rocked forward, her elbows on the table, her chin resting in her tiny fists.

"Then Zimmer and Martin will have to be stopped."

"You'd kill your own son." There was no hint of reproof or even shock in her voice, just the statement of fact. That was something Rourke liked very much about her; Emma Shaw was a realist.

"Not willingly," Rourke rasped, clearing his throat, taking another sip of his drink.

8

Dead men lay everywhere aft of the superstructure.

Two of Doring's own band were wounded, but neither seriously. Marie attended them as Reinhardt led a team to set the charges that would sink this vessel to the bottom. Such had been Doring's plan all along; the opportunity presented by Captain Dimitri's attack actually heightened the potential for effectiveness.

Gunther Brach, with two of the men, kept the remainder of the pirate crew pinned down below decks with energy weapons fire so that the demolitions party and the boat party, which Doring himself led, could go about their business unmolested.

Doring, on the floating jetty beside the rusting hull of the antique vessel, looked to the main deck and shouted up, "We are ready down here!"

"Laying the last charges now, Willy!" Reinhardt called back.

Had they been able to depart the *Vladivostok Queen* without incident, they would have lain off just over the horizon and two of the men would have gone back using scuba gear and laid magnetic charges on the hydrofoil and laterally along the underside of the hull. The effect would have been to rip the vessel open and sink it in two halves, fore and aft. The advantage provided them under the present circumstances was significant: by skillful placement of the charges, the pirate hydrofoil could be made to collapse in upon itself. It would sink faster that way and there was a vastly reduced chance of any survivors.

Doring had realized that if, somehow, Dimitri and his crew

could have seen any profit in contacting the authorities at Pearl Harbor and alerting them, that a party of Nazi commandos had quietly infiltrated the islands, they would have done so. This had been obvious from. the first. As they had crossed the Tropic of Cancer, Doring came to the realization that Dimitri, instead of seeking some dubious reward for betraying them might be contemplating a more direct assault on them.

That had happened.

Dimitri, disarmed and not yet fully bled to death from his gaping wound, still knelt on his own deck, howling curses into the night in a multiplicity of languages. Doring patted the hilt of the dagger which he had retrieved from Dimitri's crotch. The blade as an extension of his hand had done its work well.

Doring looked to the boats. All three were inflated, silent twin outboards mounted, gear stowed.

Doring ordered, "One of you stay with the boats. The rest of you, follow me up top. We get the wounded." Had his two wounded men been in serious condition, he would have killed them personally. They would have expected that, just as he would have. In the event of his death, Reinhardt had the command.

As Doring reached the main deck and swung through the gap in the rail, he saw Marie, her blue eyes wide, her skin more pale than usual. She was just completing a bandage. Women were ill-suited to anything but domestic or basic clerical duties, but a female was necessary to the operation and Marie was as good as any. Once the team became known to the American authorities in the Hawaiian Islands, security would naturally be tightened. A woman, uninvolved directly in the raids, would be able to move more freely than a man. Her English was perfect. He gave her that.

"Marie. Help put the wounded into the boats."

"Yes, Willy."

He gave her that, too; she was properly obedient.

Reinhardt approached, smiling. "The charges are set, Willy."

"Good."

"I will able to radio detonate from two hundred meters away. We will be safe from any flying debris. There are little redundancies built into the charges so that even if one of them is moderately skilled, neither can the charges be disarmed nor neutralized. So!"

"Good!" Doring nodded. Then he went to stand before Captain Dimitri. The pirate captain's body was so bent over that his forehead rested against one of the deck plates. "Captain. We must leave you now. But it was a pleasant voyage. And you shall have the ultimate sea captain's honor. I have always read that the captain must go down with his ship. This you will do."

"Fuck you!" The sound of Dimitri's voice was more animal than human now, and so low that it could barely be heard over the lapping of the sea against the hull of the *Vladivostok Queen*.

"That is a trait of which I would never have suspected you, Captain. But, if you wish to fantasize—" And Doring smiled as he walked away. He shouted over his shoulder, "Gunther! When we are safely aboard the inflatables, withdraw."

"Yes, Willy!"

9

He'd shaken her hand.

Her right arm hung limp at her side.

From the small porch, she could watch the taillights of his car as they became smaller and smaller and smaller. In another moment, they would disappear.

A wind blew strong and cold down from the mountains, tugging at her clothes, at her hair. The shawl across her nearly bare shoulders not too terribly heavy, Emma Shaw was cold. But she stood there alone on the front porch, watching the vanishing taillights anyway.

She had made the ultimate mistake any woman could make: She was in love with a man who was totally unattainable; but that was not the reason that she loved him. There was no reason to it, and that, more than anything, at once terrified her yet convinced her that what she felt was very real, perhaps her ultimate reality. And that terrified her even more.

It was unthinkable that John Rourke would suddenly take her into his arms and ravage her body as he'd ravaged her soul almost from the very first instant she'd seen him.

Emma Shaw could no longer really see the lights from his car, but she stood there anyway.

The wind raised her dress. She made no move to touch the skirt, to hold it down. Her arms hung so limply at her sides now that the shawl had slipped from her shoulders, clung to her only at her elbows. "John," she whispered to the night. She'd always enjoyed the writings of Albert Camus, the Twentieth-Century French existentialist. A story she'd always remembered was his classic, "The Unfaithful Wife," but she was not about to bare her body to the stars on the roof of some desert hovel. And, it wasn't as if she hadn't bared her body on a few occasions before.

She wanted to strip away her clothes, wear only John Rourke's arms around her. That would be enough, forever. But he wasn't here. And, he wouldn't be. "The Faithful Husband." If she were a writer, she could write a story about him, a man garbed in the righteousness of his fidelity to a wife who was all but dead.

Yet Emma Shaw could not bring herself to hate Sarah Rourke. She envied her. And that was funny, envying a woman who had slept for one hundred and twenty-five years in suspended animation, with a bullet in her brain that in all likelihood could never be removed.

And Emma Shaw shivered. The thought that crossed her mind made her feel colder and more alone than any wind or any night. John, when Sarah could not be brought back, would re-enter what he so offhandedly called The Sleep and wait with her.

While John slept with his almost dead wife, she—Emma Shaw—might sleep with others, but never sleep with him. And the great love of her life would quite literally pass her by. When he reawoke, she would be dead, gone, hardly a memory.

Or, worse.

He would reawaken, about forty or so as he was now, and she—Emma Shaw—would be alive and old and near death and John would come to visit her, laugh with her about this dinner tonight, pat her gently on a wrinkled hand, perhaps brush his lips against her cheek.

And then death would be a blessing.

She was conscious in that instant that tears were flooding her eyes. She could have turned her eyes into the wind, made them go away. But, she let them flow from the rims of her eyes and across her cheeks. She tasted the salt of her own

59

tears on her lips.

It was bitter . . .

Annie Rourke Rubenstein lay in the crook of her husband's arm. Neither of them was asleep. She was wet between her legs from him, and she nuzzled closer to him in the darkness, holding him, him holding her. "Paul?"

"Yeah?"

"I love you." His lips touched her forehead. Annie started to cry, turned her face against Paul's chest, murmured, "Hold me tighter?"

"What's the matter, Annie?"

"I was thinking about daddy, how lonely he must be? Well, I just can't—I just can't—"

"He'll get Deitrich Zimmer, get Zimmer to help her. He'll use Martin. John can do it."

"First momma, then Natalia. Daddy doesn't have anybody, Paul. He's alone every night. He's—" She could no longer speak, just hold and be held.

Paul whispered, "I know, baby." He held her and his lips touched her hair and Annie closed her eyes but didn't sleep . . .

She sat, hugging her knees close to her, her eyes riveted to the pirate ship *Vladivostok Queen.*

Willy had told her to watch.

Marie Dreissling shivered, despite the blanket one of the men had thrown over her shoulders. The wind was blowing up, making the swells roll higher and the troughs deeper and her stomach churn.

The men aboard the *Vladivostok Queen*—all of them—would soon die. Marie Dreissling knew they were enemies, but they were human beings. That was why she was glad to be a woman. Such a decision as this, to kill these men, was a decision she could never have made. That was something only a man could do.

"All right, now, watch, Marie. The explosions will have a ripple effect, sawing the damned ship in two," Reinhardt said.

Marie Dreissling watched.

Men knew about such things, determined who should live and who should die.

She blinked because the chill and the velocity of the wind were making tears rise in her eyes. And, when she blinked, she missed the first explosion. But, she could hear it, and as she opened her eyes, she saw the second, then the third.

She had expected flames, pieces of burning debris, perhaps a mushroom-shaped fireball rising into the night sky, turning the darkness to day. But there were only bright flashes and muted banging sounds and then there was a horrible groan, like the noises Captain Dimitri's bowels had made as he at last fell prone to the deck just as she had gone down the ladder to board her inflatable.

The engines of all three inflatables purred into life.

The sea churned more wildly.

The port and starboard sections, then the fore and aft sections of the *Vladivostok Queen* began to fold inward. And the vessel seemed to rise up in the water, as though it were human, drowning, grasping for one last chance at life.

The three inflatables were hydroplaning now and the rolling of the seas felt less pronounced in her stomach.

And the *Vladivostok Queen* sank beneath the waves.

10

John Thomas Rourke felt little like sleeping.

He spent some time keening the edge of the Crain Life Support System X knife, then touching up the A.G. Russell Sting IA Black Chrome's edges as well. He took his vintage copy of Ayn Rand's *Atlas Shrugged* from his suitcase and picked up where he'd last stopped rereading when other matters had drawn him away.

He read that for a time, but could not concentrate.

He thought of Sarah, and the inevitability of his future should he live long enough to meet it. By the time the day came that Sarah would be restored to him, young Martin Zimmer, their son kidnapped at birth and raised by the Nazi Deitrich Zimmer, then genetically altered to mirror the image of Deitrich Zimmer's idol, Adolf Hitler, would be dead. John Rourke would have to see to that in one manner or another. Precipitating the death of his own son, however evil and vile that life had become, would be the second most difficult thing he would ever have to do.

For all that Deitrich Zimmer had done, the ultimate responsibility for young Martin being in the world was John Rourke's, his and his alone. He alone had made Sarah pregnant with the child. And, but for the circumstances of the child's birth, Sarah might well have been beside him. They could have lived out the rest of their lives, he and Sarah, in relative normalcy.

And, together, they would be in their graves by now, knowing nothing of this future which the begetting of Martin Zimmer helped to create.

The most difficult thing, even more than taking the life of young Martin, would be telling Sarah that he had done it, and losing her forever as the consequence. She would assume, as any mother would, that somehow Martin could have been changed back, for the good. But what Deitrich Zimmer had done to the boy, through the combination of genetic surgery and the environment in which the boy was raised, was irreversible, except perhaps by surgically or chemically neutralizing the personality centers of Martin's brain.

And that would be a far worse fate than death, to live physically only. If Martin were rational, the man that he could have been, fine and strong like Michael, Martin would choose death to that.

John Rourke stuffed one of the ScoreMasters into his trouser belt and pulled on his old battered brown bomberjacket.

Then he went out into the night to walk, to think, hoping that perhaps the fresh air would make it easier for him subsequently to fall asleep.

There was a Marine walking across the quadrangle. The young man saluted. Rourke nodded and said, "Good evening." Rourke kept on walking.

His thoughts shifted to Emma Shaw. The woman was good company and a good cook. More than that, she was a good woman. She seemed to combine so many of the qualities John Rourke loved in Sarah and had loved in Natalia. If things were different, Rourke thought . . . But, they were not. Nor did he regret for a moment that he was married to Sarah, even though he knew she would leave him when she awakened to learn the fate of the child she had nearly died giving birth to, a fate John Rourke would have to fulfill.

Rourke sat on a rock overlooking the harbor area, his eyes focused far out to sea.

What he needed more than anything else now was for someone's arms to be around him; more than at any time in his life, his soul ached with loneliness.

63

He looked down into his hands. His eyes, always light-sensitive, enabled him to see in the dark. There was movement by his loafer-shod feet. It was a grasshopper, not particularly large, really nothing noteworthy about the creature. Rourke kept his feet still so that he would not inadvertently step on the creature.

The grasshopper, like all lower animals, led a much less complicated life. But, with the privilege of human thought came responsibility for thought's consequences.

The grasshopper just "hung around" for several minutes, Rourke watching the creature all the while. And then it moved off. Rourke stood up, careful to direct his feet in the direction opposite the grasshopper's path.

Life was fragile, Rourke thought, for all.

11

He had raised dogs or had helped his family to raise them since his earliest memories, so he wasn't at all upset that one of them was barking in the predawn hours. A dog might bark because it sensed danger and sought to raise an alarm, or because it experienced some sort of distress, or simply because it felt like barking.

But since his dogs didn't usually bark at this hour, he pushed aside the covers and started out of bed, just in case.

"Thorn?"

"Some barking; I'm gonna check," he told his wife, Ellie. There was another practical concern, of course. Their nearest neighbors were better than a quarter of a mile away, but their children were light sleepers—a good trait, he'd always thought—and might be awakened.

He pulled on a pair of shorts, stepped into his slip-on deck shoes and did one more thing. From the nightstand on his side of the bed, he took up his shoulder holster. He was not a firearms afficionado, but as with most people these days, carrying a gun was for him as natural as breathing, and a fine insurance policy for continuing to do so.

Although never "into guns" as a hobby, he took his marksmanship seriously and was quite careful in his selection of the firearms which he did possess. All were cartridge arms reproductions from Lancer; energy weapons had always seemed like overkill to him and required more maintenance than did cartridge arms. The charge had to be frequently checked and the contacts in this high salinity climate of Hawaii, although sealed of course, had to be kept scrupulously cleaned.

When he had purchased his guns, he'd consulted with "expert" friends, then read the literature, shopped wisely for price against value and, at last, made his decisions. All his purchases were Lancer-made reproductions. The gun which was carried in his shoulder holster was the SIG-Sauer P-226. The gun which he kept primarily for home defense was ideally suited to other needs should those arise; it was the Heckler & Koch SP-89. The design had intrigued him on an intellectual level. It was a semiautomatic shoulder stockless pistol version of the MP5 submachinegun (Lancer reproductions of these were still in use by some SEAL Team and Honolulu Tac Team personnel).

He had read that in the declining years of the twentieth century, when the SP-89 was developed, civilian ownership of selective fire weapons was frowned upon and all but impossible; these days, such was not the case, of course. If a civilian wanted to own the state-of-the-art plasma energy assault rifle that was current issue to United States military forces, or a Lancer reproduction of the Browning .50 caliber machinegun, all that was necessary was the money to buy it.

There was considerable crime, as there had been throughout history, simply because some men and women did not like to work; but, very little crime was violent, and a miniscule portion of that directed against individual citizens. Home burglaries were a novelty, as were robberies of stores, banks and the like; with virtually everyone armed if he or she chose to be, violent criminality had little chance for success.

The opposite was supposedly true in Eden, where possession of any sort of weapon by a civilian was punished with horrible severity; in Eden, cries of violence against the general population were nearly the rule rather than the exception.

Although the SP-89 was only semiautomatic, he felt no need for anything more than that, as was his prerogative. The firearm his wife carried in her purse was at once equally as eclectic and equally practical, a Taurus Model 85CH, a snubby .38 Special revolver with an exposed but totally spurless and profileless hammer.

He was not a hunter, so he owned no rifle, but kept a shotgun for emergencies, this also Lancer-made, a reproduction of the Remington 870 pump.

As he started downstairs, he looked in at the children's bedrooms. Trixie tossed and turned a bit as the barking persisted; Daniel seemed undisturbed as yet.

He took the stairs as silently as he could, grabbing his leather jacket when he passed the halltree and pulling it on over the shoulder holster and his bare skin beneath.

He walked through the house from front to rear, exiting via the kitchen door to the backyard and the dog runs beyond. Raising the oversized Malamutes was not as profitable as raising the smaller pet varieties or the Dobermans, but he had a special interest in these animals.

They were all up, awakened by the one which barked.

As he approached, the animal calmed, looked at him.

There was always one named "Hrothgar" in the family. Not that these Hrothgars were true physical descendants of the original who was the companion of Bjorn Rolvaag, of course. But, for more than a century now, someone in the Rolvaag family raised dogs and named one of those dogs Hrothgar.

Thornton Rolvaag stroked the muzzle of his Hrothgar, saying to the animal, "Something's bothering you tonight, isn't it? Hmm?" This Hrothgar, however, did carry some of the original Hrothgar's genes, and had the slightest part of wolf in him because of it.

Hrothgar stood feet planted by the door to his shelter within the run.

Thornton Rolvaag drew his hand back and walked along the fence to the entrance, opened it, went inside. Hrothgar sat before his shelter now. Rolvaag whistled softly and Hrothgar ran to him. "I should have checked for seismic activity, shouldn't

67

I? When will people learn to understand animals, huh?" He played roughly with the dog's ears—Hrothgar loved it—and gave the dog a hug.

What was called in the history books "The Great Conflagration" had one beneficial effect to a man who raised dogs; among the species wiped out was *Ctenocephalides canis,* the common dog flea.

"Hrothgar—you go back to sleep and I'll go do what I should have done in the first place, okay?"

It was odd how Hrothgar seemed almost capable of understanding, because the dog turned around, winding itself down in a descending spiral until it lay prone beneath the roof of its shelter.

Thornton Rolvaag left the run, closing the gate, stopped to give a quick look and a quick pet to each of the Malamutes, then returned to the house.

In the kitchen, he took a glass of water from the tap, drank it, then set the glass on the counter over the dishwasher. His coat still on—the night was chilly—he went toward the front of the house, to his home office.

As he had anticipated from Hrothgar's behavior, his computer link to the seismographic equipment at the University indicated the volcano was acting up again.

As if on cue, the phone rang. He tried to remember where he'd left it, found it beneath a stack of hard copy, picked it up. "Thornton Rolvaag."

"Thorn, Betty."

Betty Gilder, his professor during his postgraduate days at the University of Hawaii, was these days technically his boss, but more than that, she was a combination mother-figure and good old friend. "I've got the stuff coming in over my computer. Hrothgar woke me up."

"I think we should hire that dog of yours full-time, Thorn."

"I'll ask him and see what he says," Rolvaag volunteered.

"Think we can get around the fact he doesn't have a PhD?"

"I'll loan him mine," Rolvaag volunteered.

68

"You weren't so flippant when I was your faculty advisor, sonny."

"Yes, mother. Want me to come in?"

"No. But, do me a favor?"

"Sure. What?"

Betty sounded a little tired. "I'm bushed. Ride herd on it for a little while so I can get some sleep. Then get some sleep yourself and come in by noon, okay?"

"Fine." Rolvaag lit a cigarette. "I'll call you if there's anything anomalous."

"Kiss Ellie and the kids for me."

"How about Hrothgar?"

"Sure," Betty said.

"Get some sleep, mom."

"Right."

The line clicked dead.

Thornton Rolvaag set the phone down on the desk. He heard the rustling of clothing behind him, turned slowly toward the sound. It was Ellie, in nightgown, bathrobe and bare feet.

"Betty, right?"

"Right."

"And Hrothgar was playing seismologist again, right?" Ellie asked.

"Right again."

"Want coffee?"

He took a step closer to her and she came into his arms, leaned her head against his chest for a second. "A hug's fine."

She took his cigarette from his other hand and dragged on it, exhaling as she said, "I'm gonna go pee, then get to bed. Kids have to be at school the same time they always do. If you're asleep, what time do I get you up?"

"I'm gonna keep an eye on things for an hour or so, then hit the rack. Get me up by nine or ten; have to be at the University by noon."

"Want pancakes for breakfast?"

69

"Sounds good to me."

She leaned up on her bare toes and kissed his cheek. She had been raised on a farm on Hilo, grew up barefoot and never outgrew it. He drew her against him, kissed her lightly on the lips. "Need a sweater?" Ellie asked.

"I can get it."

"You watch your computer screen; I'll get it. And then I'll go pee."

"Think about the rolling of the surf across the—"

"Ohh, shut up!" Ellie said, laughing.

Rolvaag flicked ashes from his cigarette. When he looked back toward the doorway, she was gone.

By the time she returned with his bathrobe, his slippers and a cotton afghan in case he got cold, he had the readings coming in from the major sensors.

The Old One was restless tonight, but he'd seen her worse.

He changed—"You just wanted to see me naked, who are you kidding?"—and kissed Ellie again, then sat down at his desk.

He heard her clothes rustling again as she left.

After a few minutes, he heard one of the upstairs toilets flushing.

Rolvaag started jotting down notes.

12

Wilhelm Doring set down his suitcase.

"Why are there not separate accommodations?"

"I thought that you and the woman would be—"

Doring started to say something, but stopped as he heard Marie Dreissling clear her throat. He looked away from Stroud and looked at Marie, instead. "Yes, Marie?"

"I do not object to the accommodations if they satisfy you, Willy."

She was blushing.

Doring felt the corners of his mouth turning down. He looked back at Stroud, their contact here in Honolulu and, perforce, their landlord. "Fine. Make certain we get a good night's sleep."

"Yes, certainly Herr Sturmbannführer Doring—"

"Willy; I am 'Willy' to you and to everyone else. Is that understood?"

"Yes, Willy."

"Good. You may leave us."

Stroud, who was a contract agent to the Gestapo and was so deferential as to be annoying, left at once, bowing slightly as he backed through the doorway of his own building. The building, like many in this section of Honolulu, was largely immigrant housing. Refugees from Eden came here, as did other nationalities, Russians and Chinese in particular, and some Wild Tribespeople, because Hawaii had employment. There was a booming economy here, the jumping-off point for the Far East and Australia, where there was more employment still.

71

The population of Hawaii was largely technocratic. Consequently, laborers to handle the automated farms stretching along the Pacific toward what once was Japan and the expansive livestock and agricultural facilities on Australia were in desperate demand. The wages were good.

Every iota of data concerning the enemy had been made available to Wilhelm Doring, and he devoured it because even the smallest fact could be of benefit to him in the success of this operation.

Stroud had been waiting for them on the beach road with a large electrically powered van. The two wounded men were already stabilized before reaching the beach. Once on the beach and certain that the landing zone was secured, they had aimed the inflatables back into the shipping lanes with small time-detonated charges aboard which would take their engines and thwarts to the bottom after the synth-rubber burned.

They changed in two-person shifts (except for Marie Dreissling of course) into civilian-appearing clothing, packing their gear into more of the fabric suitcases they had brought.

Doring was taking off his windbreaker as he noticed Marie staring at him. Doring stripped away his body armor vest. Marie was still looking at him. Doring pulled his energy pistol from the waistband of his trousers. "Marie, there will never be anything permanent between us. You realize this?"

"Yes, Willy."

"Then, take off your clothes and warm the bed."

"Yes, Willy."

Doring went about the apartment, sweeping it for listening devices and optical sensors. He discerned no evidence of any of these. The structure in which they would reside, for the time being at least, was called, in the vernacular, a condominium. There were various large apartments all within the same general structure. The building itself stood some ten stories tall and occupied one side of an entire city block.

Johann Stroud, the landlord, in the employ of the Gestapo for some seven years, and considered reliable, was too obsequious to be fully trusted. And Doring was determined to act according to his instincts in all matters concerning the fellow.

The condition of this mission deep into enemy territory was a simple one: Wilhelm Doring had complete autonomy, responsible only for getting his job done; how that was accomplished was of no concern. If that meant killing the Gestapo's pet contract agent here, then it would be done.

Satisfied that the Spartan-seeming apartment was secure—it was obvious that Stroud had given them the best of those available—Doring went into the bathroom again, but this time not to check for sensors. Wash his hands. Urinate. Defecate. Brush his teeth.

Stripped to his underpants, his gun in his right hand, he walked into the bedroom.

The drapes were pulled shut and there was a bedside lamp turned on. Marie, covers pulled up to her chin, only her head and her fingertips exposed, lay in the center of the bed.

He stripped off his underpants.

Marie's eyes flickered over him, then away.

He stood beside the bed for a moment, looking down at her. She still did not look at him. But, she said "I will do whatever you ask of me, Willy."

Wilhelm Doring said nothing, but had expected no less of her. He put his pistol on the nightstand—later it would go under his pillow—and he turned off the light.

He sat down beside her, then swung his legs up as he moved the covers back.

He realized that his hands were cold. She shivered when he touched her.

Doring drew Marie's face close to his and began kissing her. Women liked their foreplay and were less responsive in its absence.

13

Allied Intelligence, while endeavoring to compromise the Eden Defense Computer Network, inadvertently gained access to the Registry of Defense-Related Personnel. It was a considerable list. Although no one in the Trans-Global Alliance had thought at the time that such information would prove more than marginally valuable, this was not the case. On at least one occasion of which James Darkwood was aware, the information from the Registry had been used to weave a blackmail plot that successfully turned one of Eden's top scientists (the man was later discovered and murdered by Eden Security Forces).

But now, the thrust of the operation was entirely different.

Darkwood spoke into his communicator. "Manfred?"

"Yes?"

"There's nothing going on here by the rear door. Why don't you start up from the front and meet me in the corridor in two minutes."

"Right."

The operation against Wilbur Nash, because of its time of day (daylight hours) and location within an Alpha Level Security Area (the housing complex for Eden Defense Plant 234), had to be weaponless.

That of itself was enough to make Darkwood's skin crawl. But what lay ahead was potentially far worse. He would exchange places with Wilbur Nash for third shift inside Eden Defense Plant 234. Once the shift ended and Darkwood was out (he hoped, alive), Wilbur Nash would be released and of-

74

fered the chance to flee Eden for New Germany rather than risk retribution for his unwilling part in the operation.

Wilbur Nash was selected because, of all the Eden Defense Workers who had access to Plant 234, he bore the closest resemblance to Darkwood. Their height was identical. Although Nash's build was slighter, Darkwood could mask that by wearing loose-fitting coveralls and slouching a bit.

Darkwood entered the residential complex and ascended the rear stairs to the third floor. As he entered the corridor, he saw Manfred Kohl, his counterpart from New Germany, exiting the elevator and turning right. Wilbur Nash's small apartment was to Darkwood's left in the corridor segment between them.

Kohl knocked on Nash's door. Darkwood watched the corridor.

He heard Nash's door opening and Manfred Kohl's fist impacting Nash's jaw . . .

Rourke slept a total of four hours, but felt sufficiently refreshed (since his last Awakening, although he still preferred to sleep at least six hours out of every rough twenty-four, he could easily function on considerably less). He decided to take advantage of the facilities at Pearl, namely the Pacific Ocean.

After a quick shave and shower, he borrowed an FOUO electric car and drove out along the beach, parked, stripped off his sweats and went into the surf. The water was cold and brought his body to life. He swam deeply, the life in the sea here phenomenally abundant, the reef which protected the beach rich.

By the black face of his Rolex Submariner, he had spent almost an hour in the water before coming up onto the beach again, towelling dry in the cool morning wind, redonning his sweats and starting back toward the main portion of the base.

Back at his quarters, he showered and washed his hair again. As he emerged from the bathroom, a towel in hand, rubbing his hair dry, he noticed that the message-waiting red diode of his answering machine was illuminated. The counter indicated one message. Rourke played it back. "Doctor Rourke, this is Commander Washington. Thought you'd like to be in on this, sir. There's a briefing at O900. It's important. I'll send a driver around in the event you get this message."

Rourke looked at his watch again. O900 was fifteen minutes away. Hurriedly, Rourke dressed. Since he had no idea concerning the nature of the briefing, in keeping with his lifelong dictum to "Plan ahead," he donned a pair of black ripstop BDU pants, a long-sleeved black cotton knit shirt and combat boots. He slipped on the double Alessi shoulder holster with his twin stainless Detonics miniguns, then slid the Milt Sparks Six-Pack with a half-dozen spare six-round magazines onto his Garrison-width belt. He slipped the A.G. Russell Sting IA Black Chrome inside his trouser band and grabbed his leather jacket.

As he did so, there came a knock at the door of his small BOQ apartment. Never one to trust to the obvious, he drew one of the little Detonics CombatMasters from beneath his left armpit, holding the gun behind his right thigh as he opened the door with his left hand and stepped back.

Standing in the doorframe was a pretty girl in khaki cap, blouse and skirt. She saluted. "Yeoman Jones reporting, sir. I've been instructed by Commander Washington to request your presence—"

Rourke smiled as he cut her off. "I took the telephone message, Yeoman. Ready to go when you are." As he slipped the little stainless steel .45 back into its holster, he told the woman, "Just finishing getting dressed."

14

The conference room was utilitarian but comfortable. John Rourke took a chair somewhere near the middle of the table while the remaining personnel—among them uniformed Naval Intelligence officers and persons in civilian attire who looked as if they had the same occupation—filed in and either sat down or hovered in corners of the room in small groups, discussing things in obvious whispers.

Commander Washington entered along with two junior officers, and just behind him was Ed Shaw, Emma's brother from the Honolulu Tac Team.

There was no military formality here, evidently this was a team of men who worked together in such close association that behind these doors—and the doors closed in almost the same instant—the superfluous was left behind. Rourke liked that.

Washington took his seat, nodded to Rourke, then looked toward the head of the table. A man in civilian clothes that seemed as nondescript as his face and manner stood at the head of the table and began to speak. "Gentlemen, ladies, we've got a more serious immediate problem than any of us anticipated. Last night, two separate landings were made in the islands, one of these apparently a large commando force similar in composition to that which our SEALs and the HPD Tac Team took out. We've got teams out looking for them.

"The second landing," the man went on, "was a total of twelve persons. That smells like something else besides a straight military unit. They landed very close to Honolulu and we have reason to suspect they waylaid a car and got into the city. What their mission is cannot be determined."

John Rourke said, "Excuse me."

The man looked at him, his face expressionless. "Yes, General Rourke?"

"Is the area where this landing took place cordoned off?"

"Yes. HPDs got it, right Shaw?"

Ed Shaw nodded.

"How about the road where you believe they waylaid a car?"

"That can be done, Doctor," Shaw answered for the man.

"If I'm not talking out of turn, then," Rourke went on, "why don't you do that. I believe the Germans have some device that utilizes a laser to bring up latent surface impressions, like a more sophisticated fingerprint detector. Maybe we could use that."

The nondescript man interjected, "That's a heavily trafficked section of road during daylight hours, General Rourke."

"A vehicle waylaid might possibly have stopped quite suddenly, whereas a vehicle waiting to pick up this team wouldn't have," Rourke suggested.

"Good point, Doctor," Shaw said, nodding. He took a small transceiver from under his windbreaker as he stood up and started away from the table.

"General Rourke, would you care to become personally involved in this?" The nondescript man lit a cigarette with a disposable lighter as he spoke.

Rourke looked at the nondescript man. "Indeed, I would." Rourke noticed Commander Washington smiling . . .

The car stopped, but Annie Rourke Rubenstein waited for the Navy enlisted man who was her driver to open the car door for her. She could get used to this.

78

Before eight, she was up and dressed and off to the hospital to visit Michael. He'd be released this afternoon, and had kidded with her that this was the most medical attention he'd ever received for something as comparatively minor. She remembered the time Michael was nearly dead and her father had operated to save his life, but she didn't mention it.

Natalia was there, too.

After talking with Michael for a while, she took Natalia down to the hospital coffee shop and they talked for a while by themselves, discussing nothing of consequence, she realized, but the time enjoyable, relaxing for them.

Then Paul had her paged and she was off again.

Her driver held the door open and she stepped out into the bright sunshine and a pleasantly cool breeze which immediately grabbed at her skirts. But she got her clothing under control quickly enough.

The enlisted man asked, "Is there anything else I can do for you, Mrs. Rubenstein?"

"No, I'm fine, thank you very much."

"My pleasure, ma'am."

He closed the door and started around toward the driver's side while Annie slowly walked toward the police line, set up to block a stretch of road along a broad curve, extending for what looked like a quarter of a mile.

There were two uniformed officers, one male and one female, standing beside the yellow tape. As Annie approached and started to introduce herself, the male officer saluted and said, "Mrs. Rubenstein, you're expected."

"Thank you." He raised the tape and she ducked beneath it, holding her dress with one hand, her hair with the other, the wind higher the closer she got to the hairpin of the curve. Beyond the road, she could see, hear, even smell the ocean.

Along the road, she saw her father and her husband, Commander Washington and Ed Shaw. A uniformed police officer was holding something which looked like an oddly shaped vacuum cleaner with a video monitor attached to it, moving slowly with it along the outside lane of the highway, nearest to the beach. The strap of her bag was starting to slip from her shoulder and she let go of her hair to fix it. Both pistols which she habitually carried—the Detonics ScoreMaster and the Beretta 92F—were too large for practical purse carry in anything of convenient size. But her father had somehow thought to plan ahead for that too. When he and Paul broke into the Retreat, their home in the mountains of American Georgia which the government of Eden had turned into a museum, among the various items they "liberated" was the gun she now carried in her purse.

"This is an Interarms Firestar," her father had told her. "Works just like your ScoreMaster or any Colt/Browning 1911-style pistol, and it's about the size of Natalia's Walther PPK/S, but instead of being a .380, it's a 9mm Parabellum. Great little gun. Keep it around if you need it." And, of course, she'd needed it, carried it now along with two spare seven-round magazines in her purse.

She picked her hair away from her face, got it under control again by wrapping her hand around it at the nape of her neck, then joined her father and her husband and the other men along the roadway.

"It's me!"

Her father looked around, put an arm around her waist and kissed her on the cheek, then turned back to business. Paul put his hands on her waist, kissed her lightly on the lips, said, "You look pretty," and turned away and went back to business.

Annie looked at the vacuum cleaner thing with the video monitor. In the monitor, she could see tire treads and all sorts of scratches and scrapes which, evidently, this gadget was picking up off the surface of the road. With the naked eye, she could see a gouge here and there or some other irregularity but nothing so detailed.

She shrugged her shoulders, opened the flap on her purse and reached inside for the scarf she carried there. She turned her face into the wind, let go of her hair for a second, then caught it up again, this time knotting the scarf into her hair at the nape of her neck. It worked the first time and now she had at least one hand free. She stepped up behind her husband, stood on her tiptoes, looked over his shoulder and asked into his ear, "So, what are you guys doing?"

"Looking for skid marks, trying to get tire impressions, give ourselves something concrete to go on."

" 'To go on'? You been watching old 'Dragnet' videos or something?"

" 'Miami Vice,' " her father supplied. "No, actually, there are footprints leading up from the beach indicating eleven men—two of whom were apparently injured but not seriously—and one woman landed here in the predawn hours."

"He's not kidding," Paul supplied.

"Come on. Advanced Man-Tracking 401's in session," her father said. He started toward the beach and Annie fell in beside him. As always when they walked together, if he detected that she was having trouble keeping up—which she was as soon as she got onto the sand—her father slowed his pace and slightly narrowed his stride.

Her shoes were the problem, flat sandals which were bogging down in the sand. "Wait a minute, daddy," Annie said. "Give me your arm." She leaned on her father's forearm and stepped out of the sandals. "There." She caught them up in her left hand, letting go of her dress. Barring a sudden updraft, the worst that could happen was that her father, who'd changed her diapers when she was a baby anyway, would see her legs.

They walked on for about twenty-five yards until they were near the edge of the surf.

"Stop here," John Rourke said. He squatted down over the damp sand. "The wind would have erased most impressions in the dry sand, but here we still have some.

She stepped into the edge of the surf, the water cold against her bare toes.

"Bend down and take a look at this, kiddo," John Rourke directed. Annie tucked her dress up close under her thighs as she crouched beside him. She saw impressions of varying sizes and shapes. He started tracing one with his finger. "They were clearer before the wind picked up and pushed the surf, but you can see there's a difference between this heelprint and that one, for example. There was one set a few yards down that was very shallow.

"The woman?"

"Good guess, but no. Hers were shallow, too, but I could tell the woman's impressions from the width of the foot and the stride. Only known four women in my life who could comfortably match a man's normal stride: you, your mother, Natalia and Emma Shaw."

"Ohh."

"These impressions merely show a number of men carrying heavy loads, probably equipment. The woman was carrying some stuff, too, either that or she limped badly. But I don't think so. Her left foot impression was deeper than her right. The two wounded men's impressions were a little erratic, but more importantly they weren't as deep." He stood up and started into the surf. She hitched up her nearly ankle-length dress and followed him into water that had to be less than an inch below his boot tops. "Right about where we're standing," he went on, "there were the marks from three inflatables. I found the impression—it's gone now, washed away—of at least two props. These guys didn't row in. They used silenced outboards. Ed Shaw's got people looking on both sides of the road, but the twelve probably set the boats out over the surf and let them go back out to sea, most likely with explosive charges rigged to scuttle them once they were well clear of the coast.

"The Navy picked up some floating debris this morning, from a Russian pirate ship—"

"Pirates! Pirates?"

"Pirates. Lots of piracy on the high seas, these days. But

they pretty much think—the Navy—the debris is from a Russian hydrofoil. Probably our twelve invaders booked passage on the pirate vessel, then had a falling out, or more likely had it planned all along to scuttle her. This isn't like those commandos we nailed the other day. I'd guess this is some highly trained, highly specialized unit. Maybe an assassination squad, maybe aimed at specific types of terrorism. Hence, the woman."

"I don't understand, daddy."

Her father looked down at her and smiled as she started back out of the surf. "The Nazis historically utilized women, but considered women secondclass citizens in many respects; that's the case with the current neo-Nazi movement. If I'm reading this correctly—and it's all supposition at this stage, of course—this group intends to blend in with the general populace on the island and they brought the woman along as a sort of liason, thinking we'd never expect them to use a woman and that she could come and go more freely than the eleven men. And the fact that two of the men were evidently wounded, of course, would dovetail nicely into the scenario concerning the wreckage from the Russian pirate vessel—injured in the battle," he concluded.

"All right, what now?" Annie asked him.

"We work with Shaw's Tac Team to hunt these people down." And he put his arm around her. She leaned her head against him as they walked. "Unlike our adversaries, we know the value of female operatives. If Natalia can be pried away from Michael, the two of you can pose as tourists—it's the same tourist mecca here that it always was—or whatever works best, maybe dig around for information."

"This is like being a cop in one of the videos from the Retreat," Annie observed.

"Investigative work; I suppose so. The important thing is that we find these people. They won't wait forever to hit their first target, whatever that is, then blend into the population. We have to end their careers as quickly as possible."

83

They reached the spot where the sand met the rock and she leaned on her father's arm again while she dusted the sand from the soles of her feet and from between her toes then put on her sandals.

They walked back side by side to the roadway. Paul was looking at the video display for the vacuum cleaner thing, Ed Shaw and Commander Washington flanking him. "Better than we hoped for, John," her husband called out. "Found some tire treads leaving the road, evidently going off to the side here. The interesting thing is that the tires are perceptibly wider once the vehicle rejoins the road. Could be it took on a heavy load."

"If it's only one vehicle, then it's probably a van or panel truck," Commander Washington said.

"Agreed," John Rourke said, nodding.

"What we want to do then," Ed Shaw said, as if thinking out loud, "is find a match to this tire tread, so we can determine the make and model, then find out what vans usually have these as factory original equipment. We can measure the distance between treads, so we can match that up with a wheelbase size. If we're lucky, we'll get a model, make, maybe even a year. And while we're running those down—

"You can check all the tire stores on the island in case these were bought as replacements," Paul said.

"My thought exactly," Ed Shaw nodded.

"Ed? Can you find gainful employment for Annie and Natalia Tiemerovna? They're experienced and they work great together as a team," Rourke said.

"Sure can. Certain sections of Honolulu have more extensive immigrant populations. If these people are trying to blend in with the general population, that's the logical place for us to start looking."

Rourke was lighting one of his cigars, managing it easily despite the wind. "The one thing we shouldn't do," he said, exhaling smoke, "is make ourselves any more obvious than we have to be. Our adversaries will be wary at any event; no sense putting them even more on guard for us."

"We'll be real discreet," Ed Shaw grinned, " 'til we bust in and nail their asses."

15

The purpose of a terrorist act, over and above its tactical objective—a bombing, a robbery, an assassination—was always and always would be to instill terror. That fundamental principle was drummed into Wilhelm Doring's head from the very first that he volunteered for the Sicherheitsdienst, the Security Service of the SS, the Schutzstaffel. His uniform, which he proudly wore on those rare occasions these days when he did not work undercover, bore both the runic lightning bolts of SS and the rounded hooked letters of the SD.

Proud as he was of his uniform, he took more pride in his work; and, he was especially prideful that, with less than twelve hours on Oahu and two men wounded, he would make his first strike.

To instill terror, make fear a constant in the lives of those who were its targets, to replace reasoned response with outraged reaction, it was necessary to strike without warning against a target no one would ever think to harden. It was for this reason that Herr Stroud's van, Gunther at the wheel, was now turning the corner into the parking lot for the Sebastian's Reef Country Day School.

The children of many of the higher-ranking officers at Pearl Harbor Naval Base, along with the children of various of the islands' officials in government, those of business leaders and the otherwise prominent attended this school. The children of a few of the islands' prominent Jews attended this school as well, and that was all the better. Doring had studied the history of terrorism, from its earliest records until the days immediately prior to

The Night of The War. Men of lesser inspiration and vision would have assaulted the school, then held its occupants hostage against some sort of impossible list of demands, then attempted an escape.

Wilhelm Doring had no demands.

His objective was terror, not getting an aircraft or large sums of money, or having some manifesto or another read on television.

The van stopped in a slot near the main entrance of the school, a smallish sign in front of the parking position reading "Visitor." The second van, its occupants local Nazi sympathizers, sincere enough in their devotion to the cause but an undisciplined, explosively violent lot according to the reports he'd been given, pulled up beside them.

Doring stepped out, pulling his hood down over his face, snapping it into position so the eye and mouth holes were properly aligned. The volunteers were already exiting their vehicle, coming round to stand between the vehicles. Doring spoke to these eight and the eight men with him who were part of his unit. "You know our mission. Shoot as many outright as you can, then utilize the explosives. We require as many dead as is possible. Understood?"

There were nods, grunted words of assent. Some of the volunteers from the second van murmured obscene remarks which were at once unprofessional and out of place. But Doring said, "Good." Doring flexed his shoulders out of the raincoat, threw the garment back into the van and strode out across the blacktopped surface of the lot. The late morning felt cool to those small portions of exposed skin remaining beneath the hood. A breeze was blowing in nicely off the ocean. Just beyond the parking lot and a stand of palms, the surf could be heard.

Doring slipped his energy rifle forward on its sling.

Doring's own seven men closed in around him, the eighth man (the driver) would wait. They hooded themselves. There were clicking sounds as they checked their weapons.

Doring looked toward the school building. A little girl stared out from the window of a lower grade classroom, where construction paper cutouts of multicolored birds were plastered to the glass.

Doring turned the muzzle of his weapon toward the window and the little girl who still stared at him from behind it.

Doring opened fire . . .

Tim Shaw's hand dropped the dash radio. Although late fifties wasn't anywhere near chronologically old these days (people were routinely working well into their eighties and living past the century mark and still thriving), some things made him feel old. The "All Cars" that was just broadcast shocked him so much that he dropped one of the dashboard radios from his hand. It would have made him feel old if he'd been twenty. Patrolman Linda Wallace, her normally chocolate brown skin gone grey, gripped her hands tighter on the wheel of the car. She muttered, "What kind of bastards would—"

Shaw snarled, "Turn the fuckin' car around. Now! Excuse my language." Shaw picked up the radio set from the floor between his legs and snapped "One Echo Twelve responding. Get every damn unit you can scrounge over to that school fast. I mean fast!" He snapped the radio back into its dashboard receptacle.

If he ever changed professions and started robbing banks, Linda had a job. Linda was a good "wheelman"; she had the unmarked squad car out of the J-Turn and going against inbound Honolulu traffic along Jacob Fellows Boulevard before Tim Shaw could wrap his fist around the grab handle. And she knew her stuff, lights only, no siren. When they were almost parallel to the next intersection, she honked the horn a few times and got them through, into the outbound lanes where they belonged.

"How quick to Sebastian's Reef Country Day, Linda?"

"Two minutes, Inspector."

"Make it a minute and a half," Shaw told her. He reached across to the rack between them; there was an energy rifle there. "When we hit the scene, you use this; I never liked these things but you're a good shot with one of 'em."

Shaw reached into the outside pocket of his black raincoat,

found the butt of his revolver, pulled the gun and checked the cylinder. The cruiser's electric motor was humming more loudly than he'd ever heard it before, but he didn't look to the dashboard panel to see if over-rev warning lights were flashing; Linda knew what she was doing and hadn't trashed a car yet, he reminded himself. This gun, like the rest of his firearms, was a Lancer reproduction; if he could have found the originals he couldn't have afforded them anyway on a cop's salary and the Lancers were so faithful that without their distinctive logo on each part, even a collector wouldn't have been able to tell the difference. This one was a Smith & Wesson Model 640, the Centennial with enclosed hammer in stainless steel, but with three-inch barrel. Loaded with 158-grain Lead Hollow Point Plus Ps, it was devastating up close and, despite the fact it was double action only, decently accurate at longer ranges too.

Shaw closed the cylinder and shoved the revolver back into his raincoat pocket.

They were turning into Sebastian's Reef now, the huge, expensive houses and fenced mini-estates going past them on either side in a blur. "Slow it down just enough so we don't wind up driving into something, Linda."

"Right, boss!"

The slipstream around them coupled with the breeze coming off the sea tore at Shaw's face. He screwed his black fedora down tighter to his head. People, mostly women, some servants, were running from the houses, some of them armed. There were sounds of explosions in the distance.

"About twenty seconds and we'll be turning into the parking lot, Inspector."

"You block the exit, then use that energy rifle, but get the hell back somewhere in case they wanna try out their explosives on a police car; don't be a hero." Shaw reached to his waist, pulling the stainless steel Colt Government Model .45 from where he habitually nested it, butt outward, between his right hip bone and his navel. He thumbed back the hammer, squeezed the slide rearward a hair, press-checking to verify the loaded chamber, then raised the safety.

As the cruiser rounded the corner, the rolling grounds of Sebastian's Reef Country Day spread out before them beyond a high, black, wrought iron fence. Palm trees swayed rhythmically, flowers bloomed everywhere. The gates to the school were opened. As they sped past along the driveway, Shaw caught no glimpse of a damaged lock or any sign of forced entry. "Just left the damn gates wide open."

As they rounded a curve in the driveway, Shaw could at last see the main building itself, flames licking upward hungrily against the bright blue of the cloudless sky. There were two vans visible in the parking lot to the far right of the building, one of them already in motion. "Stick with 'em, Linda; lemme out now!"

Linda cut the wheel hard left, the cruiser fishtailing for a split second on the gravel, then whiplashing left, the rear end skidding forward and right in a cloud of gravel and dirt. The instant the car stopped, Tim Shaw threw open the door and was out, slamming it behind him as Linda accelerated and he averted his eyes from the gravel spray, feeling the rocks pelting at him through his raincoat. The first of the two vans sped toward them, bearing down on him. Neither gun he carried was suited to stopping a vehicle, but they were both well-suited to stopping men.

Energy rifles opened fire at him from the open side door of the van. Shaw dumped four rounds from the .45 into the opening, a body tumbling out as the ground on both sides of him exploded as the plasma bolts struck.

Shaw dropped like a stone, rolling onto his left side and firing out the last three rounds. He used the old-style seven-round magazines, not the eight-round magazines brought into vogue for the big old Colt shortly Before The Night of the War; and, he observed the old gunfighter's dictum of loading from the magazine, resisting going for an eighth round.

One bullet at least struck the safety glass in the rear window of the van and spiderwebbed it.

Linda wheeled the cruiser into the driveway and was in pursuit.

Shaw was up to one knee, made a tactical magazine change for the .45 and thumbed down the slide release as he got fully to his feet. "Too old for this shit!" Shaw rasped through his teeth. But he could still run the hundred as well as the average department recruit, and the trousers from his Marine Corps uniform of better than twenty years ago still fit when he inhaled. He reminded himself of all of that as he ran along the driveway.

The second van was in motion now, starting out of the parking slot, wheeling into a tire-screeching reverse.

But electric cars could only do so much from a standing start.

Shaw was into the near edge of the parking lot now and he ran toward the first car, one of the German jobs from Argentina, so lightweight it sideslipped in a good crosswind. The body was synth-glass resin, he knew, but the engine block was steel. Shaw dropped beside the right front wheelwell, the block and the suspension system and the tire itself were all that would protect him.

As the van picked up speed, Tim Shaw punched the Colt up, bracing it on the synth-glass resin right front fender. It nearly buckled under the force of his arms. He fired, two rounds, then two more, then two more, all aimed for the center of the van's windshield over the driver's face. The first two rounds made the windshield spiderweb, the next two shattered the synth-glass, and the last two nailed the driver as the van started to swerve.

The van struck the curb edging the parking lot and bounced over it, tearing across the grass, through a flower bed, then stopping dead against the trunk of a palm tree. The van's synth-fuel load exploded, Shaw tucking back, the pressure wave blowing his black fedora from his head.

Five men piled out, a sixth man falling from the passenger side of the front seat, clothing aflame.

Tim Shaw made a tactical magazine change, eight rounds in the .45 now including the one that was left in the chamber. Under different circumstances, he would have run up to the man who was on fire, attempted to extinguish the flames. There was no chance for that now and he didn't even have the inclination to give the man a mercy shot—Shaw had his last loaded magazine up the well of the Colt.

Two of the five men fired energy weapons toward him, one of the plasma bolts striking the hood of the little German car behind which he crouched. The car vibrated with the impact, blue static charge flowing across the bumper, the only exposed part that was at least partially steel.

Shaw, still in a crouch, edged back, the .45 shifted to his left hand, the three-inch barreled Smith .38 Special in his right. He punched the .38 and the .45 forward simultaneously, firing each once, taking down one of the two men firing at him. The other three staggered away, offering no resistance.

The second man fired again, the ground beside Shaw's feet seeming to explode as the energy bolt struck.

Shaw dodged right, ran forward. As the man swung the muzzle of his energy rifle, Shaw fired both guns, then fired them again and again, drilling the man down to the ground.

Two rounds in the little .38 and five in the .45.

Shaw ran past the man he'd just shot, past the man who was screaming while he burned to death, not a bullet to waste on him.

Two of the other three were running, the third man stumbling, falling, picking up his energy rifle to fire. As Shaw got in easy range, he stabbed the .45 toward the man and fired, putting a bullet into the man's head, bone chips, blood and brains spraying out the other side. "Lucky shot for me, asshole!" Shaw shouted, running on.

The two who were trying to escape were nearly into the trees and Shaw stopped. The nearer of the two threw down his weapon and raised his hands. "I give up, man!"

"Wait here!" Shaw kneecapped him with the .38 and the man fell to the ground screaming. Shaw ran forward, snarling "Son of a bitch!" Shaw kicked the energy weapon away with his right foot, slammed the .45 across the top of the man's head with his left hand.

One man left, running into the trees and a man who'd talk if he wanted painkillers for the knee.

This last guy was dead but didn't know it.

Shaw sprinted after him into the trees, one round left in the .38, four in the .45.

The thing about energy weapons was that they telegraphed their shots. Shaw heard the crackle and threw himself flat as the trunk of the palm tree nearest to him took a hit and slivers of bark flew everywhere. Shaw was up, cutting left through the trees.

He could see fleeting glimpses of movement now as the last of the men dodged through the trees and toward the sand and the surf beyond. Shaw fired the .45, ripping out a chunk from the trunk of a palm near the man but not hitting his target. "Serves me right for usin' my left—shit!" Shaw ran forward, trying to look to his right for his quarry and look down for his footing. He tripped, caught himself, kept running.

As Shaw neared the far edge of the treeline, he saw the last man—and the man saw him. The man wheeled toward him, spraying plasma energy bolts toward Shaw across the sand. Shaw fired, then fired again, his second round from the .45 catching the man in the crotch. The man fell, but still fired his energy rifle. Shaw fired the last round from the .45, into the man's upper body between the right shoulder and the neck.

The energy rifle flew from the last man's hands and his body slumped back into the sand.

Shaw, the .45 locked open and empty in his left hand, started forward, ramming the pistol into his belt. Shaw reached with his left hand into his trousers for the little Seecamp DA .32 auto he carried in a pocket holster.

A gun in each hand, Shaw came up from the last man's injured right side. The man shouted, "You can't kill me, mother fucker! You're a cop! You figure I'll talk or somethin'. Hitler forever, man! Sieg Heil!"

Shaw dropped to one knee beside the man, raising the muzzle of the little .38 revolver toward the man's left temple. Shaw smiled. "I've already got somebody who'll sing better than you could, asswipe. Heil Hitler? Fuck Hitler! And you too." Shaw averted his eyes from the coming blood spray and double-actioned the .38's trigger.

16

Whoever this fellow was behind the wheel of the police car which had followed them ever since leaving the school compound, he was the best driver Wilhelm Doring had ever seen.

No matter the speed, no matter the turn or twist in the highway—they moved along a coastal road with hairpin curves so tight that at times Doring felt certain they would go over the side and crash on the rocks below—the pursuit car maintained a constant distance of approximately one hundred meters.

The scanning monitor set under the dashboard of the van was locking onto every imaginable law enforcement and police frequency. The Honolulu Tac Team was en route. In a matter of moments, helicopters and additional police vehicles would close on them. As if it were an omen of this, a remotely piloted video drone swept over the highway, crossing toward them. Doring took up his energy rifle and fired at it, missing, firing again, missing again. But the drone pulled back.

At last, the van turned onto a straightaway.

Doring looked into the back of the van. Hans, whose face was a mass of blood from a wound sustained when the plainclothes policeman had fired through the rear windshield, knelt beside the still-closed rear door of the van. "Are you ready, Hans?"

"I await your order, Willy!"

Doring turned around, looked at the road ahead, straightaway for another half-mile. He turned his head to his left, ordering, "Bring the vehicle to a complete but controlled stop on my command!"

"Yes, Willy."

"Hans, be ready!"

"Yes!"

Doring looked at Gunther Brach. "Stop now!" Then he shouted to Hans, the vehicle already slowing dramatically, the brakes squealing, "Fire!"

Doring twisted around in his seat. The doors at the rear of the van flew open outward. The flamethrower Hans fired was pneumatically powered and under such pressure that it could project a tongue of burning synth-fuel more than one hundred meters against a wind of up to fifteen knots.

At the moment the burning synth-fuel struck the hood and windshield of the police car, Doring stepped all the way out through the passenger-side door and onto the road surface. He brought the 40mm grenade launcher which had been between his legs up to his shoulder. He fired, then fired again and again.

Flames already engulfed the police car, making a rushing, crackling sound on the wind. And now the explosions from the detonating grenades bracketed the vehicle. Doring shifted the grenade launcher to his left hand, clicked his heels and saluted his dead adversary, a worthy opponent.

"Drive!" Doring shouted, slamming the passenger-side door shut. The van was already moving. He threw down the 40mm grenade launcher, retook his energy rifle, firing through the open window toward the video drone. But the little machine bobbed and weaved and evaded his fire. "Hans—the flamethrower. Hit the drone!"

"Yes, Willy!"

The doors at the rear of the van were still open, and Hans raised the nozzle from the flamethrower and fired. Doring looked away, shouldered his energy rifle again, firing toward the drone, forcing it toward the tongue of flame rising toward it.

As the drone banked away and Hans fired again, flame and drone met and there was a fireball as synth-fuel within the drone's tanks exploded.

"It is good!" Hans shouted.

"Quickly! Away from here," Willy ordered.

And then he started to laugh . . .

The video drone was police operated, and through its eye Tim

Shaw and two uniformed police officers had just seen Linda's car destroyed, Linda inside it.

It seemed only a second later that the drone itself was targeted and the picture was totally lost.

Tim Shaw stalked away toward the trees. He'd only had a few seconds to look inside the school before the arriving fire and emergency personnel had forced him out of their way. In one classroom alone there were fourteen dead children, the bodies of some of them still smoldering from energy bursts at what must have been point-blank range.

Shaw took off his hat. He turned his face toward the incoming wind off the sea. He leaned heavily against a palm tree, the heel of his right hand hammering against its trunk.

The little kids. Patrolman Linda Wallace.

His entire body shook with rage.

"Fuckin' Nazi bastards," Tim Shaw hissed, the tears spilling from his eyes and onto his cheeks.

17

She hadn't expected to see John Rourke, or maybe she had and that was really the reason why she'd come in the first place, why she stopped to change out of her jeans and into a sundress. Emma Shaw had no trouble getting through the police lines around Sebastian's Reef Country Day School; she'd been showing up at police investigations ever since she was a little girl and her mother died and sometimes her father had no place to leave her.

Emma Shaw was careful where she put her sandaled feet, picking her way around puddles of water, over lines of interwoven fire hose and splotches of foamy white chemical residues from fire-extinguishing equipment.

She'd seen her first dead body—aside from the ones kids always saw at funerals and her mother's dead body, of course—when she was twelve. No one had wanted her to see it, least of all her father. The call had come in late at night and her brother, Ed, was off visiting a friend and spending the night there. She'd made a pathetic little dinner for her father, which he'd made a great show of enjoying (he must have had the toughest stomach in the world in those days, she'd often thought since), and he'd just put her to bed when he knocked, came back into her room. "Hey, kid, I gotta check out a crime scene. Can ya stick right close to me and don't touch a thing?"

"Sure, daddy!"

"Pull some clothes on, fast."

The crime scene turned out to be a bar over in the immigrant section and the body she saw kind of spilled out of a synth-fuel drum someone was using as a garbage can. She'd never had bad dreams about the corpse, but she'd never forgotten it either: all grey-faced and bloodstained and the left eyesocket empty and a knife sticking out of the dead man's throat.

That was in the days when her father worked homicide, before he'd transferred to, then been asked to run the Honolulu Tac Team.

Her father, Tim Shaw, his hat low over his eyes, stood talking with John Rourke beside an ambulance that was already filled with black synth-rubber body bags.

But none of the bags seemed filled all the way from top to bottom and, with a sickening feeling in her stomach, she realized the bodies of children were inside.

Her father stood five foot nine and was a heavy man, barrel-chested and broad-shouldered, not fat. Beside John Rourke, who was well over six feet tall and seemed as trim and fit as a professional athlete, he looked short. But Tim Shaw still looked like he could lick his weight in lions with both hands tied behind his back. And Emma Shaw knew that her father could do just that if he had to because, figuratively speaking, he'd done it lots of times before. She went up to her father and as he turned around, noticing her, she put her hands on his shoulders and kissed him lightly on the lips. She took a step back, looked at John.

"Hiya, kid," her father said, forcing a little smile which faded almost instantly.

"I heard. As bad as they say?" Emma asked him.

John Rourke answered. "Worse, I'd imagine, since we don't have a final body count yet. At least eighty-three dead children so far and about fifteen adults."

"I thought you were on leave?"

Emma Shaw looked at her father, smiled, said, "I am. Can't you see?" She stuck both hands into the patch pockets of her dress and took a step back flaring its skirt as she did so. "Civvies." She let the smile leave, since there was nothing to smile about. "You get 'em?"

"You should have somethin' better to do than come here, Emma," he told her.

"I heard you were in a gunfight, so—" she left it hang.

"Half of 'em got away, okay? Killed Linda while she was pursuin'." He lit a cigarette, murmuring, "Fuckin' Nazis," under his breath.

"Did someone tell her mother?"

"That's what I'm about to do," Tim Shaw said, shaking his head and walking away.

"Come on, I'll take you for a walk," John suggested.

She let him take her elbow and start propelling her toward the palm trees and the surf beyond. There were evidence technicians working in the area, some of them people she knew who nodded to her or said "Hi" and then went back to their grim work. "Why did they do this?" Emma Shaw asked.

"Just to do it," John Rourke told her. "It was a good target for a certain type of terrorist, the kind who doesn't care about public image, just wants results. The children of some of the ranking military officers in the islands attend here, the children of a lot of the islands' social elite go here, and there was no security. It was perfect for them. They just went through and systematically shot to death everyone they could, then set explosives. If your father and the dead police officer hadn't arrived on the scene, more might be dead.

"Many of the campus's buildings were destroyed and every one was at least partially damaged. The smell from the fires was still heavy on the air in those brief instances when the breeze off the sea subsided.

"At least, thank God, there was a field trip today," John went on. "About a hundred and twenty children were away for the day visiting the Arizona monument; it could have been a lot worse."

"Dad'll get them."

"Your father took out an entire van load of the men by himself with just a couple of handguns. He's a brave man. You should be proud of him."

"I am," Emma said, nodding, "but that doesn't mean I want him risking his neck like that. He could have contained them and waited for backup."

"Possibly. Would you have?"

She felt the corners of her mouth beginning to rise in an involuntary smile. "Of course not." She lowered her eyes, watched her toes as she walked beside him.

"I rest my case," John told her as they started onto the beach. As if it were something he'd rehearsed, he said to her, "I had a nice time last night, by the way. Thanks for having me over. I must have seemed, well, awkward," he said. "Not that I was ever terrific at social functions, but I haven't had much occasion over the years to relax."

"You were fine," she said, without thinking. She licked her lips.

They were walking down toward the surf, and she wondered why he'd brought her here. Then he began to speak again, "You should be careful on your own, might even want to cut your leave short."

"I don't understand."

"This could be the group of Nazis that penetrated the island early this morning; and, if it is, that means they're quite efficient. It would only be logical for them to try to strike back at the police officer who killed their compatriots. You'd be a logical target. Do you travel armed?"

The idea was quite unsettling, that she might be a target for vengeance-minded terrorists. She swallowed, patted her purse, said, "Lancer 2570 A2 Compact right here. Same thing a lot of the Honolulu PD, Tac Team and SEAL guys use."

"A lot of the Tac and SEAL people use .45s, too. Like your father."

"I've got a .45."

"Good. Keep the Lancer handy if you need a high volume of fire; it's a great gun, even if it wasn't available in my day," John told her, smiling a little. "But you might want to have the .45 handy, too. I'm prejudiced, of course. A good 9mm Parabellum round is just about as effective in terminal ballistics as a .45 ACP, but I've always liked a bigger bullet. The point is, you're vulnerable, especially off base. So, be careful."

Even though Emma Shaw knew she should feel warm with the sun on her bare shoulders, she suddenly felt very cold. When she shivered, John put his arm around her shoulders, but he said nothing more.

18

Croenberg studied his own visage in the airliner's bathroom mirror. His normally deepset grey-blue eyes looked back at him a watery brown (contact lenses) and not so deeply set at all because of the makeup on his face. He wore a steel grey wig that was literally taped to his cleanshaven scalp beneath. The suit that he wore – pale blue – was cut tightly at the shoulders and subtly padded near the waist to help disguise both his height and his physique, making him appear shorter, stoop-shouldered and slightly potbellied. Current men's fashion made the look even easier, because jackets and trouser legs were tighter.

Croenberg checked the glued-on mustache – it was secure – and replaced the glasses. The glasses, a mild prescription and not just ordinary window glass, gave him a headache, but were necessary. He wore prosthetics of course, as well, to aid in altering his appearance, and these were uncomfortable. It was a long airplane ride from New Moscow in the Ural Mountains to Honolulu, better than an hour. In the days prior to orbital insertion flight, hundreds of years ago, air travel must have been even more maddening because of the protracted times involved.

The prostheses which fattened his cheeks beneath the makeup made the real skin beneath itch; that and the prosthesis under his shirt and trousers, covering his abdomen, which further enhanced the image of being potbellied made him perspire.

But prosthetic fingerprints alone would not have been enough to get him through United States customs passing himself off as Boris Luvov, agricultural researcher from Russia. The faces of most major figures in the SS were well-known, that of SS Gruppenführer Ernst Croenberg particularly so. And everywhere in the nations of the Trans-Global Alliance, security personnel would be watching for him and the others of the kameraden, ready to arrest or kill on sight.

Croenberg left the restroom, returned to his seat and buckled in. The sky was clear and all he could see below the aircraft as it descended was the blue of the sky and the water. Soon, the islands themselves would be visible, the foam-crested surf lapping against perfect white sandy beaches.

Paradise—to some, but only for a little while longer.

Wilhem Doring watched the television, sipped at the coffee from the cup Marie had given him.

The camera panned—in what seemed an almost sexual fascination with the wreckage of the second van—over the body-bagged men who had been its occupants. Then there was a cut, and a heavyset but fit-looking man in his fifties became the focus of attention. He wore a narrow-brimmed, high-crowned hat, the front of the brim turned down and the hat low over his eyes.

In the eyes, there was a look Doring had seen often, the look of the wolf.

This man was identified as Inspector Tim Shaw, head of the Honolulu Tac Team, who singlehandedly shot it out with the terrorists who attacked Sebastian's Reef Country Day School. This one man had killed all the occupants of the van except one, whom he "subdued."

This one—Doring bet that it was Fletcher, who had seemed the least dependable of the volunteers from the Islands—was expected to provide the police with valuable information concerning the occupants of the second van, who escaped after taking the life of Patrolman Linda Wallace.

They showed a picture of the woman, and Doring was frankly amazed that any woman, particularly one from an inferior race, could have driven as well as she did. Although she looked dark-skinned, she was probably quite mongrelized, Doring guessed, and that accounted for her skillfulness and daring.

"Can I get you more coffee, Willy?"

"No," he replied.

"What can I get you?"

"Nothing." He would get what he wanted himself, and that was to make this Inspector Tim Shaw pay dearly.

19

The man whom James Darkwood had replaced at Plant 234 — Wilbur Nash — was a quality control inspector, which made it all the easier for Darkwood to move about the plant without attracting undue attention. A quality control inspector went about inspecting for quality, and that meant looking over shoulders. There were, however, places within the plant that Nash, whom Darkwood impersonated, was not authorized to enter. Only the highest grades of security clearance were given admission there, and then only as required.

These were the places to which James Darkwood most earnestly required access.

These were the chemical mixing rooms.

It was further to Darkwood's advantage that he only needed to rely on the efficacy of the makeup with which he'd disguised his appearance up to a certain point, the makeup enabling him to make a near-perfect match to Wilbur Nash for the initial entry to the plant. After passing through a robing station barely fifty feet inside the plant entrance, all personnel here wore protective clothing which covered them from head to toe, this over their regular outer garments.

The tricky part, if James Darkwood survived that long, would be leaving the plant, because although the original facial similarity to Wilbur Nash was strong, they were nothing alike in body shape and Darkwood was taller. Again, he would be relying on the average person's lack of recognition of detail. If he was expected to be Wilbur Nash, people would see him as Wilbur Nash, unless something occurred to cause them to view him differently.

If someone who knew Nash intimately saw James Darkwood, the game would be up.

But Darkwood's immediate concern occupied most of his thoughts for now, and that was how to gain access to the chemical mixing rooms without raising some sort of alarm.

And, try as he might, he could think of no way of doing that. But access had to be gained. An entire Allied fighter group stood by, waiting for the data Darkwood could only learn by entering one of the mixing rooms. If biological agents were being produced there to be borne in chemical weapons, then Plant 234 had to be bombed out of existence. But, if they were not, the potential cost to the fighter group from Eden City's state-of-the-art antiaircraft defenses could not be justified.

For more than a year, there had been cryptic suggestions in intelligence data that Eden scientists had discovered a way of combining chemical and biological warfare methodology in a way never before attempted. Bio warfare, historically, was inefficient in the airborne context, with the potential for either covering vast and unpredictable expanses on errant winds or settling almost immediately to the ground. Furthermore, in the modern era, it was fast and relatively easy to produce massive quantities of inoculant against a specific disease or combination of diseases.

The frightening potential, if Eden possessed the rumored technology, was that chemical carriers would support the biological agent, releasing it in timed doses; and, over this period of time, the chemical carrier would act upon the biological agent, mutating it in unpredictable variations which could not be inoculated against. Some of the chemical carriers were lighter than air, hence would remain airborne for a considerably longer period of time, while some were comprised of heavier elements and would immediately fall to earth, hence again the unpredictability.

Such a bio warfare attack could not effectively be fought, so it had to be countered before it was launched.

Yet the compound in which Plant 234 was set, was placed in the center of one of Eden City's poorest and most populated areas. Precision hits would be required to prevent an attack on the plant from turning into a bloodbath of the innocent.

Throughout the first half of Wilbur Nash's shift, James Darkwood went about the mechanics of Nash's job, at the same time trying to discern what bits and snatches of useful intelligence data he could, but his thoughts were chiefly focused on what he should do. By the time the lunch break came, he had made up his mind.

20

Almost everyone at the airport was armed, it seemed, the private citizens with handguns discreetly holstered at their sides or poorly disguised beneath shirts left out of the trousers, the security personnel with energy rifles slung under their arms and Lancer 9mm caseless pistols or the somewhat more cumbersome energy pistols in security holsters at their waists.

Croenberg despised the American society which flowed around him; when citizens were armed, they were impossible to control. Superior military force could subdue them in large numbers, of course – guns were no match for tanks and missiles and gunships – but as long as there were arms there would be underground resistance, attacking from within. All of the successful dictatorships of history had begun by disarming the citizenry; such action was an indisputable prerequisite to subjugation.

Croenberg walked on, eager to get away from the terminal, to make his rendezvous.

Over the last forty-eight hours, his own handpicked team of SS personnel had infiltrated Hawaii singly or in pairs on a succession of commercial flights originating in Europe, twenty-four men in all. And the operation was totally sterile, unknown to the Wilhelm Doring unit which was doubtless responsible for the massacre at the school, about which he'd heard while watching televised newsbroadcasts from Hawaii; it was also independent of the larger, less specialized commando teams which had already penetrated or soon would penetrate the islands.

He called this specialized unit of twenty-four the Sigma Group.

The task for which he had quietly and hastily assembled them was vital to the success of National Socialism: "rescue" Martin Zimmer from Pearl Harbor Naval Base, then very quietly kill him . . .

Emma Shaw locked the door as soon as she was inside. She always locked her door before bed, of course, whenever she stayed at her little house; but, frequently, the door was unlocked throughout the day and well into the night. She had never thought about it before.

She kept her purse with her instead of setting it down as she went about her house from room to room, making certain that no one lurked in a closet, or for that matter even hid under her bed.

By the time Emma Shaw was through and satisfied that her home was unoccupied except for herself, she felt at once satisfied and silly. Still carrying her purse with the gun in it slung from her shoulder, she went to the bedroom closet and got down the box in which she kept what she sought.

She raised the lid and looked inside, There were several objects wrapped in rags. She unwrapped the largest of them. Beneath the wrappings was a .45 automatic, a stainless steel Colt identical to the one her father carried, given to her, in fact, by her father.

Wrapped in a second bundle were three spare magazines. Still a third bundle contained three more. There were two plastic boxes of ammunition, containing one hundred rounds each.

The gun would need cleaning, lubrication. She hadn't fired it, even touched it in more than a year. She could take it out back of the house and put a few rounds through it just to make certain she could still hit what she aimed at with the pistol.

With his talk of Nazi revenge, John Rourke had scared her silly.

21

There was the possibility he might be missed at lunch, that Wilbur Nash might habitually eat with a circle of friends, albeit Plant 234 did not seem much like a friendly place. On the other hand, in a short while, all ordinary plant routine would be disrupted. Then it wouldn't matter.

The chemical mixing rooms were at the center of the Plant structure, the building itself taking up two entire square blocks of Eden City, the roadway going around the facility. The building's shape, when seen in aerial photographs, was that of an impossibly large rectangle, flat-roofed and grey, like a depression in the ground on which the city itself was built, encircled on all sides by higher structures. To the north, those were the residential apartments where the higher-level employees such as Wilbur Nash lived; to the south those structures were dormitories where the factory labor slept, showered, ate. It could hardly be called living.

To the east were the loading docks and beyond those and a parking lot for trucks and cargo helicopters was the perimeter.

There was a fence nine feet high and surmounted by razor wire. This fence contained the entire facility, which occupied, including Plant 234, four square blocks. And to the west lay the metals shops, the plastics facilities and storage warehouses.

Plant 234, built on one level only, at its highest point was perhaps fourteen feet above the ground. Within the structure there were tunnels rather than corridors, allowing workers and higher-level personnel to move from one area of the plant to another without having the slightest idea what went on around them.

James Darkwood moved through one such tunnel now. There had

been a guard at the end of the tunnel, armed only with an alarm device, weaponless. James Darkwood, without a drug kit by means of which he could have rendered the man temporarily unconscious, was forced to kill the guard rather than risk having the fellow awaken and alert plant security.

Plant security personnel, dressed in voluminous black coveralls and black hooded facemasks, were indeed armed. Supervisory personnel, as Darkwood pretended to be, wore white, while laborers wore blue. Prisoners were rumored to be used here as test subjects. Darkwood absently wondered what color they wore.

Darkwood moved slowly along the tunnel toward Mixing Room Nine, hot, perspiring inside his protective clothing, smelling his own body odor; fear always smelled.

At the midpoint in the tunnel there was a ladder leading upward to a hatch, presumably set into the roof. Darkwood glanced behind him and ahead. There was no one in the tunnel, so he took the gamble. He climbed up the ladder, as carefully as he could, considering the dim ambient lighting, inspecting the hatch for any signs of linkage to an alarm system. As best he could determine, there was nothing.

Looking down first, he fixed his attention on the hatch, starting to wheel open the lock. The hatch, the tunnel itself, all served to remind him of a submarine. He shook off the thoughts, concentrating on his work.

After more than a full minute, he had the hatch unlocked. Once more inspecting both visually and by feel for signs of an alarm system and having the same happily negative results, James Darkwood very gently pushed upward on the hatch. It gave without resistance and with very little noise. He let the hatch lower into position.

Then Darkwood started down the ladder.

Back into the tunnel, James Darkwood walked on, toward Mixing Room Nine.

22

The City of Honolulu was like a glittering jewel, new and shining under the afternoon sun. There were private automobiles everywhere and the only personnel in military uniforms seemed obviously off duty. There was the occasional police car, the occasional remote video drone flying over the street to monitor for traffic accidents.

But, there was no security.

"You know," Croenberg said to the man who drove him, a particularly reliable young Untersturmführer, "considering that the Americans must know something of which Eden is about, I marvel that life merely goes on here."

The Untersturmführer—his name was Helmut Kraus—wheeled the electric car into a right turn off the boulevard along which they'd driven since leaving the airport and into a street with denser traffic. "It is like this everywhere, Herr Gruppenführer. We will crush them."

"Yes, my young friend, but first the matter for which we have all come here needs taking care of, does it not? Eden's leader and our inspiration must be freed from his jailers. Who knows what evil these Americans might plan for young Martin Zimmer at the moment we attack?"

"Yes, Herr Gruppenführer, this is true."

"You and your fellows have verified the details of the plan?"

"Yes, Herr Gruppenführer. The proper uniforms are secured, the vehicles, all is in readiness. Even as we drive to the temporary headquarters, the identity papers are being remanufactured so they will be fresh, not yet reported as stolen. We will strike, Herr Gruppenführer, tonight at the customary dinner hour for personnel of the Pearl Harbor base."

"It is good," Croenberg remarked . . .

111

Michael Rourke freed his arm almost immediately from the sling he'd had to wear when he left the hospital. The cut was already partially healed and there was very little soreness. Fortunately, the knife he'd stopped was both clean and very sharp.

Natalia walked silently beside him as they reached the beach. He'd asked her to stop the car, parking along the shoulder so he could get out and stretch his legs. A strong wind blew in from the sea and, despite the heat of the sun, the air temperature seemed quite pleasant and cool. "Were you ever in Hawaii, Natalia?"

"What? Before The Night of The War? No. Never. It is very beautiful."

"Yes. People used to refer to Hawaii as Paradise—I can see why. Boy, if Adam and Eve got kicked out of a place like this, told they could never return—" He didn't finish the thought. Instead he took Natalia's left hand in his right and they walked across the sand. Natalia was barefoot, holding her sandals in her other hand.

"The sun feels good," Natalia remarked. "I remember going to the Black Sea a lot with my uncle when I was a little girl. I wish you could have known Uncle Ishmael, Michael. He was so kind and good and strong."

"From what my father has said about your uncle, I think dad took a liking to him from the first."

"He was a soldier, you know?" Natalia went on. "And he had his duty as a patriotic Russian, and he did it well. But he never lost sight of his humanity. That came first and he shaped his sense of duty around that."

"I think he was a pretty good surrogate father, too," Michael told her, letting go of her hand and putting his arm around her shoulders. Natalia leaned her head against his chest. "You were lucky to have him."

"Michael?"

"Yes?"

"When this is all over, can we just go somewhere? Anywhere, even one of the out islands, but just the two of us?"

"Sure we can, sure," Michael said to her, touching his lips to her hair. It was soft, and smelled like fresh flowers. He stopped walking and so did Natalia. He turned her around to face her. He raised her chin and looked her in the eye. "I love you. Want to marry me?"

"Uh-huh," Natalia whispered, then just leaned her head against his chest again, her arms limp at her sides . . .

"Your drivin' gives me the creeps," Tim Shaw told his son, Ed.

"Why? You taught me how to drive when I was a kid! You always said I was a good driver."

"No, it's not the way you drive; it's what happened to the last person who drove me. Pull up over here."

Shaw's son, Shaw's own second-in-command in the Honolulu Tac Team, was the best police officer Tim Shaw had ever worked with. When Ed's slot came open, Tim Shaw wrestled long and hard with putting him into it, however, because it would look like nepotism. For a while, after Ed was in the job and just getting settled, there had been some talk of that, a father putting his son into a better-paying more responsible position that would eventually lead to the son's taking over the father's job when the father someday retired.

But once Ed proved himself in the job, the talk stopped.

Tim Shaw was proud of that – that Ed had made the talk stop by just doing his job better than anybody else could.

Ed cut off the engine.

Tim Shaw picked up a radio unit, spoke into it, "Give call sign. Leaving the car at Fifth and Mauna Kea. Shaw and Shaw Out." He dropped the radio set into the left hand pocket of his raincoat (his revolver was in the right pocket) and stepped out of the car. Ed was already out on the street side. Along Mauna Kea Drive, for a half-mile in either direction from where they stood, was the immigrant section of Honolulu, a self-made ghetto. Most immigrants to the islands – and there were thousands of them each year – made a place for themselves, got decent jobs, good housing. But there were some – like the ones surrounding Fifth and Mauna Kea – who brought their old lives in the reforestation camps of Brazil, in the tent villages of France, in the Reactionist communities of Russia, and all the ills of everywhere else, and they lived the same way they always had.

Volunteer charitable organizations, church groups, everybody and his brother tried making Fifth and Mauna Kea and what surrounded it just an unpleasant memory by stretching out a helping hand; but not too many here took helping hands; they would rather cut them off.

Mauna Kea Drive was, aside from being the most dangerous part of Honolulu, almost as much a tourist mecca as Waikiki. Every street leading off Mauna Kea was like another country; the people who lived here had brought both vice, and a good sense of marketing. A tourist who made it through the area without being rolled had a really good story to tell when he got back to New Germany or Russia or China or Australia. One street was a Russian sidewalk bazaar, another like a Chinese market, another as bawdy and loud as one of the reforestation camps.

"So, who are we lookin' for, Dad?"

"Russian guy by the name of Yuri. Runs designer drugs all along Mauna Kea. He's half German, usually hangs out along Sugar Street." Sugar Street was the toughest of the mini-neighborhoods along Mauna Kea. Germans, Russians, some Eden refugees, all of them at one time or another filtered through the reforestation camps in Brazil where it seemed like living in another world, if living was the right word for it. Eight years earlier, Tim Shaw had flown to Brazil to serve extradition papers on a man wanted for murder in Honolulu. He never brought the man back to Hawaii because the guy escaped from the Brazilian jail before Shaw got there. Tim Shaw traveled around for a week with a Brazilian police inspector, a German guy named Klein, just to see if the murder suspect could be recaptured. In that week he saw more of the reforestation camps than he ever wanted to see again.

There was no morality, no law, and the scum of the earth worked there, slogging through the mud, planting trees, moving on, planting more. Some of the terrain was so rough that no machinery could get in and manpower alone was the only solution. And no one clamped down on the reforestation camps because as the earth's population grew almost exponentially now, without a new rain forest, in another hundred years or so the oxygen levels would be so depleted that life would be imperiled. Anyone willing to live in the reforestation camps – and spend an eight-hour shift sometimes in mud up to one's knees just planting seedlings – was cut a lot of slack, no matter how rotten the person was.

Kids didn't grow up wanting a job like that; men and some women went into those jobs, into those camps, because of what happened in between. As a kid himself, Tim Shaw read a story once about the French Foreign Legion in the years Before The Night of The War. In the story, which was about some brothers who joined the Legion because of a theft, one of the big points was that men enlisted to get away from their pasts. The reforestation camps were that way now; they were a place to get away from a past better forgotten.

But escaping the past was like taking a vacation; it was impossible to leave yourself behind.

Tim Shaw opened the rear door.

Before he helped her out, he said, "You sure you wanna go through with this, Mrs. Rubenstein?"

"You need a tourist, right?"

"Yeah, but if you get hurt, your father and your husband are gonna be all over my ass. Excuse the language." Annie Rubenstein stepped out of the car, pushing down her miniskirt, Ed getting the streetside door. Tim Shaw looked across the roof of the car at Angie Fargo's pretty face. "Hey, Angie, you keep this civilian outa trouble, huh?"

"Got it, Inspector."

"You guys start walkin'. And first sign of trouble, just remember, I can almost hear ya breathin'." Tim Shaw put the receiver into his left ear. He looked at Annie Rubenstein. "You remember one thing Mrs. Rubenstein. This guy Yuri, he's a tough little shit. Mean. Wouldn't matter to him if he slit your throat to get five bucks, right? And he's tight like this—" Shaw held his first two fingers up, then squeezed them together, "—with the Nazis. He's an Eden agent, gotta be. Eden's his drug connection."

"Then why haven't you arrested him?" Annie Rubenstein asked him.

She looked so sweet and innocent when she looked at him like that—she reminded him of his own daughter, Emma. "Would you believe we got nothin' on him? Everybody knows he deals designer drugs, everybody knows he deals information. Now, it isn't like it was Before The Night of The War, where there's a law tellin' you how long to hold your breath and which way to fart—excuse the language—and these days it's basically the Constitution and a few laws to help implement things, but we still can't nail a guy 'cause we think he's wrong; we've gotta have evidence."

"So if he tries to rob us or something—"

Shaw grinned; for a girl who'd done so much with her father and her brother and her husband, she was an innocent when it came to the streets. "He's not gonna go for ya; but whoever does'll probably be able to lead us to Yuri."

"Then what? I mean, if you still can't arrest him."

Shaw smiled, pushed his coat aside so she could see the .45 tucked in his waistband. "This is an extraordinary situation Mrs. Rubenstein. It requires extraordinary measures. Those Nazi creeps that killed all those kids can't be left hangin' around to do more of the same. That's why Ed's with me. And Angie over there, her father and I were in the Marines together and used to work the streets together, too. She's a good guy. I figured you were a good guy, too." Tim Shaw smiled at her. "Know what I mean?"

"You're taking the law into your own hands," Annie Rubenstein said, smiling at him.

"Right you are, little lady. Got any problems with that?"

She smiled again. She really did remind him of his daughter. "Not a one. My father always said the only real law is personal morality; with it, a code of laws is superfluous and without it a code of laws is a joke."

"Your old man's got the ticket, Mrs. Rubenstein. Now, go be a good little tourist."

She took his hand. "I like you."

"I like you, too, so don't go gettin' yourself killed or somethin', okay?"

"Wouldn't dream of it." She looked across the roofline of the car. "Ready Angie?"

"Ready, Annie."

Shaw watched as the two women walked along Mauna Kea toward Sugar Street, about three blocks down. Without looking at his son, he said, "We're gonna get that Yuri bastard, Eddy. Make him tell us where those fuckin' Nazis that hit the school are hidin' then maybe we'll have a moral dilemma."

"A dilemma?"

"Yeah. A dilemma."

23

He'd stood outside the door to Mixing Room Nine for several minutes, listening. There were mechanical noises coming from beyond it, some sounds which might have been from lab animals. He could tell nothing else.

Armed not at all, James Darkwood had no choice but to open the door and hope he wouldn't walk into a black-clad security man with an energy weapon.

The door was like a watertight doorway on a submarine.

He spun the locking wheel.

He opened the door.

He stepped over the flange, a synth-rubber gasket surrounding it, evidently to seal Mixing Room Nine in the event of contamination.

Beyond the doorway was a narrow walkway extending in both directions and, beyond it, nothing. Darkwood stepped across the walkway to the railing and looked down. Contrary to all the intelligence data the Trans-Global Alliance had concerning Plant 234, the facility was not entirely on one level. Below Darkwood, stretching off well beyond the perimeter of the building, out to run beneath the loading and storage areas outside, was an assemblage of huge pressurized vats. Piping led from one to another and to storage tanks in the distance on either end. At the center of the area, almost just below him, were structures looking like hermetically sealed field accommodations or tents. But they were transparent.

And there were men inside these, naked as Adam except they were tied hands behind them and there were stickball gags in their mouths. Some of the men just stood in the centers of the tents while others threw themselves against the transparent walls, falling down, struggling to their feet, throwing themselves at the tent walls again.

After a few seconds, the men started to collapse.

These were test chambers and the men inside the chambers were being used to gauge the effectiveness of Eden's biological weapons. As James Darkwood realized this, he began to retch. Turning away from the rail, he saw a black-clad figure with an energy rifle coming toward him along the catwalk. "Who are you!"

James Darkwood slumped against the still open door.

"Why is this door open?!"

Darkwood stood there, his left knee against the door.

"Answer me or you will be shot!"

"I took a wrong turn, man."

"That is not the correct answer!"

The security man was very close now, almost close enough. Darkwood doubled over, coughing as he said, "Maybe my suit has a hole in it. I feel sick, man. Maybe we're all contaminated."

The security guard took the one step Darkwood needed him to take, and James Darkwood threw his entire body weight against the door, swinging it hard against the face and upper body of the security man, kicking him against the wall. Then Darkwood was on him, Darkwood's right knee smashing up into the testicles, Darkwood's left hand pinning the energy rifle, his right fist hammering across the mask-covered face, hammering at it until his knuckles felt as if they were broken.

When he stopped hitting the man and looked at the man's face through the blood-smeared faceplate, he could see that the man was unconscious or dead.

Darkwood released the energy rifle, drew his left fist upward, then hammered downward for the guard's throat, crushing the larynx. If the man hadn't been dead before, he was dead now.

Darkwood leaned back, still straddling the body.

Before he changed uniforms with the dead man, he would change faceplates in their masks. He started dragging the body off the catwalk, over the flange of the airtight doorway and into the tunnel.

Soon the man he'd killed at the entrance to the tunnel would be discovered, and the guards patrolling Mixing Room Nine might have to make regularly scheduled check-ins. All in all, time was running out. Granted, he already knew enough about Mixing Room Nine to recommend the air strike against the facility. And, if he had been the agent he should have been, he would have left immediately.

But there was something else he'd seen below the catwalk. There was a pen on the far side of Mixing Room Nine, like a large animal cage with shining metal bars that were probably electrified. Inside the cage were at least two dozen bodies, crowded together, naked, no one touching the bars.

They were the victims for the next test series.

In a few minutes or a few hours – it didn't matter, really – a few of them would be taken out, tied and gagged and put into the tents to die.

James Darkwood had a duty more immediate than his report to consider.

24

Even though most of the other women she saw – and Angie the policewoman, too – were dressed in miniskirts and high-heeled plastic-looking boots, Annie Rourke Rubenstein still felt like a hooker in an old videotape. That a woman could possibly want to dress like this amazed her. When she sat down, no matter how hard she tried, there was nothing between her bare behind and whatever she sat on except her panties. If she bent over – she would not unless her life depended on it! – her panties would be all there'd be between her bare behind and the eyes of whoever happened to be looking her way and under her skirt.

And the top she wore stopped just below her breasts, leaving her midriff exposed. These days, it was fashionable for people to see a woman's belly button because the waistband of her skirt didn't even rise to her natural waist.

A thought suddenly crossed her mind and, as she and Angie navigated a narrow alleyway still one block away from Sugar Street, she asked the woman, "Have you read anything about Lydveldid Island lately?"

"Lydveldid whatland?"

"Lydveldid Island – Iceland, you know!"

"Ohh! Every once in a while there's something in the papers, I mean."

"About women's fashions there?"

"No."

"Well, I just couldn't imagine the women there dressing like this."

"What's wrong with dressing like this?" Angie retorted.

120

"Well, nothing I guess, but when we lived there I used to wear these wonderful long skirts and these blouses with long puff sleeves and cuffs and necks up to—" She started gesturing what she meant, but Angie was just looking at her oddly. "What's the matter?"

"Why would anybody want to dress like that!"

Annie shut up, kept walking. She liked dressing that way. If Angie didn't—

"Hey, look sharp Annie," Angie hissed through her teeth.

Annie felt her eyes narrowing slightly as she followed Angie's gaze into a store window. The window displayed lingerie, and not the kind that a woman would buy for herself, she thought. Hot pink bras with black bull's-eye cutouts so the nipples could protrude, panties with fur trim and cutouts at the crotch. But, reflected in the glass, she saw two men, staring at them, not the lingerie. "Think they work for this Yuri guy?"

"Doesn't matter. If they hit us, Tim and Ed'll get 'em, and they're bound to know where Yuri is. Yuri's got his greasy little fingers into everything in this part of town. Keep walking, Annie."

Annie slipped her hand into her purse, cocked the hammer on the little Firestar 9mm and raised the safety. Although, like her father and her husband, she didn't like a cocked and locked carry. Under the circumstances, if she needed to use the gun, it would be faster. As she withdrew her hand from her purse, she held a handkerchief, dabbed at her nose with it, then replaced it in the bag.

Angie rasped, "Don't jump the gun, Annie. Remember, we want them set up so Tim and Ed catch 'em red-handed."

"They can hear everything, right? Inspector Shaw and his son?"

"I sure hope so. Two of those guys we can handle, but around this part of town, they usually strike in larger groups. These guys are probably just scouts for a gang. Six or eight guys, probably."

"A gang. Wonderful," Annie said, nodding. Like most women, she felt, she had always considered combat grossly unpleasant, however necessary it sometimes was. But if there had to be fighting, it was much better to have it out in the open. This business of living in a city and playing by artificial rules just did not appeal to her. If these men were about to attack them, logic dictated taking out her weapon now, letting them know she could fight back and would. Then, the men would have the choice of leaving or fighting. There would be no waiting.

Instead of taking out her weapon, she left it inside her ridiculously small purse, the purse hanging from her left shoulder. This was madness. With the high-heeled boots, she couldn't even run properly and the flimsy stockings she wore would shred the first time she dropped to cover. Better a pistol belted at the waist, an ankle-length full skirt of good honest fabric and stockings with some body to them and sensible combat boots.

Annie shook her head, walking on beside Angie, eyeing the two men who were quite definitely following them. She could see them every time a suitable piece of window glass was available.

Annie Rubenstein and Angie reached the end of the block, Angie stopping to look into a shop window. A uniformed policeman walked past, Angie turning away. "He knows me," she whispered. "If he stops to say hello we'll lose the guys tailin' us."

There were magazines and books displayed in the window, all of the printing in Cyrillic alphabet and unreadable to her. "A Russian bookstore?" Annie asked.

"More or less," Angie said, laughing softly.

Annie looked more closely. Interspersed among the books and magazines were a variety of items, some of which she recognized; others were objects she had not only never seen before but could not guess at a use for. "Is this a —"

"Sexual aids, that's all. Welcome to Sugar Street." The beat cop passed them and Angie turned her head down the side street. Annie turned away from the window display of books, magazines, dildos and whips, following Angie's gaze.

"Sugar Street," Annie repeated. The sidewalks were all but obscured by carts and booths and the scruffy-looking men and scantily clad women who hovered about them hawking their wares. Some of the stalls were apparently outgrowths of the stores they fronted, while others just occupied sidewalk space. And, there wasn't much of that. The street was packed with gaily clad tourists weaving their way among the stalls, and persons whom Annie assumed were denizens of Sugar Street itself, men and women even more unsavory in physical appearance than those operating the sidewalk bazaar.

There was two-way traffic on Sugar Street, but it moved very slowly because pedestrian traffic zigzagged and crisscrossed from one side of the street to the other. Annie wasn't quite certain what was going to happen, but she felt whatever it was would occur relatively

122

quickly, because as they entered Sugar Street, they picked up two more tails.

Miniskirt notwithstanding, Annie felt suddenly naked. Her gun was in her purse and her purse was suspended from her shoulder by a thin strap that could easily be cut. Under normal apparel, she could have worn a thigh holster or leg holster. Under what she wore now, she was lucky to conceal herself. If her purse were "snatched" — as the old expression went — she would be weaponless. Even though that wouldn't make her defenseless, it wasn't a condition she would relish.

Annie Rubenstein remembered her father's oft-spoken words then, "It pays to plan ahead." She did that now. She'd learned concealment techniques at her father's knee, her brother beside her, years ago, as part of his general survival curricula in the five years he'd spent with them before returning to The Sleep. "There are various objectives in concealment. Sometimes, you may be required to conceal a firearm or knife in such a manner that nothing short of electronic devices or a disrobed search will reveal it. And don't think the subject of concealment under the present circumstances is merely academic. If men do return with the Eden Project, if the world grows again, well, one of these days there will be cities again. Maybe I won't live to see that day, but hopefully you guys will. Not that cities are that terrific, but they're necessary. And, even if laws are sensible enough that carrying weapons openly is perfectly acceptable, sometimes it will be necessary to be armed so that your weapons aren't seen. Now, when you don't have to make the gun or knife or whatever all but invisible, when instant access is more of a requirement, then you have to remember one basic fact about human nature: people generally see what they expect to see. If you can disguise your weapon in such a manner that they still see what they expect to see, you'll be all right."

Annie Rourke Rubenstein did that now. Bending over a stall filled with tacky-looking shrunken heads made out of coconuts, she let her purse fall forward, pressing it against her naked abdomen as she picked up one of the coconut heads. "Isn't this cute!" Annie remarked. When she looked at Angie, Angie looked back at her with an odd expression. As Annie put down the shrunken head and clasped both hands to her bag, her left hand flipped the catch on the flap. As she straightened up from looking into the stall, she drew the Firestar with her right hand and slipped the cocked and locked pistol down into the waistband of her skirt.

The metal was cold against her skin, and she shivered slightly.

As she walked, holding her purse close against her, the purse obscured the portion of the gun sticking up over her waistband. As long as she kept her purse covering the area between her navel and her left hipbone, the gun wouldn't be seen.

Annie walked on, four men following them now, two behind and one on either side of the street.

The sounds, the smells, the press of people around her was almost overwhelming to her. But she was in it now and there was no turning back.

25

Energy rifles were peculiar devices, and objectively much more efficient than cartridge weapons; despite that, James Darkwood would have much preferred his .45 automatic to the arm he now carried as he moved along the catwalk toward the nearest apparent means of descent to the lower level, a wide-treaded metal ladder.

The ladder touched the floor about twenty-five yards from the presumably electrified holding pen where the human prisoners were held until their turn arrived to play laboratory test animals.

There was one advantage to the energy rifle for which Darkwood was quite grateful: he could fire it into the circuit box that controlled the fence and the electrical discharge from the plasma bolt would short the entire pen. Then he could free the prisoners.

What he would do before reaching the pen and afterward, with a group of naked, half-starved prisoners at his heels, he wasn't certain. With luck, any of the personnel in Mixing Room Nine who tried to prevent him from carrying out his self-appointed task would be personnel important to the very operation of Mixing Room Nine, and killing them would bring about catastrophic delays in Eden's bio warfare program. Or, at least that was a pleasant fantasy to mull over while he descended the ladder.

So far, he had seen no other black-garbed security personnel, but he knew that wouldn't last. And, as he looked below him, he saw two. They waited, flanking the base of the ladder. But their weapons were still casually slung just like his, not at the ready.

"Dave. Where were you?" The words were shouted up to him as he reached the midpoint on the ladder.

125

Darkwood, presuming he was supposed to be Dave, coughed, cleared his throat, answered, "The door wasn't secure. I checked it." That matched enough with the truth that if one of the two security men had seen the door open or closed Darkwood's words wouldn't instantly precipitate an alarm.

"What took you so long?" The second voice held both an edge of authority and suspicion.

Darkwood was nearly at the bottom of the ladder and nearly at the point where he'd have to commit to action, one way or the other. "Well, a funny thing happened—" Darkwood shoved himself back and dropped, his right hand grabbing the forward thrusting energy weapon of one of the two men, his left arm flailing outward into the facemask and chest of the second man.

As the man to Darkwood's right started to struggle to get his weapon free, Darkwood let go completely. The result was just as Darkwood hoped, the man falling off balance, sprawling across the floor. Darkwood wheeled left, hammering his right fist into the chest of the man on his left side. In the next instant, Darkwood dropped away, buckling his right leg, snapping his left leg out, catching himself on his hands as he rolled right, leg sweeping the already stumbling man to the floor.

Darkwood came out of the roll and onto his knees, the untried short-barreled energy rifle in his hands. He fired, a plasma bolt striking the first man square in the chest. Darkwood swivelled right, firing at the second man, a chest shot, then a shot to the head. The faceplate smoldered as the man fell back dead.

Darkwood was up, firing a second burst into the first man, just to make certain. Darkwood was beside the nearer of the two men in a single stride, unravelling the sling of the dead man's energy from the man's right arm and shoulder. Darkwood slung the weapon to his left side, his eyes shifting from side to side as he moved, waiting for the first reaction from the knot of men near the tents.

Darkwood was nearly beside the other dead man when that reaction came. A man shouted, "What the hell are you doing?"

"Security has been breached, sir! But I'm on top of things. Stand back in case there's more trouble," Darkwood shouted. He took the rifle from the other dead man, slinging that to his left shoulder as well.

Three men not wearing white protective clothing emerged from beside the test tents and started toward him, one of them opening his suit and reaching under it. "Gun," Darkwood said to himself. He fired the energy weapon that was in his right hand, knocking the man back into the other two, the man's chest smoldering from the center of mass shot, the fashionably skinny necktie worn beneath the protective suit on fire. The necktie had to be polyester.

The other two men raised their hands. "Don't shoot us!"

Darkwood looked at the man who'd spoken. "You put men into those tents and then flood the tents with biological agents and you ask for mercy? You're nuts!" Darkwood pulled the trigger, killing the man, then swung the muzzle right a few degrees and killed the other one.

There were more men in motion, but not coming directly at him, and an alarm began to sound, loud to the point of being earsplitting.

Darkwood ran for the pen where the prisoners were kept, shouting to them as he ran, "Stay as far away as you can from the fence. I'm going to short it out and that'll make an arc. Understand?"

There were some grunted sounds, some nods, but mostly looks of bewilderment, none of these people – men and women ranging from early teens to well past Darkwood's own age – apparently able to instantly handle the idea of a man dressed in the uniform of the plant security forces coming to their rescue. Darkwood stopped a few feet from the junction box.

"Now, don't look! Protect your eyes!" Darkwood fired a full charge burst, letting the bolt strike at the target while Darkwood still kept the trigger depressed. If it had been his only energy rifle, he wouldn't have done it because the weapon – it was grounded and a current backlash wouldn't harm him – might get shorted out itself.

The junction box exploded, shards of metal flying upward in an arc.

Darkwood stepped back. He swung the muzzle of the rifle toward a wooden skid not far from the fence. He fired. The energy rifle's circuitry wasn't fried.

Darkwood approached the fence. Blue waves of electricity still moved across it, the prisoners within the enclosure huddling in fear.

The frequency and apparent intensity of the energy discharges visibly diminished over the course of a few seconds, Darkwood's concentration already on the lock for the gate. If everyone within the enclosure had seemed in good shape, they could have climbed over the fence. But the people looked half-starved to death and some of them had quite visible limb fractures and dislocations.

James Darkwood warned again, shouting over the blaring alarms, "Stay away from this side of the fence. I'm going to shoot off the lock." Energy rifles didn't exactly shoot off chunks of chrome and steel reinforced titanium but they could melt it.

With an eye toward both the catwalk and the two sides of the lower level, Darkwood shoved two of the rifles forward, raising them to shoulder height. Energy weapons had no perceivable recoil, so it was easily possible to fire two at once. He did that, energy bolts from both weapons striking at the massive locking mechanism. Electricity flowed from it, across the bars of the enclosure, Darkwood shouting again, "Stay clear!"

He shot a glance to his right. No security guards were on the catwalk. Just the distance to be run down the tunnel would consume several minutes, but men from near the testing tents were forming up, would any moment charge toward him.

The locking mechanism on the enclosure glowed almost white hot, then exploded in a brilliant flash of light. Darkwood let the weapons fall to his sides on their slings. Some of the prisoners were starting toward the fence. Darkwood shouted, "Wait until I clear the charge!"

He looked from side to side, found a piece of apparatus, perhaps something utilized in mixing the chemicals – he wasn't certain. But it looked like metal. Hefting it, there was enough weight. He hurled the object toward the fence.

It stuck against the fence as though magnetized for an instant, then fell away in a shower of sparks.

Darkwood ran to the gate, took a step back, kicked at the gate and the gate bounced back toward him.

Then he told the people inside, "Take these rifles, use them, get clothes from the ones who were going to kill you and meet me on the catwalk! Understand?"

There were shouts of assent. A naked woman somewhere in her twenties but exhausted and emaciated looking, her right shoulder severely dislocated, dropped to her knees at his feet, hugged her arms around his legs, kissed his knees. Darkwood stepped away. "It's all right. No time for that. Come on!" Darkwood tossed one of the energy weapons to a man of about fifty, but strongly set in his face and fit enough looking to be able to use it. He gave the second weapon to a man in his late teens.

The two armed men flanking him, the rest of the freed prisoners around and behind them, Darkwood started toward the catwalk ladder.

Some of the workers who tested the bio warfare materials, who mixed them, were running for the catwalk ladder themselves. Darkwood opened fire, cutting down two of them as they started up, the others running back to shelter. "Remember. Get clothing. You'll need it."

Darkwood fired at two workers running toward him with huge wrenches in their hands. He shot down both men.

Darkwood reached the ladder.

It was hard climbing that way, but he kept the rifle in his right fist and started up.

26

They were two blocks into Sugar Street, the tourists fewer and fewer, the merchandise that was for sale in the grimy windowed shops and the precarious-looking stalls seemingly raunchier and raunchier. A woman—she was from the Wild Tribes but had brilliant blue eyes—came up and offered them drugs. Then, apparently she'd noticed the men following Annie Rubenstein and Angie, and she ran off like a frightened animal.

There was less vehicular traffic now, too, most of the cars having turned off Sugar Street at the intersection just past. Annie spotted two more men watching them, making for a total of six. "Just how close will Inspector Shaw and his son be, Angie?"

"Close enough I hope," Angie hissed through her teeth.

They were directly opposite a small store front, the windows filled with packing crates and grated over, the door open, a hot, musty smell emanating from inside. The two men Annie Rubenstein had just spotted started walking quickly toward them.

Annie looked back. The man on the far side of the street was coming across. The three men behind them were closing up fast. "They're trying to herd us into the store," Annie said, hugging her purse against her abdomen to cover the butt of her gun.

Angie turned around, looked into the store. "Doesn't look like there's anybody inside, which probably means the place is loaded." Angie made a great show of looking at the men, gesturing to Annie, then started a mincing run into the store front, saying under her breath, "No guns yet, kid."

Annie resented the appellation "kid"; aside from the fact that she had been born more than six and one-half centuries ago, in chronological age she was no more than a couple of years younger than Angie.

She followed Angie nonetheless, but with a long-strided walk, her purse still clutched to her abdomen over the butt of her gun. As soon as they were inside the store, Annie realized this had to be a mistake. There was the smell of body odor, dust, mildew. Two light fixtures only illuminated the entire length of the deep but narrow building, all the narrower-seeming because of the boxes that were stacked floor to ceiling on both sides of them.

The interior of the store was tailor-made for an ambush, a box canyon, but man-made.

Angie was talking, but evidently not for Annie's benefit, but so that Tim and Ed Shaw would clearly understand that the hoped for robbery or mugging attempt was happening. "Do you think those men who are so close behind us want to hurt us, Annie?"

"Could be. What a yucky-looking store, and right here in the middle of the block. You'd think they'd do something about it, whoever owned it. Let's see if we can find the owner."

"The owner of the store? That's a good idea," Angie enthused with admirable dramatic fervor.

They were halfway along the store's length now and as Annie looked back she saw the six men from the street, two of them standing in the doorway, the other four walking after them. And when she made eye contact with one of them, first that man then the other three started whistling, shouting, "Hey, chickie! Wanna party? Or you jus' wanna gimme all your money and jewelry and clothes and maybe I don' touch you, huh?"

There was laughter, dirty-sounding.

From deep within her, memories surfaced, of a helicopter ride more than one hundred twenty-five years ago with a man from the Eden Project who was really a Soviet agent, a man who'd bound her into the seat of the helicopter and much later tried to rape her.

She shivered.

As she looked ahead, she saw that Angie was stopped dead in her tracks, bare hands in the air. Annie sidestepped so she could look around Angie. Poking out from between two stacks of boxes was an energy rifle, a pair of enormous hands holding it and a skinny upper body and animal-like face. "You bitches move, I

131

blow your fuckin' heads right off. All I'd screw myself outa's the earrings and I could live with it."

This couldn't be part of Angie's plan, to have someone get the drop on her. Even if Inspector Shaw and his son arrived in only a minute, both of them could be dead by then.

"Let go of the purse," the man with the energy rifle ordered Annie.

"This purse?"

"Let go o' the fuckin' purse!"

Annie glanced over her shoulder. The four men who'd entered the store after them were fewer than a dozen feet away, but no weapons drawn. Annie said, "So, I'll let go of the purse." She let it fall away, twist-drawing the little Firestar from inside the waistband of her skirt, wiping down the ambidextrous safety with her left thumb as she shouted to Angie, "Hit the floor!" and fired.

Tim Shaw heard the shot and kept running, his ear ringing with the sound. The listening devices both women wore were ultrasensitive and Shaw ripped the plug from his ear before another shot deafened him.

He glanced across the street. Ed was running diagonally from the corner, gesturing wildly with his left hand toward the store front at the center of the block, Ed's .45 in his right hand.

Tim Shaw was about a minute ahead of his son, nearly to the front of the store now, his own .45 coming into his fist, his badge in his left hand, clipping it to his belt. "Police! Outa the way, damnit!" People spread away from him in waves, to right and left as Shaw's feet hammered the last few yards of pavement toward the store front. He thumbed back the Colt's hammer.

He saw a face peer out then pull back.

There were more shots from inside the building.

As Shaw started to slow, two men darted from the front of the store, one of them holding an energy pistol, the other holding a knife.

Shaw stabbed the .45 toward the one with the energy pistol and shot him twice in the back, sending him sprawling face-first into the gutter. If the bullets didn't kill the guy, Shaw thought, the stuff floating around in the gutter sure would. The one with the knife kept rabbiting into the street.

Shaw shouted to his son, "Eddy! Get the little bastard!"

"Right!"

"Got a shiv! Be careful!" Shaw shouted, reaching the store front, pulling a loaded spare magazine from under his jacket, clamping it tight in his teeth.

Shaw dropped into a crouch, trying to take advantage of what little cover there was below the level of the plate glass and the gratings as he charged the doorway. People in Sugar Street were running everywhere, the few tourists here screaming or shouting, the locals just escaping.

More gunfire emanated from within the store.

Shaw edged forward toward the open doorway. Shots, directed toward him this time, the plate glass near him shattering, huge shards of it crashing downward. Shaw could stay where he was and risk getting cut in half or try to make it inside without taking a bullet. He ran inside, firing his .45, aiming high so he wouldn't hit Mrs. Rubenstein or Angie.

Shaw hit the floor behind some crates and dropped to his knees, buttoning out the partially spent magazine up the butt of the pistol and replacing it with the one clamped in his teeth. "Police! Throw down your weapons, damnit!"

"Fuck you!"

Shaw shrugged his shoulders.

He heard Angie's voice, shouting, "Tim! Four guys in here! Got us—" Gunfire again, rapid and heavy Shaw screwed his hat down tighter on his head. Angie shouted again. "Got us pinned down, but we've got the back door cut off."

"Fuckin' wonderful," Tim Shaw said under his breath "We got 'em trapped."

Shaw thumbed up the safety on the Colt, setting it down onto the floor beside him, pulling the little three-inch barreled Centennial out of the pocket of his raincoat. He shifted the revolver into his left hand, putting the .45 back into his right. He thumbed down the Colt's safety. "All right you guys, listen up. We can do this the easy way or the hard way; don't mean shit to me! All I want's information. You gimme what I want, you drop your weapons, you walk.

You don't, you might die. What's it gonna be? I don't have all day, huh!"

Nothing for a few seconds. Then the same guy who'd shouted, shouted again. "Yo, cop!"

"Yo, shithead! Whatchya want?"

"What information ya want?"

"I gotta talk with a schmuck by the name of Yuri. Know him?"

"Never heard of him!"

Tim Shaw shrugged his shoulders, called back, "Gee, that's too bad, ya know. Now I'm gonna have to kill all you guys, ya know? What a bummer, huh?!"

"Hey, dad!"

Tim Shaw shot a glance toward the doorway and the sound of the voice. Behind what little cover there was, he saw Ed, a .45 in his fist, his right knee on the neck of the guy who'd rabbited out of the store, the guy's hands cuffed behind him.

"Way to go, Eddy!" Shaw shouted to his son. Then he turned his head and shouted toward the interior of the store: "The reinforcements are here, guys. Start rememberin' Yuri or start gettin' whacked. What time you had just ran out."

It was as if everyone waited for a beat. The only sounds were the street noises, and those far away, outside of the building, the street as empty as a ghost town in an old western movie.

In about another thirty seconds, there'd be sirens; in about two minutes there'd be uniformed cops. Tim Shaw needed at least a minute to get the information he wanted and then let these guys walk if they played ball.

Then the same voice came back: "Whatchya wanna know about Yuri, cop?"

"His favorite fragrance so I can buy him a gift, asshole! Throw your piece out and get your buddies to do the same, then stand up, hands up and where I can see you guys. Then ya tell me what I wanna know and ya walk. Not before."

Without exposing himself to hostile fire more than he had to, Shaw could see most of the corridor between the crates, almost all the way back to the rear of the store. And he saw a gun—just a regular, good old-fashioned gun and not an energy pistol—skate across the floor and come to a stop against a packing crate.

Then there was another one, just like the first. Both Lancers, either stolen from an armory or from a well-off citizen; punks like these didn't buy guns, at least not from legitimate gunshops. There came an energy pistol, then another energy pistol and an Eden bayonet.

"I'm touched, guys," Shaw said "Step out with your hands up. Mrs. Rubenstein, Angie—keep 'em covered."

"We got 'em, Tim!" Angie called back.

Shaw could see the four men now, coming out, hands high over their heads. If he hadn't given his word, he would have popped them and rid the world of four scumbags. But he shrugged his shoulders and stepped into the little corridor between the boxes and crates, a handgun in each fist. Sirens were growing louder on the air. "So, before I forget my part of this, tell me where to find Yuri. And if you guys aren't makin' tracks before the uniform guys get here, there's no deal. So, talk fast."

"Yuri's over on Maui, man, with his little sister; she's real sick."

"And you give me a pain in the ass, junior," Shaw said, grinning. He walked up to the one who'd talked, a man of about twenty or so, his hair so greasy-looking it shined, his trousers so tight they looked like they were spray painted on. Shaw laid the muzzle of the Smith & Wesson up against the man's right temple. "Play it straight and you walk; lie to me and if I don't catch it now and blow ya away, I'll hunt ya down and do it then. You can't hide from me, not ever, got it?"

"Yeah, yeah, all right."

"Where's Yuri—and just so we don't labor under any misapprehensions here, the Yuri I want is the guy who sells designer drugs and is all pals with the Nazis. That Yuri. Know him?"

"Yeah, man."

"I'm old enough to be your father, God forbid. Don't call me 'man'."

"Yes, sir."

"Better. Where's Yuri?"

"1322 Lanai Avenue, apartment 63."

"Truth?"

"So help me, man—sir!"

Shaw flexed his fist on the butt of the Smith & Wesson. "One other little thing. This goes for all four you guys, right? I ever catch any of you tryin' a mugging again, you go down; not to some luxury jail cell, either. You really go down, six feet under good old Hawaiian soil. We understand each other?"

"Yes, sir."

"Get into a job training program or somethin'—just get outa my life." Shaw lowered the revolver and looked past the four toward Annie Rubenstein and Angie. "Okay with you girls these guys split?"

Annie Rubenstein smiled, nodded her head.

"Whatever, Tim," Angie said.

"Step aside, ladies, and let these guys take a hike the back way." Then he looked at the four. "You guys wanna do that?"

"Yes sir," said the only one of the four who'd yet spoken.

"Remember. Let your consciences be your guides and if you cross me I kill ya. Hit the road."

The four started edging away. One of them started to reach for his gun, but not in any way that was threatening. Shaw laughed, "Be serious, huh!"

As the four ran along the corridor between the rows of boxes, the sounds of the sirens got so loud they had to be just outside the front entrance. Shaw walked back toward the two women.

There was a dead man with an energy rifle in his fists, nested in some of the boxes, two neat bulletholes in him, one in the chest and one in the thorax. "Those shots were pretty close together. Microphone picked it up as one shot. Which one of you charming ladies, uh—"

Angie grinned and nodded her head toward Mrs. Rubenstein.

Tim Shaw just shook his head. "Angie, stay with Eddy and help him out. Mrs. Rubenstein, wanna come with me to 1322 Lanai, apartment 63?"

"I was hoping you'd ask."

A gun in each hand, he nodded toward the rear of the store. "Shall we?" Once he found Yuri, he'd have a line on the Nazis that hit the school. He thought he should warn Mrs. Rubenstein, and as he slipped his revolver away, the .45 in his left hand now, he said to her, "You realize you might be an accomplice to a killing?"

"A killing?"

136

He held the door for her as they entered the alley. Garbage and empty boxes were everywhere, but the four bad guys weren't anywhere to be seen. "Well, Yuri isn't exactly your model citizen, and if I find out he knew about the school thing, well, he'd get a lawyer and eventually he'd walk because I don't have any probable cause."

"Then the law's as screwed up as my father said it used to be in the Twentieth Century?"

"Ohh, no. But some people get around almost any law. Yuri's one of those guys."

"The killing thing?"

"Yeah?" Shaw responded.

"Only if you have to, huh?"

"Believe me, Mrs. Rubenstein, that's the only way it'd ever go down. And I like your style lady."

27

From the top of the catwalk, James Darkwood saw the true meaning of the word "revenge" more graphically than he could ever have imagined it. The men and women whom he had liberated from the cage were killing everyone on the lower level, shooting them or bludgeoning them to death, ripping clothes from the bodies of the dead to cover their own nakedness, running on.

Darkwood looked to the lower level only occasionally, his eyes and his weapon on the tunnel, waiting for the inevitable. He gave things another minute at the maximum.

And this time, as he turned to look over the catwalk, he shouted, "Let's get out of here! Now! I'm leaving! Anybody who wants out with me comes now!"

To the casual observer, Darkwood realized his actions in freeing these captives might have appeared to be altruistic in nature. But they were not. Quite selfishly, he wanted to free those people because it would make him feel good to do so; and, any of these people he could get away with him might well provide highly valuable intelligence data concerning the experiments going on in Mixing Room Nine of Plant 234.

Darkwood took one last look back. People were already starting up the ladder for the catwalk. James Darkwood stepped into the tunnel, starting forward at a good pace, his energy rifle trained on the far end of the tunnel for that inevitable moment when the first security forces would come storming through.

He was almost right under the overhead hatch leading to the roof when the door at the far end of the tunnel opened.

138

It was too long a shot for an energy rifle, but Darkwood fired anyway and the door slammed shut. About another minute and they'd try again, probably with gas that the standard masks like the one Darkwood wore wouldn't filter out. "Up here!" Darkwood shouted, gesturing to the ladder with his free hand. And then he started up the ladder. "And hurry!"

The going was slower, holding his weapon, just as it had been on the ladder leading up to the catwalk, but he felt better holding it. If the security people were good, there'd be a reception waiting for him and the escapees on the roof. He hoped the security people weren't good.

At the height of the ladder, Darkwood hooked his left forearm through the second from the top rung and grasped his rifle. With his right hand, he shoved upward on the hatch, letting it fall over open.

No plasma energy bolts lit the darkness.

Darkwood started up through the hatchway, the escapees clambering up behind him. "They're coming!" a voice shouted.

Darkwood was onto the roof, no security personnel in sight. "Hurry it up. Take deep breaths and hold them until you're on the roof. They'll use gas," Darkwood called back down into the tunnel. Partially naked men and women were piling out of the hatchway, half crawling over one another. Darkwood pulled off his protective hood and the mask, throwing it away, the night air assaulting his nostrils, his lungs, making his blood rush with its cool freshness, giving him the sensation of lightheadedness.

Darkwood stepped back, closed his eyes, tried adjusting to the lower light level.

There was only one hope of getting out alive.

That was to make it to the loading docks and steal a cargo helicopter. He thought of his ancestor, Jason Darkwood. In Jason Darkwood's later years, memoirs were penned. In them, Jason Darkwood told of his first flight aboard an aircraft, how it had at once frightened and exhilarated him.

What would Jason Darkwood have thought if he'd known that one of his descendants was qualified as a pilot, on both fixed wing and helicopters?

139

James Darkwood smiled. Jason Darkwood would probably have enjoyed it.

"That the last?"

"Yeah—that's all of us," a woman shouted back to him.

"You two guys," Darkwood ordered two of the younger men. "Get the hatch closed and try to jam up the mechanism for the locking wheel. Buy us some time. You with the rifle," he told the older teenager, "Stay with them just in case." Darkwood looked around. Several more of the escapees had weapons they'd acquired in the lower level of Mixing Room Nine. "Anybody with an energy weapon, stick close to me. We're going over to the edge of the roof. Any resistance we encounter near the loading docks, we have to take care of quickly, then we're stealing a cargo chopper and flying out of here. Any questions?"

The older man to whom Darkwood had given a rifle asked, "You fly?"

"No, but I know how to run machines that do," Darkwood grinned. "Let's go!" And James Darkwood started running in the direction of the loading docks.

28

They encountered no resistance on the roof of Plant 234, but by the time they reached the west side of the structure, overlooking the loading docks and the parking area beyond where over-the-road transfer trucks and cargo helicopters were parked, there was considerable activity.

Eden Military Police cars were in sight converging on the complex. In no time at all, James Darkwood realized, there would be helicopters as well. Then his luck, which had been running rather well and better than he had any right to expect, would run out. The cargo helicopters were slow, lumbering beasts to get airborne. Once airborne, because of the great engines required to handle the enormously heavy loads they usually carried, they maneuvered slowly, but they could cover straight line distances quickly.

There would be a chance, a very decent one, to escape.

If, however, gunships closed in on the loading dock and parking area, one of the cargo choppers would never get airborne and Darkwood and the men and women he'd freed would be doomed.

There was no time left to consider alternatives or ponder his fate should he fail. "Follow me!" Darkwood commanded, clambering over the edge of the roof and dropping to the sloping roof which covered the loading dock, skidding along its surface toward the roof of a cargo trailer. Darkwood hit the cargo trailer's roof hard, rolled, caught his breath. Some of the freed prisoners were already following him.

Darkwood hauled his energy rifle up on its sling as he climbed to his feet.

Dockworkers shouted at him. Black-uniformed plant security personnel turned their weapons toward him. James Darkwood, still on the roof of the trailer, fired his energy rifle at the nearest armed man, cutting him down. Energy bolts impacted the roof of the truck, crackling across its metal framework, melting the plastic where the bolts struck. Darkwood jumped to the loading dock, rocking the butt of his rifle into the jaw of one man, hammering the muzzle down over the skull of another. He stepped back, firing into a knot of men coming for him.

Energy weapon fire came from the roof of the trailer, the older man whom Darkwood had armed cutting down some of the dock workers and security personnel. Darkwood jumped from the loading dock, shouted to the older man, "Rally everybody and follow me toward the choppers!"

"Right!"

James Darkwood ran. Two plant security personnel came up on his left and before they could fire, Darkwood fired. He kept running. He felt no remorse at having fought with the dock workers; these were not slave laborers and they have to realize they worked at a chemical weapons plant. If they could sacrifice their morality, he could sacrifice their lives if necessary. He ran on, nearing the far end of the parking lot.

A military police car was driving toward him at high speed.

Darkwood brought the energy rifle to his shoulder, stopping dead, firing at the windshield. The plasma bolt struck and the windshield shattered, the Eden Military Police car swerving, spinning, rolling over.

Darkwood ran for the nearest of the cargo helicopters. "Please, God!" Darkwood murmured as he reached for the door handle. The machine wasn't locked. "Yeah!" Darkwood climbed up, looked aft, saw no one, went forward, dropping into the pilot's seat. He flipped the toggle switch for power and the control panels began to light. He'd never flown one of these, but all the controls were marked in English and the basic design of

142

the cargo helicopters was similar to that of military transports, and he'd flown one of those on several occasions just for fun.

This was not fun.

The helicopter fuselage began to vibrate as he started the main rotor. He started the tail rotor then. The wheels on which the chopper stood were self-chocking; he'd checked that as he boarded. He left his wheels chocked, his eyes on the tachometer diode readouts for the main and tail rotor engines.

Time was his greatest enemy. At any second, Eden gunships might close him off, or military police vehicles cross into the lot and open fire.

As he looked through the windscreen, James Darkwood could see his band of half-naked evacuees, running, hobbling, some helping to half-carry others, coming toward the machine. Gradually, only a little more quickly than he should, Darkwood started building RPMs. Oil pressure and temperature gauges were showing well, the ambient temperature outside in his favor there.

At the far end of the parking lot he saw a military police car, then another, then another. "Shit." Darkwood checked his gauges. He couldn't get airborne yet even if he tried. But he could move.

Darkwood activated the controls unchocking forward wheels, then aft, the chocks folding up into the wheelwell housings. Oil pressure and temperature were rising. He checked pitch controls. He had full response. James Darkwood released front and rear parking brakes and adjusted main rotor pitch, increasing tail rotor RPMs. The cargo helicopter started to move forward across the parking lot, not like an aircraft but like some huge lumbering bus with undersized wheels instead.

The military police cars were closing. Those few of the escapees who were armed opened fire on the vehicles, crippling one, but the others were still coming.

Darkwood opened the portside vent window, shoving the energy rifle which leaned beside him through the open port. It was no good, though, because he could not get low enough to take a sight picture and still remain in the pilot's seat. He left the muzzle of the weapon to protrude through the vent anyway, concentrating full effort on the aircraft.

He was almost afraid to look up beyond the immediate area surrounding the craft, afraid that he might see gunships and it would all be finished.

Behind him, he could hear the escapees clambering aboard. "Strap yourselves in. Keep that portside door open in case we have to fire."

All but five or six of the freed prisoners were aboard now, Darkwood confirming that he had sufficient pressure and temperature, had sufficient RPMs.

"Everyone is aboard!" The voice which called to him was that of the younger man. "We can use the energy rifles and—"

"Don't engage a target once we're off the ground unless you have to. We need to get away, not wreak devastation!" "Wreak devastation," Darkwood almost verbalized—crashing into something important was the most damage of which they would be capable.

Darkwood changed pitch and increased main rotor speed. The machine started airborne, sweeping upward with all the perceived grace of a giant rock with stubby wings. But, they were up.

Darkwood throttled out still more, climbing and slowly accelerating.

He saw something over the horizon and his heart nearly stopped. But the light pattern, as he realized in the next second, originated from a fixed wing craft. Not even Eden Security Forces would be stupid enough to send in a fixed wing fighter aircraft, because it could do nothing except bomb and strafe a ground-based target and there had been no time for the security forces to get a fighter scrambled.

His eyes still on the horizon for gunships, Darkwood praying all the while he wouldn't see one, he turned the chopper toward the mountains north of the city. He could ditch in the snows there and get help. Darkwood operated on a big assumption, of course, that Eden City's considerable air defense system, which was designed to keep enemy aircraft from successfully reaching the city, would be essentially ineffective at preventing an aircraft from leaving. Eden City was, after all, much like a prison.

"We made it!" It was one of the women shouting the words, then shouting them again. "We made it!" There followed a chorus of cheers, mostly for him, people patting him so vigorously on the back that once he nearly lost control of the throttle. Then the singing started, patriotic songs to the United States.

Eden, on the other hand, had its own national anthem; but it was terrible to listen to.

29

There was another landing of a commando group, some forty or so men strong, but John Rourke, Paul Rubenstein and Commander Washington and his Pearl Harbor SEAL Team reached the beach site on the other end of the island of Hawaii too late to intercept them. The Honolulu Tac Team hadn't accompanied Rourke, Washington and the SEALs, busily engaged instead in tracking down the unit responsible for the attack on the Country Day School at Sebastian's Reef.

As Rourke went airborne again in one of the SEAL Team helicopters, intending along with the other choppers to make a grid-by-grid aerial search, a radio message came in from Michael. Rourke flipped to the proper frequency as he was notified, saying, "Go ahead, Michael. Over."

"Dad, there's something big going on at the University. You'll want to be in on it. Over."

"What? Another terrorist attack? Over."

"Negative that, thank God. A briefing. All I know is it's supposed to be really important, something to do with an impending volcanic eruption. And you'll be interested in meeting the college professor doing the briefing. His name is Rolvaag. Ring a bell? Over."

Bjorn Rolvaag had saved Annie's life more than a century ago, then fought at their sides thereafter. With his faithful dog Hrothgar and his mighty staff in his powerful hands, Rolvaag, ever silent, ever placid had been both friend and ally in the very best sense of those words. An Icelandic policeman who spoke no English and preferred the windswept Arctic wastes to civilization, Rolvaag was the sort of man John Rourke had always respected as a true hero. "This professor, if he's a descendant of Bjorn Rolvaag, has a lot to live up to. I'll be there. When? Over."

"In about twenty minutes. Rolvaag and this other scientist, a Dr. Betty Gilder, are supposedly still assembling data. Meeting's at the University science center. Your pilot should know how to find it. Over."

"Hang on a minute. Over." Rourke moved the microphone away from his lips and shielded it with his hand as he shouted to the pilot beside him. "Can you get me to the University science center in twenty minutes?"

"Sure can, General. Land you right in the quadrangle, sir."

Rourke nodded, flipped the microphone back in front of his mouth. "I'll be there. See you. Out."

Rourke waited for his son Michael to sign off, then switched back to the intraship frequency. And he stared at the mountains. They seemed distant right now, but under the wrong set of circumstances, they might seem all too terribly close.

30

The repository for the cryogenic chambers in which Sarah Rourke, Deitrich Zimmer's son Martin's natural mother, and Colonel Wolfgang Mann slept so touchingly side by side had been recently moved to enhance security—greater precautions required, it was presumably felt, in the light of the imminence of warfare between Eden and the rest of the world.

For the purposes of what Deitrich Zimmer intended, the new location was vastly better than the old one.

Immediately upon learning of Martin's capture, Deitrich Zimmer pulled the best of the best among those who proudly wore the Sigrunen, the top men to be had from both the Sicherheitsdienst and the Sicherheitshauptamt; the only one from this former unit unavailable to him was Wilhelm Doring, since Doring had already left for his assignment in the Hawaiian Islands.

In the end, however, Deitrich Zimmer had thirty-six superbly trained and totally dedicated officer and enlisted SS SD personnel.

They stood before him now in this small auditorium within the SS complex beneath the glacier, bounded to the southeast by the vast icefield of Great Slave Lake, to the northwest by the subglacial Mackenzie River. The very existence of this facility was known only to the SS and to each man who, because of a need to know, was told of the facility's existence. It was called, simply, "Hafen."

The thirty-six, as well as Deitrich Zimmer's aids and advisors, held their upraised right hands in salute, their voices responding in Greek-like chorus, "Sieg Heil! Sieg Heil! Sieg Heil!"

Deitrich Zimmer raised his eyes, from the beautifully shining faces of these men, looked above them to the ceiling of the hall, the cross which was poised to roll forward on its right angled legs, set in white on a field of red.

And, behind him, set into the black marble wall, the Totenkopf, in highly raised bas relief of finest silver, itself the symbol of purity.

And now Deitrich Zimmer raised his hands palm outward, extending them from the podium as he smiled beneficently on these his stalwarts.

After several minutes, the chorus subsided, the black-uniformed men took their seats and Deitrich Zimmer spoke, his voice soft, low, beautiful, he knew. "My fine young men. After these all too brief moments together, you will go forth on a mission of incalculable importance to Aryan destiny. You will attack the cryogenics facility in what is so obscenely called "New Germany." You will find inside this heavily guarded enclosure the worst of all traitors to the Reich, Wolfgang Mann; and, sleeping beside him, whore that she is, the woman who is mother to our beloved Martin, herself the wife of the greatest of all enemies of the Aryan people, John Rourke.

"The temptation will be great, my fine young men, to go beyond the carefully defined parameters of your mission; do not yield to such temptation.

"Once your historic quest has been realized, the way will be clear for the inheritors of the power and the glory of Adolf Hitler—Sieg!"

"Heil!" The chorus thundered toward him, every man to his feet, right arm outreaching, hand thrust forward.

Deitrich Zimmer motioned for the young men to be seated and they were. All was silence. Then Deitrich Zimmer spoke again. "The way will be clear at last for the Aryan race to bring order to the chaos of this hideously mongrelized planet. As your beautiful children and devoted wives one day soon walk in peace and in sunshine, it will be because of what you do. There will be no fear that your mothers and wives and sisters and daughters will be bestialized by their inferiors, no longer will the bastard servant dare raise hand or voice against his biological master.

"The dream of our glorious Führer whose blood flows in the very veins of my son Martin will be at last realized and the epoch of mankind's greatest achievement will have begun. And it will flourish for a thousand thousand of years! Sieg!"

"Heil!"

"Sieg!"

"Heil!"

"Sieg!"

"Heil!"

Deitrich Zimmer brought them once again to order. "You will soon go forth to your destiny! And the greatness that is the true Aryan Germany is in your hearts and shall be there forever and forever!

"Heil Hitler!"

The auditorium walls, the platform on which he stood, his very eardrums rang with the chorused cheers.

31

There was a mountain trail she liked to walk when she wanted to think. This property, not the house, had been her parents' property when she was a little girl and Emma Shaw had walked this trail the day she learned her mother was dead. She'd walked it again before deciding that instead of doing policework or something else that was still today a more normal occupation for a woman, she wanted to be a Navy fighter pilot. She'd walked the trail again when Hank Walsh had asked her to marry him and she thought she might be pregnant with his baby. She hadn't married him and she hadn't been pregnant, either, just very late.

Emma Shaw, the .45 chamber empty and stuffed into the waistband of her blue jeans, her T-shirt covering its presence, walked the trail again. It wasn't a steep trail, nor was it any more or less picturesque than anywhere else in the mountains here, but it was hers.

Her father had wanted to give her the property when she'd told him she wanted to build a house here, perhaps feeling sorry for her that she might end up an old maid and trying to show his love for her. But she'd purchased it from him instead, and at a fair price, too. But she'd taken his offer of simple interest.

Her trail was really her trail, even to the point of being paid for.

John Rourke.

Midway along her trail's length, Emma Shaw sat on her rock.

She took a cigarette from the pack stuffed into a hip pocket of her jeans, took her disposable synth-fuel lighter, fired the cigarette and inhaled.

There were certain times in her life she'd felt downright stupid being a woman, like the time with Hank Walsh and the baby that wasn't. If she'd married Hank—he was nice, kind, considerate—just because she was pregnant, she would have been trapped by her biology. If she'd had an abortion, which she felt people had a right to choose for themselves (she chose to think it was not for her), she would have been trapped again by her biology.

If love for a member of the opposite sex was a function of biology alone, which she didn't think it was, she was trapped now. She'd considered the concept of love quite often, as she imagined all women did, or at least the ones she knew. Love was a combination of biology, spirituality, the mind (whatever that really was) and factors she didn't think anyone really understood at all, least of all herself.

Emma Shaw loved John Rourke.

The sun was setting and she could see it a little bit from her rock on her trail on her portion of the mountain. By craning her neck, in the morning she could watch the sun rise, and at dusk watch it set.

Loving John Rourke was even dumber than considering marriage to good old Hank Walsh. She just flat out hadn't loved Hank. Maybe her situation was dumber now because she was in love. And John Rourke was like no one else. He was married, and that wasn't a problem easily surmounted under ideal circumstances. That his wife lay in a coma in cryogenic freeze, never aging but with a bullet lodged inoperably in her brain, made matters even worse. Emma knew that even if she hadn't had a conscience—which she did—the situation was impossible.

Add to it John's very nature, the fabric of his being.

Love him, yes, but be blind to him, no.

When she was growing up, she tried living up to the image, later the memory of her mother, to her father's hopes and expectations and dreams for her, then to the other pilots, the really good ones. She'd had her heroes, her role models. John Rourke, although he wasn't conscious of it, was his own hero and role model. He lived up to himself.

Either as cause or effect—Emma Shaw wasn't certain—John Rourke saw himself as an objective entity, not subjectively. John Rourke did or didn't do something because John Rourke should or shouldn't do that thing. Then, he did it or didn't do it, depending on what John Rourke should or shouldn't do. He analyzed, evaluated.

Emma Shaw stubbed out her cigarette (filterless, there was nothing to police that would spoil the environment) and lit another, something she almost never did. She liked Natalia very much. Natalia was gutsy, pretty (prettier than Emma Shaw had ever been on the best day of her life), everything a man would want in a woman, especially a man like Doctor Rourke. John had loved Natalia, Natalia had loved John. They probably still loved each other, but Natalia was Michael's woman (Emma Shaw at once hated and envied the idea of "being someone's woman," as if somehow a woman were transmuted into property).

Why wasn't John more—Emma Shaw verbalized her thoughts. "Why wasn't he pissed off?" But neither the setting sun which shone down over her trail and her rock in long purpling orange streaks nor the fiery gold clouds nor anything at all answered her.

Granted, Michael Rourke was John's son, but still and all, she thought, John could at least have been angry at the situation if not at Michael and Natalia.

So, here he was, born over six hundred and fifty years ago, living by his own measure (she liked that, even though it irritated her), abandoned by the woman he loved and faithful to a wife who was just this side of dead.

But John's problems were in the real world, at least.

153

Her problem was her own stupidity. As Emma Shaw exhaled smoke through her nostrils, she started to laugh. At least now if she became an old maid, she had a reason, pining for a love she could never have.

32

The helicopter descended through the deepening shades of purple into darkness, landing on a grassy patch at the center of an enormous quadrangle that was the exact center of the University complex. All about the four sides stood buildings modeled in Greek Revival style. Fog rolled in from the sea, not heavy, almost ghostly, and the columns, the statuary, took on what was almost the aspect of another time and place. The rotor blade downdraft made the wisps of fog curl back upon themselves, rise, then dematerialize, ghostly-seeming that way as well.

Paul Rubenstein was the first to jump down, ducking needlessly beneath the swirling blades from force of habit, John Rourke just behind him.

Standing well away from the chopper, Paul saw his wife, his brother-in-law, the woman who would, it seemed, someday be his sister-in-law, Natalia. And Tim Shaw and his son, Ed, both from the Honolulu Tac Team were there as well.

Paul smiled to himself, wondering if these men were ever off duty. John and he never seemed to be off duty, Paul Rubenstein reflected.

The Schmiesser in his left hand, Paul fell in step beside John, walking toward John's daughter, his wife, taking her into his arms, kissing her quickly. "How'd that stuff work out today with helping Inspector Shaw?"

"Ohh, it was very interesting; I got to see some really neat parts of Honolulu and we may have gotten some leads on this man named Yuri who's a Nazi sympathizer and a drug dealer, too, you know? It was very interesting."

"Great. Sounds like you had a lot more fun than we did," Paul told her, smiling good-naturedly, folding his arm around her.

After a round of handshaking, they walked along the north edge of the quadrangle, the science hall, looking like an enormously proportioned temple, rising out of the fog ahead of them.

"We'll be passing my car," Tim Shaw said. "You guys wanna drop your reachers in the trunk or somethin'?"

"Reachers?" Annie repeated quizzically, before Paul could ask what Shaw meant.

John laughed. "1930s gangster slang for a rifle or any kind of long gun, really." And John raised his HK-91 in his right hand for a moment. "My 'reacher'!"

They stopped beside the trunk of Tim Shaw's unmarked police cruiser, Shaw opening it, John putting the HK-91 inside, Paul resting his MP-40 submachinegun next to it. There were several other long guns inside, as well as attaché-sized high impact plastic cases, likely for handguns. A hardplate flak vest, a riot helmet and shield, a bullhorn and more miscellaneous police-related gear filled out the rest of the trunk space. "Ready for anything, huh?"

Tim Shaw laughed, saying, "Well, ya never know what might go down, Mr. Rubenstein. Take today, for example. We could have needed some of this gear if it'd gone down differently."

Tim Shaw closed the trunk lid. They returned to the quadrangle and resumed walking toward the science building. Michael and Natalia, who hadn't gone to the car with them, stood on the steps, waiting. Every time Paul saw the two of them together, he could not help at once feeling happy for them and sad for John. John had planned it this way, of course, from the moment they entered the cryogenic chambers at the Retreat on the morning of The Great Conflagration. Perhaps he'd planned it well before that; it was something he and John had never discussed in that regard.

Knowing that a significant possibility existed that the shuttle

156

fleet which comprised the Eden Project, the hope of mankind then, might never return to Earth after its five-century voyage to the edge of the solar system and back and unaware or at least uncertain that anyone else on the face of the planet survived, John had planned for the only thing practical. He would allow his then-young children, not even teenagers then, to awaken before the rest of the sleepers, John spending five years working with them, teaching them, preparing them, then himself returning to The Sleep.

John had planned for Annie to marry his best friend; that occurred. He had planned, however reluctantly, for Michael to wed Natalia. That had not taken place. When the Awakening came, Michael was away from the Retreat, investigating what he thought might be a sign of the returning Eden Project. Instead, Michael discovered a survival community and met beautiful, sweet little Madison.

They eventually married. She was murdered by a KGB Elite Corps suicide squad during an attack on the Hekla community at Lydveldid Island. And, when she died, her—and Michael's—unborn baby died with her.

All the while, John and Natalia loved each other, but John would never be unfaithful to his wife, Sarah. It seemed as if Sarah and John patched things together, were making their marriage work. Sarah became pregnant by John. After the war with the Soviet Union at last ended—the world was full of life, as it turned out, and just as full of the same old causes of violent death—a commando unit of neo-Nazis attacked John's hospital at Eden Base, now the site of Eden City. They nearly killed John. In essence, if not in fact, they did kill Sarah.

The child Sarah carried picked that moment to be born. Sarah, facts indicated at the time, had given birth to the baby entirely unaided. She was shot in the head, the bullet lodging deep within her brain—inoperably deep. Her child, the boy who grew up to be Martin Zimmer, was kidnapped.

Deitrich Zimmer tampered with the infant child's genetic makeup, in some manner or another which Paul did not fully understand, grafting genes taken from the body of one of Adolf Hitler's blood descendants to the boy's own. And Zimmer raised young Martin, who was thought to be dead, as his own son and taught him racial hatred, how to use terror, how to be the perfect Nazi. Through the use of cryogenics Deitrich Zimmer and Martin Rourke Zimmer survived to an era suitable for young Martin's iron-fisted rule.

Allied doctors determined that the only chance John Rourke had to survive, to keep him from dying as he slipped ever more deeply into trauma-induced coma was to return to The Sleep. As for Sarah, she was physically alive, but could not be revived with medical means available then. Perhaps Deitrich Zimmer could have done it then, and perhaps he could now, genius that he was. His abilities in microsurgery were then unrivaled and were since unequaled.

John began to emerge from his coma and was revived. Paul and his wife, Annie, Michael and Natalia took The Sleep as well so they could all be together someday in the future.

The future was here. Michael and Natalia at last became lovers in the period between John's and Sarah's near deaths and their returning to The Sleep. Paul and Annie postponed having a child. John awakened. Sarah did not.

John was alone.

John stubbornly believed that Sarah would someday be restored to him, while the rest of them—Michael, Natalia, Annie, Paul himself—hoped. If belief in something could make it so, then Sarah would be restored. But how would she be? What damage had the projectile lodged in her brain really done? How much could the brain's natural recuperative abilities and the curative side effects of The Sleep be counted upon to save her?

Through knowing John Rourke, Sarah, Michael and Natalia, Paul Rubenstein had learned of another kind of love beyond that of child for parent, husband for wife; it was the love that true friendship is. And he loved John and Sarah too much as his friends to see one unintentionally inflict grief and suffering upon the other. If Sarah were restored in body alone but not in mind, Paul never questioned for an instant that John's devotion to her would be unfailing. The thought of John Rourke spending the rest of his days caring for the mindless husk of a human being that had once been a living, vibrant person, made Paul Rubenstein tremble with rage and disgust.

And the thing of it was—as he held his wife Annie's hand so tightly for a moment that she said, "Ouch!" and then leaned up only to kiss him softly on the cheek—he would do the same for Annie and she for him, refusing to believe that the person inside the body would never come back, was gone forever, was dead while yet clinically alive.

"This world sucks sometimes," Paul said to his wife, his voice a low, rasping whisper.

"Thinking about dad, aren't you? Dad and mom?"

"Were you reading all my thoughts?" Paul asked her. A peculiar result of the cryogenic sleep for Annie was that it had heightened her mental powers, scary sometimes. She could read the minds of people she loved during periods of intense emotion and/or stress, could empathically experience their pain, their suffering, whatever danger they might be in. "Were you?"

"I didn't mean to," Annie whispered, leaning her head against his shoulder as they ascended the steps. "But, I love you, too."

Paul touched his lips to her hair, held her for an instant before they went on.

Then they continued past Michael and Natalia and into the science building, John Rourke walking ahead of them, alone.

33

His audience was as mixed a group as he could ever have imagined. There were government officials wearing expensively tailored business suits or understated high-fashion dresses, naval officers in their dress white uniforms, miscellaneous civilian women in trendy miniskirts or floral print sundresses with enormous flowing skirts, police officials wearing everything from uniforms to casual sportclothes to seedy-looking street attire, the young and old, the important and their aides who someday themselves might well be important, personal representatives of the President of the United States (who was at Mid-Wake) and the Mayor of Honolulu and the Governor of Hawaii, Her Honor and His Excellency in personal attendance. Scientists, male and female, from every discipline within the university were present, too, but the scientists were in the minority. Everyone had a Sigma Security Clearance and, for one reason or another, a need to know.

The only group not represented was the press.

And that was for very good reason.

Thorn Rolvaag, his palms slightly damp, gripped the sides of the rostrum and began. "I'm Doctor Thornton Rolvaag, Regents' Professor of Vulcanology here at the University of Hawaii. What is said here tonight will be learned — unavoidably — by everyone in the islands within days at the most, perhaps only hours. But, until then, I am instructed by various persons to tell you that the information I will share with you tonight cannot leave this room. After what I'm afraid will not be a very brief statement and may, at times, be a bit abstruse — scientists

160

aren't always that great at simplifying things—I'll answer any questions that I can."

Rolvaag cleared his throat.

"Being half Icelandic, perhaps I have vulcanology in my blood. And the study of indigenous volcanic activity in these islands is not really all that much removed from the study of the volcanoes of my ancestral homeland. There are several classifications of volcanoes, and those of Lydveldid Island and Hawaii are coincidentally of the same type. They are shield volcanoes.

"Shield volcanoes," Rolvaag went on, reminding himself as his eyes would drift to his notes, to keep it simple because he wasn't speaking to scientists in the main, but to laymen, "have an angle of slope between three and eight degrees and at their summit there's almost invariably a crater with very steep walls and a flat base.

"Where the difference arises between the volcanoes of Iceland and those of Hawaii is, putting it simply, in size. Icelandic volcanoes range from a little over three hundred feet in height to well over three thousand feet, with base diameters correspondingly twenty times the height.

"Hawaiian shield volcanoes are the largest on earth, possibly the largest that have ever been. Kilauea on Mauna Loa, for example. When one considers the portion of Mauna Loa which is underwater, it has a height ten times greater than the largest of the Icelandic volcanoes—roughly thirty-three thousand feet, or about six miles. Its base is two hundred and fifty miles in diameter. Hawaiian volcanoes have an average angle of slope which is no more than six degrees and the summit is most often a plateau, quite expansive.

"To put this into perspective," Rolvaag said, "consider how the Hawaiian Islands came to be. We're all familiar with the concept of plate tectonics, how solid masses float across the earth on a plastic-like surface of molten material. Protocontinents—Pangea and Gondwanaland—existed at least twice in geologic history, only to break up subsequently into their separate

161

land masses. The jigsaw puzzle was assembled, then broke apart. Some forty-three million years ago, the Pacific plate began moving in a northwesterly direction, creating the Hawaiian ridge and the islands where we stand. The youngest of these islands, and the most geologically active, is the big island, Hawaii.

"All shield volcanoes are formed almost totally of basalts, are rich in calcium, magnesium. Although the ancient peoples of Hawaii credited the eruption to the restless feet of the Goddess Pele, as scientists today we credit eruption to something perhaps just as unpredictable as a female goddess, the movement of magma and gas beneath the earth's surface. When too much pressure builds up, there is an eruption. For the traditionalists who may be among us, I suppose it could always be theorized that Pele causes these buildups," Rolvaag said, smiling.

"There are two types of lava with which we are concerned," he said, continuing. "In Hawaii they are called pahoehoe and 'a'a. Pahoehoe is fluid, moves rapidly, while 'a'a is much rougher-textured and more violent in appearance.

"The temperatures below the ground can easily reach two thousand degrees Fahrenheit. That's not warm at all when compared to the sun, where it's a balmy twenty-seven million degrees Fahrenheit." There was a faint ripple of laughter. "Within the context of metallurgy, however, two thousand eight hundred degrees is considered the high end limit for combustion heating. What lava is, then, is wildly hot liquified metal, stating it most basically. Anything it touches, it destroys or covers over, sealing it.

"Plate tectonics, of course, are responsible for a wide range of phenomena, everything from mountain building to earthquakes to the crisis we now face. Doctor Betty Gilder and I, along with a staff of graduate students and in discreet consultation with other experts in the field from among the nations of the Trans-Global Alliance have confirmed, ladies and gentlemen, that Kilauea is about to erupt in a manner unprecedented in recorded history." Murmurs went throughout the auditorium, some restless shuffling of feet, turning of heads. "What this means, in part at least, is that the big island, Hawaii, must be evacuated. Those plans, I understand, are already under way and the actual full-scale evacuation effort will begin within hours, hopefully soon enough. The evacuation will be locally announced—" Rolvaag checked the Steinmetz on his wrist. "It will be announced on the big island and initial efforts begun within the next ten minutes.

"Normally, ladies and gentlemen," Rolvaag went on, his voice low, "our volcanoes could well be classified as "gentle giants," capable of great destruction, indeed, but in modern times responsible for little if any loss of human life. That will not be the case in this instance.

"When Kilauea erupts, we are predicting a violent burst of gas and ash, forming a cloud which may well obscure the sun for some time. We further predict a lava flow of such proportion and violence that the plateau will sink and the slope at least partially disintegrate, thus spilling both types of lava, pahoehoe and 'a'a, more rapidly and in greater volume than ever experienced before in a populated area.

"This sudden introduction of lava in such immense volume, and the upthrust and subsequent collapse of the undersea portion of the mountain will precipitate tsunamis and high tides of levels and strengths significantly greater than ever experienced in these islands. Earth tremors, to include those which may be felt on the ocean floor, will be experienced as far away as the Chinese First City and Port Reno in North America. Mid-Wake itself, as well as the Russian-American subsurface complex, largely a manufacturing area, will experience quakes. As of yet, the actual strength of these quakes cannot be predicted.

"You have been asked to come here, ladies and gentlemen, in order that you be informed. I understand that each of you, in one manner or another, will be involved in the efforts which will be required to minimize as best possible the effects of this natural disaster. Now, I promised to try to answer any questions I could."

There was a flurry of hands.

Rather than try to guess who was the most important, he went to the first hand he'd seen. "You, miss, in the print dress."

The woman stood up. "I'm Annie Rubenstein. I wanted to know if there is anything which could be done to divert the effect of the eruption, even partially? That's probably a naïve question, but my science is a little behind the times."

One of the Rourke Family herself. Rolvaag had read accounts in old letters and the like concerning the involvement Rolvaag had with this girl; it was hard to imagine she had been born six and one-half centuries ago. "That's a good question actually, Mrs. Rubenstein. A very good question. The lava has to go somewhere, of course, the pressure relieved; and there's been a theory for some time that—with a volcano as immense as the one we're discussing here—it might indeed be possible to find a point where a lava flow might produce significantly less damage and the pressure buildup might be relieved more gradually. I can't go into all the details here, but I'd be happy to discuss the process in greater depth with you and anyone else interested at a later date.

"Suffice it to say, however," Rolvaag continued, "this is only theoretical. The basic methodology would involve utilizing high-speed torpedoes or missiles which would be fired in series and essentially drill through the rock over one of the tubelike structures within the volcano through which lava flows. Puncture the tube and the lava will flow out at the site of the puncture. Do this with several of the larger tubes and it would be analogous to what would result with a human being, for example, if one suddenly diminished arterial blood flow. The eruption could essentially die."

Thorn Rolvaag wondered if indeed it might work . . .

John Rourke sipped at a cup of coffee, his eyes focused beyond the rim of the cup, on the computer animation of the anticipated effects of the volcanic eruption. The video screen on which it was displayed dominated the far wall of the conference room, its proportions as large as the motion picture screens of the Twentieth Century.

Watching this animated holocaust brought back bitter memories, of watching video screens much smaller from within the confines of The Retreat more than six hundred and twenty-five years ago when the ionized atmosphere reacted to the heating of the sun and the skies caught fire in what came to be called The Great Conflagration.

If that was a disaster of truly Biblical proportion, this would be near to it in scope, although more localized.

John Rourke had never been one to just sit around and wait for the inevitable. Perhaps Fate could not be conquered, or perhaps it could. But Fate could be contested, at least. Annie's seemingly naïve question was provocative. In theory, at least, what Dr. Rolvaag said about tapping into the arterial flow of the volcano was fraught with promise. The technology available for such an attempt might not be equal, however, to the task.

Its logic was inescapable. Rather than let the volcanic matter pour out violently through one hole, relieve that pressure so the material would instead dissipate through a series of holes, and the volcanic matter would waste itself on the sea floor.

Something Rolvaag hadn't mentioned bothered John Rourke as well. Would this eruption, unprecedented in recorded history, be so massively violent that it would in some manner or another affect the geothermal vent? Both Mid-Wake and what was formerly the Soviet Underwater Complex—and was now a Russian-American manufacturing facility—derived electrical power from it?

Without electrical power in massive kilowattage, the domed facilities would not be able to maintain the required air pressure and would have to be evacuated. Mid-Wake was the seat of the United States government, still the major repository for "American" culture. Thousands of persons would have to be gotten to safety; if there was insufficient time for that or an inadequate number of vessels, thousands of persons would instead suffocate in their own waste air while those few who might still cling to life would be crushed as the sea finally collapsed the domed cities.

Dr. Thornton Rolvaag appeared without warning at Rourke's elbow. "You move quietly, Doctor," John Rourke observed.

"Thank you, Doctor." Rolvaag extended his hand. "A pleasure to meet the man my ancestor thought so highly of."

"A pleasure to meet Bjorn Rolvaag's spiritual descendant," Rourke said, taking Rolvaag's hand, smiling. "It's hard to imagine a Rolvaag, however, without a staff in his hands or a great dog at his heels."

Rolvaag smiled. "I have several dogs, raise them as a matter of fact. One is even named Hrothgar. Looks a great deal like the original Hrothgar, really, as far as I can tell from photographs; you'll have to meet him and see for yourself. And my Hrothgar carries a little of the original Hrothgar's blood. As to the staff, well, I'm afraid I'm not much of a weapons man, although like almost everyone I own a few firearms and I've learned how to use them with at least a modicum of skill."

"Your predictions, Doctor, do they take into account the fate of the geothermal vent from which Mid-Wake derives its power?"

"They're hardly predictions in the crystal ball sense, of course. They're probabilities based on the interpretation of identifiable available data. There is that possibility concerning Mid-Wake, obviously. We're working on a computer model even now concerning that so that we can try to arrive at some meaningful projections relating to the geothermal vent. For the moment, it's a wait and see situation. I liked your daughter's question. On the surface, it sounded a bit—"

"Naïve? On the surface, one might be tempted to think so, yes; but, Annie isn't the sort of person to let grass grow under her feet waiting around helplessly for the inevitable. And she provoked an intriguing response, you'll have to agree, Doctor Rolvaag."

166

"You know weapons and explosives far better than I. Do you think it could work, Doctor Rourke? I mean, utilizing some artificial means by which the pressure within the volcano can be relieved?"

"Both the United States and New Germany have new conventional explosives, more powerful than anything which existed in my time," Rourke said. "I think the possibility bears serious investigation, serious and rather rapid investigation, actually. You might save an incalculable number of lives and prevent terrible devastation."

Rolvaag smiled a little. "Would you help me talk with the Navy?"

"Yes, certainly," Rourke nodded. "Let's do it right now." In the far corner, nearer to the screen, he saw Admiral Hayes. Immediately, Rourke began walking with Rolvaag toward the woman. The computer animation had reached the part where the side of the mountain collapsed and immense quantities of molten rock spilled forth. The video presentation was fascinating, but John Rourke didn't want to see life imitate art.

34

When the telephone rang, Emma Shaw had been doing something she considered inherently foolish, putting her hair into ultrasound rollers. When she picked up the receiver, she had only one roller left to go. Curls and waves of the natural kind originated within the molecular structure of the hair follicles themselves. When curls were made artificially, the molecular structure was bent. In centuries gone by, chemicals and/or heat were the medium for bending the hair. By accident, when ultrasound showers were designed for field use in arid climates (Northern Australia, the Gulf Coast fringe of North American Eden, etc.), it was discovered that hair follicles were affected. Over the last fifteen years, ultrasound rollers had replaced almost every other means of curling one's hair.

The telephone call, from the Officer of the Day for the unit to which she was temporarily assigned, had told her that all leaves were cancelled and she should report with all speed to unit headquarters at Pearl. She hung up, finished putting in the last roller and threw together her gear, out of the house in under eight minutes.

Ultrasound rollers did their work in less than fifteen minutes, so when she was ten minutes away from Pearl, on the straightaway where she figured she could get away with it, she kept one hand on the wheel and freed her hair of the rollers with the other. Without brushing it out, she looked in the rearview mirror and was reminded of Medusa. But she managed to brush her hair reasonably well before turning into the access road to the main gate.

Past the security checkpoints, she went immediately to her fighter wing. There was traffic everywhere, on the ground and in the air. For the last several minutes of the drive, she was able to observe the huge C-6000 Skyjumpers taking off, not roaring into the upper atmosphere on their enormous jet boosters for intercontinental atmospheric insertion jumps, but flying low and slow, almost afterburnering it by comparison to their usual thrust. Island hopping? She wondered.

She parked in a vacant slot for the wing and crossed the field toward Wing HQ. A stiff wind blew in from the sea, cold, too, the wind feeling good in her hair, the collar of her bomberjacket turned up against its cold on her neck. The one time in God only knew how long she had curled her hair, she was going to be packing it under a helmet.

Shore Patrol was guarding the entrance to Wing HQ and, even though she had her I.D. badge clipped onto the left breast pocket flap of her jumpsuit and the two guys at the door with energy rifles knew her by sight, it was still necessary to have a more positive I.D. She did the palm print thing with the panel on the door (that palm and finger prints could be prosthetically altered these days hadn't filtered down to Navy security yet) and was at last given access . . .

For an officer of his rank to participate in a field exercise was, of course, sheer madness. But, it was necessary. And his English, when he was cautious, could be accent-free. So was the English of the men with him. It was one of the reasons they were chosen for the operation.

There was a certain thrill in the blood on a mission such as this, almost like a sexual release when it was over. Croenberg had plenty of sex when he wanted it, but somehow commando work was even more satisfying; perhaps its edge of death was the reason.

Several of the others were already on base, Croenberg and a

169

fellow named Rauph, a good young man and particularly so with any sort of edged weapon, were driving together. Rauph showed his I.D. at the main gate, as did Croenberg and, without further ado, they were inside Pearl Harbor, the greatest base of military power of the United States.

It was that easy.

Hopefully, this simplicity would be the hallmark of the mission itself, to rescue young Martin . . .

Ed had a family, wife, kids, but Tim Shaw, although he had a son and a daughter, had no home responsibilities. But he did have his work. With the coming disaster, the Nazi commando team responsible for the attack on Sebastian's Reef Country Day School would be in a better position to wreak havoc than they could ever have expected. So, it was more important than ever to stop them.

Yuri hadn't been at the apartment when Tim Shaw had gone there earlier with Annie Rubenstein. What a neat girl, he thought, smiling just thinking about her. She had spunk, just like Emma did, living proof that someone could have balls without having testicles.

His hat low over his eyes, his coffee steaming the windshield of the unmarked cruiser, Shaw sat behind the wheel and watched the building while he ate his dinner. Indigestion and divorce were the two chronic problems of the police officer. He'd never experienced divorce, his wife dying as the result of a freak accident. Indigestion, on the other hand, was inseparable from the territory. But the cheeseburgers at Bingo's were usually at least edible, sometimes pretty good. This—his second, but it was dinner—was a pretty good one. Half-devoured, he put it aside and grabbed a few french fries, munching on them as he watched for Yuri to either enter or leave.

Most likely, Yuri was not home, no lights in his windows, no car in his parking slot.

It was possible that Yuri'd picked up word on the street that the cops were after him and knew where to find him, hence might never come back here. But that wasn't likely. The kids who'd talked up Yuri's address were scared, maybe just scared enough not to try crossing the cop who would have put them away.

Anyway, it was too early to give up and go home.

Shaw sipped at his coffee again.

The cheeseburger, a little greasy, went down easy. One thing he liked about Bingo's was the tomato was always fresh, the cheese always real rather than synth, the meat real meat and not mostly soy protein like some of the chains used these days. And the hamburgers were wrapped in waxed paper. Somehow, they tasted better that way.

Cheeseburger number two down for the count, he continued with the french fries. The usual thing, it seemed, was that the subject would show up while the food was still being eaten, ruining a perfectly good (at least sometimes) dinner.

No Yuri.

French fries gone, Tim Shaw broke open the pie. Whereas the chain places had these little pies that looked like squished loaves of bread and tasted fried, Bingo's had real pie, sliced right there in front of the customer, packaged on the spot.

Apple pie (his favorite), Shaw took a bite, then sipped at his coffee again.

A good dinner enabled a man to do his best thinking.

Rather than the matter at hand—Yuri would take care of himself, either showing up or not—Tim Shaw considered the obvious look in his daughter Emma's eyes when she looked at John Rourke. Ever since she'd been old enough, he'd wanted her to fall in love with somebody, get married, raise children, do all the natural and normal things. If she was in love with John Rourke, aside from the fact that Doctor Rourke was a larger-than-life living legend born more than six centuries ago with children Emma's age and a wife who was neither dead nor alive, as best Tim Shaw could make of it, Rourke would be a bad choice on other grounds.

According to what his son and Emma's brother, Ed, said, Doctor John Thomas Rourke was the best man he'd ever seen in combat. And the times that were coming—war with Eden—would demand a great deal from a man like that. Assuming that everything else was somehow taken care of, what would Emma do with the guy she loved off all over the globe fighting and her at home worrying?

Tim Shaw didn't have any answers, and he wondered if maybe he even had the right questions. Emma going head-over-heels for John Rourke, somehow, just seemed like a no-win proposition for her, something which would only bring her unhappiness.

Like every father from the beginning of time, Tim Shaw imagined, he wanted his daughter to have a life full of happiness, not sorrow. And Doctor Rourke, however neat a guy he was—and Rourke was all of that and more—was also trouble.

Finished with his pie, as Tim Shaw glanced across the street again he saw a car pulling up, German-made with an internal combustion engine, one of the cars patterned after the classic vehicles of the Twentieth Century. Essentially hand-built, running on synth-fuel instead of storage batteries, they cost a fortune. As a boy, Tim Shaw had been fascinated with both antique guns and antique automobiles, alert for every new book with photos of the antiques that were uncovered in archeological digs. And Shaw recognized this car, a red and white 1957 Chevrolet dripping with gleaming chrome, as readily as he recognized the guns of the Rourke Family.

There was a woman behind the wheel of the Chevy.

Yuri sat in the front passenger seat.

As Shaw's own father would have put it, Yuri and the woman began to "swap spits" there in the front seat. Shaw's mind raced. When was the best time to grab Yuri? Now? When Yuri exited the Chevy? When Yuri went up to his place?

Tim Shaw decided. The street had more possibilities. Shaw grabbed a radio out of its niche in the dashboard and dropped it into the left outside pocket of his raincoat.

His car was parked almost directly opposite the Chevy.

Taking a last swallow from his coffee, Shaw hit the kill switch

172

for the dome light as he stepped out of the car and into the street. The brim of his fedora was still low over his eyes.

Tim Shaw started crossing the street, looking both ways, but not just for traffic. It was always possible Yuri was setting him up, but doubtful. Shaw's course was a diagonal. By the time he was on the other side of the street, he was behind the Chevy. He took the curb, walked up from behind the Chevy and, as he approached the passenger side—the window was down—he did two things. He glanced into the back seat to make certain it wasn't a setup for him and he snatched the .45 from his trouser waistband.

His left hand went to the door handle and Shaw slipped in just behind Yuri, thumbing the .45's hammer back to full stand as he laid the muzzle behind Yuri's right ear. "Hey, don't let me stop yas," Shaw said low, almost under his breath, grinning as Yuri's body stiffened. "A full body erection! Whoa, you passionate guy you!"

Yuri stammered, "You mother fuck—"

"Shut your face, you worthless sack o' shit."

"Yuri? Who is this—"

"Tim Shaw, ma'am. I'm a police officer, so rest easy."

"You got no fuckin' warrant, you—"

Shaw shoved the muzzle of the .45 a little harder against Yuri's mastoid sinus. "I need a warrant to arrest ya, Yuri, but I can kill ya without a warrant."

Yuri passed gas, loudly and violently and his face went pale. The woman's brown eyes went wide and there was just the hint of a laugh at the corners of her pretty mouth. She was black, maybe about twenty-five, her face really pretty and what Shaw could see of her figure making him wish he could see more. Shaw shut the door and the dome light went out. "What's a nice girl like you doin' in a place like this, kid?"

"It's my car!"

"And a gorgeous car it is, babe. You won't mind if Yuri and I finish our business outside, huh? After all, wouldn't want blood—" (Yuri had gas again) "—or somethin' worse, huh?

173

Wouldn't want it all over your upholstery." Shaw tapped Yuri with the muzzle of the .45. "Tell the young lady good night, dirtbag. Tell her!"

"Good night."

"Tell her ya had a nice time."

"I had a nice time."

"There ya go! Stick with me Yuri and you'll be a killer with the broads." Shaw looked at the girl. "No offense."

"I betchya he could learn a lot from you," she said, smiling, her eyes even prettier than before when Shaw opened the door and the dome light spotlighted her face.

"You'd be surprised, miss." He gave her a wink and jerked Yuri out of the car and onto the sidewalk, Yuri just managing to stand. "Good night!"

"Good night," she said. Full lips, wide mouth, killer smile.

Shaw told her, "It sure would be." And he slammed shut her door and she pulled the Chevy into the street.

Yuri said, "You gonna pay—"

"No, I don't like payin' for information. You're gonna give it to me for free. And then maybe, just maybe, I won't croak ya." Shaw started propelling Yuri toward the car. "Go rabbitin' on me and you're whacked."

"Whatchya want, man?"

"Nazis, the mothers that hit Sebastian's Reef Country Day School today."

"I don't know nothin' about no Nazis, man!"

They were at the middle of the street. It was a quiet neighborhood as far as street traffic went. Shaw grabbed Yuri by the collar and turned him toward the corner. "Walk."

"Where you takin' me, man?!"

"Walkin's good for ya, Yuri. And after a good walk, there's nothin' more relaxin' than lying down for a good rest."

"What?"

They reached the corner and Shaw stopped Yuri. "Time to lie down."

"What?"

"Down!" Shaw shoved Yuri to his knees. "Flat on your face in the street! Now!"

Yuri went flat. Shaw took his radio out of the pocket of his raincoat and flipped it on. "Patch me through to the Fire Department."

"Fire Department? What the—"

"Shaddup!" The Fire Department dispatcher's voice crackled back at him. Shaw spoke into the radio. "Yeah, this is Inspector Shaw with Honolulu Tac. Who'm I talkin' to?"

"Bill Bradley, sir."

"Bill, I need a Commander. Get me one on this frequency, okay?"

"Sure thing, Inspector. Stand by."

Shaw put the radio under his arm, fished out a cigarette and lit it, the muzzle of the .45 still in line with Yuri's head. "Whatchya want the damn Fire Department for, man?"

"Relax, Yuri. Do I look like the kinda guy who'd set ya on fire?"

Yuri didn't answer and before Shaw could say anything else, the radio crackled. "This is Commander Irving."

"Yeah, Commander. This is Tim Shaw, Honolulu Tac. Look, for this operation I got goin' down here, I need a fire truck, see." He gave Commander Irving the address. "I need a truck to come right around the corner fast as it can, comin' right down Brixton Street, make that turn, plenty of speed, plenty of sirens. You guys do that?"

"I need authorization, Mr. Shaw."

"It's Inspector. And I run the friggin' Tac Team. That enough?"

"Well, yeah, I guess."

"Faster your guys can make that turn, the better."

"I'll dispatch trucks right away."

"How soon before they get here?"

"Two minutes or a little over."

"That's perfect; consider yourself owed one, Commander."

"Right."

Shaw clicked off the radio and dropped it back in his pocket

175

"Hear that, Yuri?"

"What the hell you need some damn fire truck—"

"I don't need a fire truck. Any truck'd do. See, you're gonna keep lyin' here in the street and when the fire truck turns the corner—a buddy o' mine used to call 'em drunken painters 'cause they're always runnin' around and haulin' ladders—anyway, when the fire trucks turn the corner, they're gonna run right over ya, Yuri. Tragic, huh?"

Yuri started to get up. Shaw put a bullet into the street right next to Yuri's head and Yuri froze. "You crazy, man!"

"Well, to tell ya the truth, Yuri, that thing at the school really upset me, ya know? All those kids and everything? I gotta take it out on somebody. If I had the Nazis that did it, I'd kill them. But, all I got's you."

Yuri passed gas again, long and loud. "Lemme up, man. I don't know shit."

"Sure ya do, Yuri. It's that brown stuff that's gonna be fillin' your pants soon as ya hear the first fire truck comin' around the corner. Probably gonna be a hook and ladder, the real big long ones with all those axles and those big truck tires, ya know?"

"I don't know no Nazis, Shaw!"

"Golly, what a shame. And I'll probably feel real guilty after those trucks grind ya into the pavement just thinkin' about that."

"Then lemme up!"

"Get up and I shoot ya; you'd be just as dead either way."

"Man, I don't know no fuckin' Nazis!"

Shaw flicked ashes from his cigarette into Yuri's hair. "I don't really care what the Nazis' sex life is like, Yuri. I just wanna know where to find 'em."

Yuri stammered. "Okay! They got a place at the waterfront on—"

"I don't think you're sincere, Yuri. Doesn't sound like where these guys'd hang out. You're lyin'."

"I ain't lyin'!"

Shaw snapped his cigarette butt to the pavement, a couple of inches away from Yuri's face. "Wow, I'm gonna feel real bad, I go

176

down to the waterfront and find 'em then, you run over by all those trucks and everything."

"It's the damn truth, man!"

Sirens could be heard in the distance, growing louder.

Shaw didn't say anything.

"I don't know where the hell them Nazis is, man!"

Shaw didn't move the .45, didn't say a word. The sirens were loud now. As Shaw figured the time from the sound, the first fire truck would be coming around the corner in about forty-five seconds. "Yuri, look, I'll wait on the curb, huh?"

Yuri visibly filled his pants.

Tim Shaw stepped up onto the curb. "Where are they, Yuri? And if it doesn't sound like the truth, you got the choice of a bullet or a fire truck."

"Stayin' with Stroud, over in immigrant village, in the condos Stroud owns. There's twelve of them and they got a special assignment, ain't tied with none of the other commando groups. All they do is terrorist shit, man. Got guns, explosives, all the good shit. Heavy hitters. The big building on the corner across from the fish markets. I don't know no address, man. Lemme up!" Yuri was screaming in order to be heard over the wailing of the sirens.

There wasn't time for Shaw to let Yuri get to his feet. At the far left edge of Shaw's peripheral vision, there was a blur of motion, a streak of red. Shaw was already jumping from the curb, grabbed Yuri by the shirt collar and dragged him back. The first fire truck rounded the corner almost in the same instant, its slipstream ripping the black fedora from Tim Shaw's head, the sound of its siren momentarily deafening.

Yuri was crying, screaming, holding onto Shaw's leg.

Tim Shaw shook him loose. Yuri stayed there, on his knees, eyes turned up toward Tim Shaw's face. Shaw held the muzzle of the .45 inches from Yuri's right eye. Despite the evening's breeze, the smell from what Yuri had done to himself was almost overpowering. Shaw whispered, "Go and sin no more; or next time ya die."

177

Tim Shaw upped the safety on the .45 and walked the few paving squares to where his hat had landed, picked it up, struck it against his thigh a few times and snapped down the brim. He looked back at Yuri and told him, "Sorry I messed things up with you and the babe."

35

It was ultramodern here. There were no bars, but if he attempted to pass through the ordinary doorway leading from his cell – it was more like a very small apartment – he would be stopped. There was a powerful electrical field there that would shock, stun, or kill, depending on how one interacted with it. A touch, a shock. A partial body contact, a stun. If he threw himself through the field, the voltage would likely stop his heart permanently.

The power of the field was demonstrated to Martin Zimmer when he was "locked" in. An old tennis ball was used. After passing through the plasma energy field, it was half disintegrated, what remained of it blackened, crisped.

Martin Zimmer was adequately convinced. He stayed where he was put. Since he was a VIP, the accommodations, however Spartan, had some amenities. There were books (he hated reading), there was radio (he found music boring) and there was television (the news bored him and he hated most of what was broadcast, particularly the westerns, which seemed to dominate dramatic programming).

He played solitaire and watched soap operas throughout the day. After dinner – filling but bland – he continued playing solitaire and paid halfhearted attention to a documentary on the life of Nathaniel Darkwood, scientist and explorer, one of the founders of Mid-Wake. Martin Zimmer cared not a whit for Darkwood from a biographical standpoint, but the underwater photography was diverting enough.

When it came to the part about how, through the efforts of

Darkwood and others, Mid-Wake the underwater scientific research station became Mid-Wake the city state, surviving the holocaust of the surface, Martin Zimmer, despite his dislike of music, turned to MTV. As far as he was concerned, it would have been better if Mid-Wake had perished on The Night of The War. There would have been no United States, no Pearl Harbor Naval Base, no jail cell in which to be incarcerated.

Martin Zimmer suspended his game of solitaire; he couldn't find a red nine without prying beneath the rows of face down cards and that took concentration in order to do it artfully. And his favorite group was on television with their latest video, Gimme Head and the BJs doing "Deep Penetration." He read all the fanzines from New Germany, the United States and Australia—books were a waste of time—and he knew everything there was to know about Gimme Head and the BJs. He'd been planning to have them do a private performance at Eden City before all this with the Rourke Family had come up; and, someday he'd still have them.

This particular video was filmed inside an atmospheric insertion jet specially rigged out with all the seats removed so when the jet intentionally went to zero gravity—that was unnecessary in atmospheric insertions, of course—they could all roll around and play their guitars at the same time. And the girls with them in this video were so gorgeous-looking that Martin Zimmer got an erection just looking at them and fantasizing himself with Gimme Head and the BJs and the girls weightless and flying naked.

When the video was over, he started searching for his red nine . . .

The radio transceiver was exceedingly artful. It was hidden inside his left cheek where, if he'd still had a wisdom tooth, that would have been. It slipped in and out easily. Natural acids within his saliva powered the battery. Voice quality for the receiver was always poor, however, since much of actual speech occurred in combination with tongue, teeth and lips. But, when one whispered carefully, the transmitted speech was intelligible. Sound, when receiving, was transmitted along the jawbone directly to the inner ear. Built into the system were compensators which would prevent a sudden high-decibel incoming noise from stunning the ear.

The members of the commando team were in place, some by the guard station at the helipad serving the Fleet Admiral's base headquarters, others near the brig, still others near the motor pool synth-fuel dump located on the far side of the base.

His driver—young Rauph—beside him, Croenberg, his Naval Commander's dress whites sparkling, approached the two fatigue-clad Marines who stood guard at the doorway to the Pearl Harbor brig.

They saluted.

Croenberg returned the salute and started for the doorway.

"Begging the Commander's pardon, sir, but I'll have to ask for a palm print check, sir!"

Croenberg had not expected this, because it was not usual base security procedure, nor had this practice been instituted as little as two hours ago.

Croenberg started to move his right hand toward the palm print identifier panel, set like a plaque beside the doorway. The young Marine Lance Corporal stepped back. Even though Gruppenführer Croenberg had not anticipated this, he had planned ahead for the unexpected.

The concept of a weapon carried up the sleeve of a garment was nothing new. Nor was the principle of mechanically assisting the retrieval of such a weapon. In most cases, to actuate some sort of spring-loaded device, some sort of arm movement was required. The inherent difficulty and danger, of course, was that somehow such movement would be performed inadvertently and the weapon released; conversely, to prevent such from happening, one might even subconsciously avoid a certain range of movement, thus attracting the attention of the curious or detail-minded.

The device Croenberg wore, in order to guard against both such contingencies, required two rather irregular movements to be performed in sequence. As he moved his right arm now, as if to touch his hand to the panel, Croenberg cocked his right wrist back to maximum extension, thus performing the first motion and moving his hand out of range. Croenberg wheeled toward the nearer of the two Marines, rotating his arm downward and outward, then up and in.

At the instant he completed the rotation, the 7.65mm single shot pistol – it was about the size of an ordinary carpenter's mechanical tape measure, the barrel just under six centimeters in length – fired. The bullet struck the young American Marine at the bridge of the nose, glanced along the bone and into the left eye. The barrel was surrounded by sound baffles, absorbing the expanding gases, muffling all sound above that of a light cough.

At the same instant, Croenberg heard the sound of Rauph's knife ripping fabric and flesh and the second Marine started to fold.

Croenberg grabbed the body of the man he'd shot before it fully hit the level of the small synth-concrete porch. Rauph was already trying the door as he clutched the second dead man's body against him.

The door swung open. Croenberg shoved the body through the doorway and drew his pistol. Then Croenberg stepped through the doorway after the dead man.

As expected, there were no guards in the antechamber between the exterior and interior doors. Croenberg shoved his dead man in the nearest corner, relieving the body of its energy rifle. Rauph had already done the same. One of them on either side of the interior doorway, Rauph turned the knob.

As expected, it opened.

There were two guards on the other side, both of them seated at desks, one on either side of a narrow, sterile-looking green corridor. They started for their sidearms but never made it, Rauph firing his suppressed pistol, Croenberg doing the same, Croenberg and Rauph firing across each other.

Both Marines went down, the one on the left whom Rauph had shot slamming into the wall, slipping down along its length leaving a blood trail from the bullet's exit wound at the back of his neck. The one Croenberg shot—a neatly placed bullet above the right eye—fell against the wall, then jackknifed forward over his desk.

Croenberg rasped, "We are inside. All is well. Hurry." The others, posted near the brig, would follow them in. But Croenberg and Rauph did not wait, crisscrossing as they passed through the doorway, momentarily taking cover behind the two desks.

As expected, there was no resistance.

They started down the corridor, toward the VIP cell block where Martin Zimmer was housed . . .

Ordinary solitaire was too easy, and after several hours of playing it Martin Zimmer tired. He wasn't ready for a nap, and nothing else of interest presented itself. He took up the cards again and shuffled them well, then dealt twenty-five cards face down. He set the remaining twenty-seven aside, then picked up the twenty-five.

Fanning these out in his left hand, he started picking cards, deciding to try to form full houses first, then work back from that. The game was called by various names, his father Deitrich Zimmer who had taught it to him had said, but most commonly "poker solitaire." The object—statistically almost impossible and in actuality difficult to perform—was to make five pat hands in poker, straights, flushes, straight flushes, full houses.

When he was in practice, which he was not, Martin Zimmer could do it about one in ten times. Getting four pat hands was almost absurdly simple, but then breaking up those hands and reforming them in order to produce a total of five was the frustratingly difficult part.

As he started building a diamond flush, the plasma energy shield could be heard to crackle on the other side of the door.

Martin looked at his digital wristwatch. It was too early for the evening security check and he'd already had dinner (terribly bland).

The door opened.

Martin Zimmer dropped his cards to the floor and stood up. "Croenberg!"

"Martin! We have come to rescue you from these enemies who wrongfully imprison you."

Martin Zimmer started to laugh.

36

There was a detailed physical profile of each of the prisoners in the Pearl Harbor brig and the closest physical match to young Martin happened to be a black man with the first name of Adolph. The whole idea appealed to Croenberg's dark sense of humor. To get Martin out of the brig without a major battle erupting the moment someone happened to spot him, they would disguise him as this black man who was serving time in the brig for running a dice game.

A digitized photographic representation of Adolph Langley was obtained and enhanced into three-dimensional perspective, then a life mask prosthesis constructed, as well as hand coverings.

Martin Zimmer protested, of course, but Croenberg—very respectfully—pointed out, "This is the only way to get you free, Martin. I know it is a sacrifice to disguise yourself as this person, but you make this sacrifice for the greater glory of National Socialism. It is the lot of the hero to give of himself."

That last remark apparently convinced Martin.

With Rauph and two others helping—Croenberg elected to watch the corridor rather than help dress Martin—Martin Zimmer was ready to travel in seven minutes, except for one detail. As they brought Martin to the door, Croenberg reached into the case from which the clothing had been taken and produced the restraints. "I am afraid you will have to wear these, Martin, in order that this should look convincing."

"The things I do for my people," Martin said, shaking his head, smiling.

185

From Croenberg's detailed analysis of Martin Zimmer over the years, including sexual habits, he doubted seriously that Martin was anything but excited by the prospect of being in chains. The belly chain was locked at the back, then Martin's wrists put into the cuffs, holding his hands at waist level. Croenberg wanted to say something, but didn't. Instead, he directed Rauph with a nod to lead Martin away.

As the last man exited Martin's cell, Croenberg reactivated the plasma barrier . . .

The only thing Tim Shaw liked about electric cars was that they ran silently. Three cars had already pulled up behind the fish market, the only noise they made the soft humming of their tires over the pavement.

Ed and most of the rest of the Tac Team had energy rifles. Fortunately, although every once in a while he heard rumors that the Germans were working on developing one, no one had yet to invent an energy shotgun. Like the rest of Tim Shaw's firearms, the shotgun he held in his right hand was a Lancer replica, this of the Remington 870 police shotgun from six hundred and twenty-five years ago. Like all Lancer replicas, it was faithful to the last detail, even using ordnance steel that was blued as opposed to stainless. In the climate in the islands, that meant more care, but the 870's smooth action made it all worthwhile.

Beside him, Ed said, "The three cars behind the condos are in position. The only way they'll get outa there is if they can fly."

"Don't be too cocky," Tim Shaw advised his son. He turned away from staring at the condos and looked at the twelve men. "All right. This is kind of a funny operation. We don't have a warrant, don't have probable cause beyond an informer's tip—and my ass'd be in a sling if anybody knew how I got it—and the idea isn't so much to arrest these bastards as to stop 'em. If we can take 'em alive, terrific; we'll get good information out

186

of 'em. But if it's a choice between killin' the mother fuckers and lettin' one of 'em get away, we kill. Any questions?"

There were a few grins from the Tac Team guys, but there weren't any questions.

Ed would run things tactically because he was better at it, so Tim Shaw told his son, "Give 'em the word, Eddy."

Ed gave the word . . .

Aside from Croenberg and Rauph, dressed as officers, the other men of the squad infiltrated to Pearl Harbor Naval Base were uniformed as enlisted personnel. The two with them, as they entered the car now, wore Shore Patrol armbands.

Martin was sandwiched between them in the rear seat of the sedan, Croenberg sitting in the front passenger seat, Rauph driving. An enlisted man behind the wheel would have looked better, but that would have necessitated a fifth man for this element of the operation and that would not have worked.

Rauph started the electric car out of the slot marked "Visitor" and turned the wheel into a hard right, cutting across several of the vacant slots as the vehicle angled toward the street.

There was a considerable amount of traffic, but as yet no alarm was raised. "Nice and slow, well within the speed limit, Rauph," Croenberg ordered. The more easily they reached the Fleet Admiral's personal helicopter, the better . . .

After attacking the Sebastian's Reef Country Day School, the plan was to drive to the opposite end of Honolulu and carry out a similar operation against one of the City of Honolulu's largest public schools where children from the immigrant community and the children of other of the island's poorer elements attended. Because of the short span of time between reaching the island and pulling the first raid, however, there had not been sufficient opportunity to prepare the required number of explosive charges.

Hence, the container which housed more than seventy-five percent of the team's detonators was brought along. For safety, the explosives were kept in one van and the detonators in the other. The van which was intercepted was the one carrying the detonators. The second assault was scrubbed and now Wilhelm Doring faced a critical shortage of proper detonators.

While he mentally kicked himself for the price of his haste, Wilhelm Doring's eyes never left Marie as she spoke with the old woman at the lunch counter. The other six men who had accompanied them were watching the street, two from the opposite side, two at either end of the block on the same side as the restaurant. The transceiver in Doring's mouth would alert him should there be any potential trouble.

At last, Marie's seemingly interminable conversation with the old woman ended and she—Marie Dreissling—started back toward the doorway where Doring stood, waiting. "Well?"

"Willy, she—"

"Do we have the detonators or not?"

"Her husband did not tell her. He said he would be late and we should wait here for him."

That infuriated Doring, that a local Nazi sympathizer would assume that an officer of the Reich should be kept waiting for a mere nobody. Partly because of the positioning of the radio device within his mouth and partly because he was angry, Wilhelm Doring all but growled, "The girl and I have to wait here. Keep your positions. I will be in radio contact as necessary. Doring, Out."

"She suggested we come and sit at the lunch counter, Willy. She will give us free food and coffee!"

He could have strangled Marie for her complacency concerning the detonator shortage and her enthusiasm over the offer of coffee and food. Instead, Wilhelm Doring smiled at her, saying, "That sounds pleasant enough." He took her elbow and started toward the counter with her, careful that the tips of his fingers didn't crush her arm.

It was a cardinal rule of any clandestine operation that meet-

188

ing times were to be met exactly, neither early nor late; if a predetermined appointment could not be kept, the meeting was scrubbed.

But, because he needed the detonators, Wilhelm Doring would wait.

37

Fleet Admiral Wilma Hayes's helicopter was the finest and fastest of those made in the United States, equal to anything found flying for Eden City. The helicopter's top condition-one speed was 500 miles per hour and it was nearly as maneuverable as a fighter aircraft, could outrun any helicopter gunship in the air arsenal of any of the world's powers.

It was precisely because of its excellence that Gruppenführer Croenberg had included the machine in his escape plans. Rauph, driving the sedan, was as good with a helicopter as he was with a knife; he had flown Eden's most comparable machines (almost as fast but vastly less maneuverable) and was completely versed in the literature of the Laimleer X11A. All that was necessary was to neutralize the Marine Corps personnel guarding the Admiral's helicopter, then get it airborne and away.

For the former task, standard procedures would suffice — security measures were rarely able to frustrate the intentions of those who were truly bold — and, for the latter, there was the planned diversionary action at the motor pool fuel dump. Had Croenberg selected the synth-fuel storage area which served Pearl Harbor's fighter and gunship response groups, there would have been a substantially greater guard force with which the men he had detailed to the operation would be required to deal.

Rauph turned the sedan into the side drive running parallel to the Admiral's headquarters complex, the two Nazi saboteurs catching up to and throwing themselves inside, the helipad just beyond, not even a fence separating it from the rest of the compound. From the back seat, Martin began to ask,

"Can't we just drive off—"

"If we drive, Martin," Croenberg explained, without looking over into the back seat, "the moment your escape is detected, every helicopter, every car, every remote in the area will be watching for us. The chances would be substantial that we would be captured, you recaptured. And, we must get off the island. Were we to evade initial response efforts, every place of exit from the island would be sealed, coastal patrols increased, etc. It would be necessary for us to swim out to a rendezvous with a vessel. Possibilities for success would be doubtful at best and the very act would be fraught with peril to you.

"But, by stealing the Admiral's helicopter," Croenberg continued, "we not only escape the base in an aircraft which will be almost impossible to catch but we escape the island as well. By the time fighters are scrambled in pursuit of us, we will have arrived at our destination, the helicopter will be set on auto pilot and dispatched over the open sea. As the helicopter is intercepted, it will be destroyed, by us. Therefore, there will be some resultant confusion as to whether or not you lived or died. That is to our advantage."

"I cannot wait, my faithful Gruppenführer, to be rid of this disguise."

Croenberg looked over into the rear seat now, saying, "I assure you, Martin, that soon all of your vicissitudes will be at an end." Indeed they would be. Croenberg added, "Forgive me while I confer with the personnel waiting to institute the needed diversion." The sedan was fewer than one hundred meters from the helicopter and the guards surrounding it. Croenberg, his voice sounding low and guttural as he spoke for the benefit of the microphone concealed within his mouth, said, "This is Rescue Leader. We approach Objective Beta. Initiate action against your objective, then commence escape sequence. Out."

Fifty meters now, the sedan slowing.

Croenberg had already reloaded the 7.65mm sleeve pistol . . .

Thorn Rolvaag's wife, Ellie, fed both Rolvaag and Betty Gilder a hastily prepared late supper of spaghetti with meat sauce, garlic bread and red wine. The children, Daniel and Trixie, were already fed, off in the nearby recreation room watching their favorite interactive television program. Ellie picked at her food; waiting to eat with her husband, as had been her custom ever since they were engaged, always seemed to destroy her appetite.

And she was as pretty as ever, Rolvaag thought, just looking at her.

Ellie brushed a lock of dark hair away from her forehead with the back of her hand as she raised her wine glass. "So, you really have to go up there tonight?" Ellie asked.

"I tried talking your stubborn husband out of it," Betty said, smiling at Ellie, frowning at him, "but it's that old Viking stock, I guess, makes him bullheaded."

"Not that I want to," Rolvaag said, picking up a piece of garlic bread. "But Doctor Rourke took me over to see all this Navy brass and I told them about Betty's and my Diversion Theory and—"

"I had nothing to do with it," Betty said, slightly reprovingly. "You're the brains of the operation. All I said was that I thought the Diversion Theory was brilliant, that it would indeed be possible to redirect lava flow and reduce the force of the actual eruption."

"If Kilauea is about to erupt, Thorn," Ellie began, "you don't have to be up there. You can monitor everything—"

"No, see, I need pressure readings, sweetheart," Rolvaag tried to explain. "Pressure readings have to be taken in situ. It's just like taking somebody's blood pressure; you can't do it without touching the arm." His wife had been a nurse so she should be able to identify with that.

"You can get an accurate blood pressure reading by other means than putting a cuff on somebody," Ellie pointed out.

"Well, I can't test vent pressure without being there. There's a chopper taking me up. They drop me off and pick me up a couple hours later and I've already called my data back and it's crunching through the computer. Simple."

"He's not going alone," Betty said in Rolvaag's defense. "Carl Bremen—the graduate student?—he's going to go along."

"What about all these Nazi terrorists, Thorn?" Ellie insisted. "I don't like the idea of you being God knows where with all these—"

"There's no reason in the world why any Nazi terrorist would be on the volcano," he told her, cutting off her argument he hoped. Thorn Rolvaag felt as if he were the object of attention at an inquisition, except in this case the intentions behind the questions were loving. "I've got constant radio contact ability and I carry a pistol."

"Take your other gun."

"The shotgun's too cumbersome to lug around when I've got the monitoring equipment."

"Then the other one," Ellie—who knew less about firearms generally than he did—insisted. "The one that looks like a submachinegun but isn't."

"The SP-89; fine, I'll take that." He could sling it to his shoulder and get it out of the way easily enough, and with two thirty-round magazines clipped together he wouldn't have to burden himself with bringing spare magazines along. "And Carl carries a gun, too."

"I don't know much about guns, but I know graduate students can't afford good ones," Ellie said, then sipping again at her wine.

Thorn Rolvaag didn't know what kind of gun Carl carried, but with any luck he wouldn't have the occasion to have to find out, either.

Above the noise of the television broadcast, Thorn Rolvaag could hear Hrothgar and some of the other dogs barking from the kennels. But animals could often sense things men could not, sense impending earthquakes, volcanic eruptions, other natural disasters, even storms. Rolvaag took a last sip from his wine, not finishing the contents of the glass. Tonight he would have to be very clearheaded. And he tried to ignore the barking of the dogs, because he knew what caused it . . .

The walkway between the buildings was narrow, as if space were at too great a premium to bother with convenience. But, casual observation from above would be more difficult, so Tim

Shaw didn't complain about it. Instead, three of the Tac Team men with him, he made his way along the walkway, staying as close as they could to the building wall, to further frustrate any chances of being detected.

When, at last, they reached the rear of the building, Shaw signaled a halt, then rasped into his radio, "Okay. We're at the back. Eddy, remind your guys one more time we got maybe twelve bad asses in there, so be cool." Using infrared sensing from a video drone flyby—he'd had a buddy in narcotics call it in—they were able to tell from body heat signature registers that only the third floor had any apartments with more than three people in them. It stood to reason that the Nazis would stay together, Shaw hoped. At the near side of the third floor, the drone gave a reading in excess of three persons. Beyond that, because of the materials used in the building, it was impossible to get a precise figure. There could have been ten people in the apartment.

And, of course, the apartment could have been occupied by a family of four. In that case, back to square one. But, Shaw didn't think so. Yet, because of the chance that there weren't any bad guys in the apartment at all, it wouldn't be practical to break in and start shooting. A check of the package boxes in the lobby showed nobody at all living on the third floor; that was suspicious in itself since housing in this part of town was hard to come by and this character Stroud, who owned the building, probably wanted to keep it rented so he could make money.

But maybe Stroud made his money by renting to special clients.

The third floor had all the earmarks of a Nazi safe house.

Tim Shaw said into his radio, "We're goin' in. See ya up top." Then he signaled the three men with him and started around the corner toward the fire elevator. They didn't dare activate it, because it might be noisy and creak, since the machinery was old. But they could scale the ladders flanking it on either end, and by that means reach the third floor. After that, whatever went down would be a crapshoot that he hoped wouldn't turn into a turkey shoot with him and his men as the targets . . .

The Marine guards lay dead and Rauph sat at the X11A's controls, the main rotor increasing revolutions. Through his transceiver, Croenberg monitored a garbled mixture of breathing and occasionally intelligible sounds, while his men attacked the motor pool fuel dump, planting demolitions, suppressing resistance. These men not only aided Croenberg's own escape along with Martin, Rauph and the other two SS men accompanying Croenberg, but they aided their own escape as well. If all went well, the fuel dump explosions would alert base security, then if Martin's absence was not already detected, it would be. Someone would realize the Admiral's high-speed helicopter was missing and all attention would be focused on that. Meanwhile, Croenberg would be getting away in the helicopter and his men who attacked the fuel dump would escape in the confusion, then dissolve into the Nazi commando units already in place on the island.

An unexpected assist to Croenberg's intentions was coming from the heavy volume of air transport takeoffs, wholly unanticipated but entirely welcome. The more crowded the air space surrounding Pearl Harbor, the more difficult it would be for the Naval authorities to scramble a fighter squadron, even given that virtually all fighter aircraft were jump capable, could take off and land vertically.

Young Martin was still shackled – "There is no time now, Martin. You must be patient, I implore you!" – he occupied the copilot's seat. Croenberg, despite his rank of Gruppenführer, did not consider himself above the task at which he was currently employed. He assisted two SS men in deploying the helicopter's door gun. It was a PEM-7, the finest in power, range and accuracy of the light plasma energy cannons in the arsenal of the Trans-Global Alliance. The door gun on the other side was being treated similarly by the two men picked up at the gate.

Mounting it between the doors as they did, there was a full 360 degrees of possible rotation, allowing them to cover and cross both sides of the helicopter's fuselage.

With any luck, they would never need it.

Rauph's voice came to Croenberg through the intraship communications channel, the receiver for this in Croenberg's left ear. "It is my pleasure to report that the aircraft is prepared for take-

195

off, Herr Gruppenführer, awaiting your order."

"Very well. Get us out of here, Rauph."

"Yes, Herr Gruppenführer!"

And the aircraft slipped forward and began to rise. In what seemed like a mere instant, the helicopter was airborne, skimming over the Fleet Admiral's Headquarters Building. Further inland, Croenberg could see the smoke and glowing bright orange fires from the synth-fuel dump against the night sky, where base firefighting equipment was racing toward it.

38

John Rourke drove the borrowed For Official Use Only sedan with only the scantest portion of his concentration. The Nazi attack on the school bothered him greatly, not only in its actuality as an act of heartless brutality but as a symbol of the times. After more than six centuries, what had actually changed?

The Earth's population was the merest fraction of what it once was, yet human life was valued more cheaply than ever.

When he someday was able to restore Sarah, what sort of a world would he be giving her?

As he buttoned down the driver's-side electric window, the sirens he'd heard for some time while approaching Pearl Harbor's main gate became suddenly piercingly louder. "I wonder what's going on," Annie asked rhetorically. To his right, from the direction of the motor pool, there were explosions, and heavy black smoke rose into the darkness, obscuring the base's artificial lighting. Fire equipment raced along the intersecting street just beyond the main gate.

After Doctor Rolvaag's briefing on the impending volcanic eruption, they had spent their time discussing with Admiral Wilma Hayes the role the Navy's submarines could play in implementing Rolvaag's Diversion Theory. Rolvaag himself left, for a quick meal and the gathering up of his gear, then a helicopter ride to the volcanic summit. Admiral Hayes introduced Rourke and his family to various Naval personnel and civilians whose expertise might dovetail into the project.

Rourke showed his I.D. and those of the others with him to the sentry computer; and as he did so, one of the Shore Patrolmen on

197

duty there saluted, spitting out a stream of words so rapidly that Rourke had to concentrate in order to follow him. "Begging the General's pardon, sir, but I have orders from Commander Washington to respectfully request that the General come to the Base Brig at once, sir, where it has just been discovered, sir, that the VIP prisoner held there has escaped, apparently aided by a commando team which has stolen the Admiral Hayes helicopter and sabotaged the motor pool synth-fuel dump in order to create a diversion."

"Martin, free, damnit!" Michael hissed.

"Thank you," Rourke told the breathless-sounding Shore Patrolman. Then he took back the proffered I.D.s for himself, Paul, Michael, Annie and Natalia, and he stomped the electric car's accelerator pedal to the floor as he threw the cards onto the seat between him and Paul. If Martin escaped them, all hope of forcing Deitrich Zimmer to perform the operation Sarah needed so desperately would vanish with him.

John Rourke just missed a fire truck as he took the hard left turn . . .

Her helmet radio started blaring simultaneously with the radio in the transport vehicle. The entire briefing just ended had dealt with the rescue operation—for persons on the big island, Hawaii—from the impending volcanic eruption and her adopted Wing's part in it. And Emma Shaw had been assigned to co-pilot a fighter aircraft of no use in the operation. But the radio instructions caused the transport driver to crank the wheel of the vehicle in which she rode into a tight right turn and head toward the other end of the field, near the side runways where porters were already readying the takeoffs.

She ran her fingers through her just-curled hair and pulled on her helmet so she could talk. "Commander Shaw to Pearl Angels Three. Commander Shaw calling Pearl Angels Three. What's going on? Over."

"This is Pearl Angels Three control, Commander Shaw. Admiral's helicopter stolen by suspected enemy commando unit. The Wing's going after it. Martin Zimmer may be aboard. You'll receive instructions once you're scrambled. Now, get off the air!

Out."

Emma Shaw pulled off her helmet, the wind tearing at her hair again. If Martin Zimmer had escaped, John's plans to save his wife might be dashed. She shouted to the driver over the slipstream, "Hurry it up, damnit!" But if she were ordered to shoot down the machine, could she do it? Because killing Martin Zimmer would seal Sarah Rourke's fate, perhaps forever. If she fired at the aircraft and missed, would it be intentional, however subconscious?

"Shit," she said.

39

Information was already coming in that a black prisoner had accompanied the men in dress whites who had boarded and off-lifted Admiral Hayes's helicopter. That there was no reason for the murder of the man they found in the cell was obvious; the Nazis had simply done it.

"They wanted Martin to look like Seaman Langley, but why this?"—Washington asked. John Rourke looked at Commander Washington, then back at the body of Seaman Langley. "He would have been out of the Brig and back to duty in another day, for God's sake. What'd he do to them?"

Langley's throat was slit from ear to ear and his eyes stared glassily toward them across the floor where his body lay beside his bunk. "Not a thing. They just like killing people."

Rourke stood up from the crouch, walked over to the dead man and stood beside him. "Will your Shore Patrol investigators mind if I close his eyes?"

"I, uhh, I don't think so."

Rourke nodded only, bent over the man, closed the mans eyelids, murmuring under his breath, "Rest in peace." Rourke rose to his full height again. He looked at the others standing there with him inside and just outside the cell enclosure. "If they've taken Admiral Hayes's helicopter, they're making a run to one of the other islands. And surface vessels large enough for them to land a chopper on would be too easily spotted and neutralized. They may be daring, even reckless, but they're not stupid, our adversaries, so they won't be likely to try ditching in the ocean and making a submarine pickup. And the comparatively few subs that Eden has are small and wouldn't be any match for the United States fleet head on. If the Nazis are planning on using a submarine to get away, it would have to pick them up after they were safely landed and some time had passed. They'd know that right now we'd have every aircraft and every submarine at our disposal looking for them and an Eden sub wouldn't make it through the grid.

"That means," John Rourke continued, "that we have lost custody of Martin Zimmer, but we haven't lost him permanently, or at least not yet." Rourke began to pace the cell. "The Admiral's helicopter. Tell me about it, Commander Washington."

"Well, it's a fast, very fast machine. It can outfly any chopper in the air, and give a good accounting of itself with some types of fixed-wing aircraft. It's that fast at top speed and it's exceedingly maneuverable Admiral Hayes uses it when she has to get from Pearl to Mid-Wake. She can land on one of the surface platforms there after just four hours. It burns through fuel fast, though, and it's light, so there isn't the weight to spare for a large fuel load. Cruising range is maybe 2875 miles. I'm no expert on aircraft."

"Fine. We assume," Rourke said, nodding, "that the men who took Martin Zimmer will be clever, will have planned this phase of their operation as carefully as the rescue itself, right down to the fuel dump fires. They'd want to get out of the air as quickly as possible. I assume the Admiral's chopper can be flown on autopilot like the other helicopter's I've encountered in this time?"

"I guess so," Washington answered. "That's checked easily enough."

"But in a moment, shall we?" Rourke went on. "Assuming it can fly on its own, without a human pilot at the controls, the logical thing for the commando team to do would be to set the machine down quickly in some relatively safe location, then get it airborne again and send it out on remote through the weakest portion of the United States sensor net, but keeping in mind they have to make it appear that the craft has an actual, practical destination. Then, they simply blow it up.

"So," Rourke said, taking one of his thin, dark tobacco cigars from the pocket of his jacket, "we should first confirm that the Admiral's helicopter was carrying its maximum fuel load before it was taken, then determine maximum range from Pearl, not bothering to deduct the amount of flying time needed to reach one of the other nearby islands because they could top off the tanks easily enough before the craft goes airborne again. Pick likely landing sites—not that they would really use, but that they'd like us to think they'd use—within range from here. Collate the data in conjunction with a computer analysis to determine the thinnest coverage of the U.S. sensor shield. We should be spotting a blip in that area within a reasonably short period of time, and find wreckage from the helicopter.

"They'll blow it up, of course," Rourke said matter-of-factly. "Once that happens, we'll know we're onto their plan. In the meantime, we methodically begin a search of the most likely remote landing spots nearby. Meanwhile, we analyze these possible LZs in light of our suspicion that they'll be waiting for a subsurface pickup once the heat dies down. That should give us a limited number of sites which can be thoroughly searched. We've got a chance!" John Rourke declared. At least he hoped they did.

40

Tim Shaw thumbed back the hammer of the .45. If the Nazis were utilizing audio-triggered silent alarms, they would already be alerted to the Tac Team's approach. There was nothing to lose with a click either way.

For the past several minutes, he'd been listening to the conversation inside the condo. It was in German and he could not understand it. But once he heard mention of Sebastian's Reef Country Day School, and he picked out at least three separate times when SS Rank was referred to. And he detected the word "Juden," which he knew meant "Jews," followed by laughter. If there weren't Nazis inside the condo, he'd have a lot of explaining to do. But in his guts, he knew they were.

Tim Shaw moved the microphone away from the wall, flipping power off as he removed the earpiece. The bugging device was ultra-compact and slipped easily into the side pocket of his suitcoat.

Shaw took off his shoes, stuffing them into his raincoat pockets after first transferring the little three-inch barreled .38 Special revolver to his trouser band. Then he donned the glasses and started moving again, as silently as he could. On stockinged feet he moved along the catwalk servicing the ladder leading to the escape elevator. The light from the condo's nearest window flowed in a yellow wash over the synth-aluminum treads. Unless these Nazis were living back in the Stone Age, they'd have Interrupters laid out. Interrupters were low-frequency laser carrier beams designed to be used with mirrors, establishing a series circuit. When the beam was interrupted by something passing through, the low-charge plasma energy on the carrier beam was unable to reach the next mirror. This momentarily interrupted the power for an alarm circuit, triggering the circuit and activating either one or several of a number of responses – an audible alarm, a flashing alarm light, a computer video warning, etc.

Shaw moved ahead, feeling stupid with the glasses over his eyes, and with them it was harder to see here than ever. The glasses were nothing sophisticated, but the guys in robbery encountered them all the time. Merely sunglasses with exceedingly dark lenses, burglars used them to help spot the pale red light of the laser beams.

And, as Tim Shaw was about to take his next step, he saw a beam and he froze.

He exhaled slowly as he drew his foot back. The presence here of Interrupters almost clinched it, that the Nazi terrorist unit he sought was one with the German-speaking persons he'd heard laughing over references to the Country Day School and to Jews. There was one other important feature of Interrupters; they were terrifically expensive. No rich person would be living in a building like this. But the Nazis would have them for perimeter security.

Shaw backtracked several paces along the exterior landing. A wind was blowing in across the city from the coast and it was almost cold here, the wind itself a mixture of smells of the sea and smells of the city.

He turned up the collar of his raincoat as he leaned against the wall. From his raincoat pockets, Shaw took his shoes, putting them down softly on the catwalk, slipping his feet into them. He removed the sunglasses, stuck them into the breast pocket of his suitcoat. Then he took his radio from the same pocket where one of the shoes had been. "Listen up, Eddy, rest of you guys on both teams," Shaw barely whispered into the device. "Found Interrupters. I can feel it. These are the people we want. Eddy, you and your guys be ready at the front. We're goin' in back here in about sixty seconds. If ya hear guns, it's the bad guys. If it's the wrong condo, I'll be on the radio fast. Out."

His three Tac Team men were already moving up to join him, had heard the message he'd broadcasted just as the men with his son Ed had heard. There was no need to repeat anything.

Shaw looked at his watch, barely able to see its face. He gave up, counting off seconds in his head. There was no way to get past the Interrupters, because if they were laid out at all properly they would be positioned at differing heights and maybe a burglar going against an undefended target had the time to climb through what amounted to a spiderweb of laser light without touching anything, but armed men going after a group of suspected terrorists, more heavily armed than they, certainly did not.

Tim Shaw's rough calculations made it that nearly a minute had passed. He rasped to the three men, "Billy, Mick, get on the other side of the friggin' window and cover while Sam and I go in. Be fast, cause you're gonna hit an Interrupter beam about three steps from now and they're gonna know we're out here." And, with any luck, they'd head for the front door of the condo and walk right into the rest of the Tac Team guys that Ed had waiting for them with shotguns and energy weapons, then surrender because they knew they were trapped.

But there was a better than even chance they'd go down shooting, and Tim Shaw was ready for that, too.

Shaw pulled his fedora from his head and stuffed it into his raincoat pocket, crushing it but there was nothing else he could do. Beneath his raincoat, slung crossbody from right shoulder to the left side of his chest, was a gas mask bag. He took the mask from inside the bag and pulled the mask over his head, popping the cheeks to make a seal. "Go," Shaw snapped.

Billy and Mick ran the length of the catwalk. As Billy reached the spot where Tim Shaw had seen the Interrupter, an alarm began to sound from inside the condo, barely audible but distinct enough that Shaw was certain what it was. Shaw, Sam beside him, was already moving, the .45 in his right hand, the .38 Special in his left.

As they neared the window, Shaw stepped aside, flattening himself against the wall as Sam fired a tear gas grenade from his launcher, the grenade shattering the window. If there were innocent people inside, there'd be a lot of explaining to do. And, there was always the possibility someone could get hurt from flying synth-glass, but there was no other way.

The tear gas round exploded as the second round was fired.

Shaw stepped away from the wall, kicking in the rest of the glass.

Gunfire tore through the opening and Shaw stepped back, bullets whining past him, pale blue energy bolts flickering and hissing across the night air. Billy announced over a bullhorn, "This is the Honolulu police. You are ordered to lay down your weapons. Surrender and you will not be—"

205

There was a loud clanging sound and Tim Shaw saw a grenade hit the catwalk surface. Shaw reached for it, to scoop it up and flip it over into the walkway below them, but Sam shoved him back as Sam reached for it himself. Shaw couldn't react fast enough to stop him.

The grenade was in midair when it exploded, Sam thrown back against the wall of the building, pieces of shrapnel peppering the wall and peppering Sam's left arm and left leg, too, blood stains growing. Sam shouted, "I'm all right! Get the fuckers!"

Tim Shaw shouted to Billy and Mick, "Throw that damn bullhorn away and cover me!"

Before either man could answer him, Shaw threw himself through the shattered window opening and into the cloud of gas beyond. Shaw fired the .45 in his right hand and the .38 that was in his left, his eyes trying to pierce the clouds of tear gas for targets. From behind him, he could hear Billy and Mick entering. Shaw stumbled over something, fell to his knees, pushed himself to his feet and realized that what he'd fallen over was a body.

As the nightwind blowing in through the shattered window swirled the gas cloud, Shaw could see the condo's front door. The door was open. Shaw shouted, "Mick! Hold the position by the window. Billy! Stick with me, right side."

Shaw reached the doorway, three shots left in the .45, the little .38 Special with only one.

Billy held a riot shotgun at high port close against his chest, ready to snap the muzzle down to action. Tim Shaw upped the safety on the .45, locked it under his armpit, dumped the cylinder for the Centennial and pocketed the empties along with the still-unfired cartridge, ramming a speedloader against the Smith & Wesson's ejector star, five fresh rounds in place. The .38 Special revolver went into his belt as he transferred magazines in the Colt, a fresh one up the well.

"You shoot, but keep it at an angle. Then I roll out and you cover. I'll signal for you. Be careful and don't fuckin' shoot me by mistake."

"Thanks a hell of a lot, Tim!"

"Yeah, so shoot already."

Billy fired a high one into the ceiling of the corridors and Tim Shaw went through in the same instant. Billy jacked out the empty. Shaw fired the .45 that was in his right fist twice, but high and at a steep angle because he had no target and didn't want to kill an innocent who might be in the corridor above.

That left six in the Colt and five in the Smith.

There was gunfire in the stairwell below and Shaw shouted to Billy, "Control the corridor and don't let anybody down after me! I'm gone!" Shaw hit the steps, taking them down two at a time, the tear gas clouds here wispy thin and nearly dissipated. There was a flash from an energy weapon, then another and another and Shaw stabbed his .45 toward the origin of the gunfire as he threw himself right against the stairwell wall and fired, then again and again and again.

There was an explosion, the energy weapon firing into the stair treads, plasma energy flickering along the handrails. Shaw took a jolt and fell.

There was the sound of shotguns from below, then more energy weapons, then shotguns again.

Shaw lay across the stair treads just up from the landing, the right side of his body shaking.

A man's form appeared over him. In thickly accented English, the man snarled, "American policeman is shiess!" And the man turned the muzzle of an energy rifle toward Tim Shaw's chest.

Tim Shaw's right hand still tingled so badly he could not close his fist tightly enough around the butt of the .45 to fire it.

But there was nothing wrong with Tim Shaw's left hand which punched the Smith & Wesson .38 Special toward the Nazi's face and double actioned the trigger five times fast. The energy rifle fired into the steps less than a foot from Shaw's head and Shaw rolled, the man's body rocking back, the energy rifle firing again as a scream started from the man's lips but never made it, dying halfway out.

Shaw thrust the emptied revolver into the pocket of his raincoat, took the .45 from his still semi-useless right hand. He clawed his way to a standing position beside the rail. The gas was almost totally dissipated. Shaw's right hand was good enough to rip the mask away from his face.

Immediately below him, halfway down the next flight of stairs, one of the Nazis fired his energy rifle into the already fallen body of Jim Thundercloud, one of the Tac Team guys.

"Fuck you!" Tim Shaw shouted and, as the Nazi looked up, Tim Shaw emptied his .45 into Thundercloud's killer's face.

41

The ground shook beneath Thorn Rolvaag's feet, the mountain's very fabric trembling. The voice of Carl Bremen, who was beside him, seemed to tremble slightly as Bremen asked, "Isn't this more activity than you expected, professor?"

"A little bit more," Rolvaag said, lying. When he'd last checked seismic readings just moments before leaving the house, a Naval escort there to take him to the nearest open field where a helicopter waited, readings had indicated nothing like this. And Rolvaag was afraid now (although he said nothing to young Bremen) that the eruption might have gone too far for his Diversion Theory to have any practical effect, if indeed it could be implemented.

The reason Rolvaag had waited—taken the time to have a quick dinner, etc.—was that high observation thermal-image photography of the volcano was not yet ready. He had to know which pipes within the volcano had the greatest magma buildup and the greatest potential for violent discharge, then have them mapped to the base of the volcano which lay beneath the sea.

The initial photography had been excellent, but only so far as it went. The aircraft, which was airborne now over the volcano at over fifty thousand feet, was utilized for submarine surveillance. Its instruments, with any luck, would accurately map the heat signatures of the major pipes to their base where the pipe reached the level of the ocean floor. It was at this point that the Diversion Theory would be tested.

Cracks in the shield surrounding the crater were already appearing, brightly glowing yellow-orange lines of liquid fire oozing from between the rocks.

Both Rolvaag and Bremen carried masks with independent oxygen supplies, but the fumes were not yet so severe as to require them.

They were less than a half-mile from the summit of the volcanic shield, beyond which lay the crater itself. He was reminded of the ancient Hawaiian superstitions. Kilauea did indeed seem all-powerful and it was no aspersion on the lack of scientific knowledge of an ancient people to suppose that an angry deity threatened. There was a story — known to all vulcanologists — of King Kamehameha casting a lock of his hair into the flowing lava of Hualalai as an offering to Pele and unlike modern efforts which Rolvaag proposed, Kamehameha's effort was documented. No one else in history had attempted to divert the eruptive power of a volcano, or if they had, nothing existed to document their success or failure.

Actual Hawaiian blood, centuries-diluted, flowed in the veins of exactly three living people, the decendents of three original members of Mid-Wake. Thorn Rolvaag was not one of these but perhaps his Icelandic heritage drew a blooded Norseman spiritually much closer to the ancient Hawaiians than might readily be thought. Had he considered it even remotely likely that casting a lock of his hair into one of the almost imperceptibly growing trickles of lava near him, as he and Bremen trod along the shield — he would have done so. The important thing was to find some means by which to evade the volcano's destructive force. How that was accomplished, whether by means physical or spiritual, was of no consequence.

They moved toward the site of the largest pipe and with the instruments available to them, it was his hope to measure the pressure of magma and gas so that he could calculate whether or not his intended diversion would have any hope of working, or indeed might precipitate greater catastrophe. Thermal imaging photography had already revealed heat buildup in excess of what Rolvaag had anticipated and the movement of the rock on which they walked grew steadily in violence. The eruption of Kilauea was stacking up to be of a force equal to or surpassing the greatest eruptions of reported history.

Hawaiian volcanoes generally tended to be slow and predictable, although lava had been known to plume to phenomenally great distances, but this eruption seemed erratic and could not be described as languid.

Thorn Rolvaag was worried.

He had already determined that they would take measurements

from this largest discernable pipe only, then flee. Going on about the shield to take additional measurements would bring him little extra data and could well claim his life and Bremen's.

He kept moving. The ground shook exceedingly violently and Rolvaag stumbled, catching himself on his left hand. Bremen was either not so quick or not so lucky, falling almost flat. As Rolvaag started to stand he faintly heard the noise of a helicopter. He looked up and saw a machine rising over the artificial horizon of the cone. It was not the Naval helicopter which had brought them here and waited now some distance off shore to be called back for pickup. But as they had flown out here, Rolvaag, despite his immersion in his own efforts, could not have avoided even if he had tried, hearing of the theft of Admiral Hayes's helicopter and the rescue from captivity of Martin Zimmer by Nazi commandos.

As Carl Bremen slowly and evidently in some pain started to his feet, Rolvaag said to him, "We have to get up toward the height of the shield, the summit. That helicopter."

Bremen asked, "What is it? What is wrong, professor?"

Rolvaag stared toward the cone, never looking at Bremen as he said, "Remember what the pilot said? Our pilot. That Doctor Rourke had instructed all aircraft in the area to look for signs of the commando unit having landed, that the stolen helicopter might be put on autopilot and flown away as a diversion?"

Immediately after the theft of Admiral Hayes's helicopter all communication frequencies had been altered to guard against Nazi interception. "What if that commando squad landed here with Martin Zimmer? That helicopter looked like it was taking off not just passing overhead." By now, ever since the capture of Martin Zimmer, almost everyone on the islands with any sort of official connections knew that Martin Zimmer was not only of strategic value to the United States as a potential bargaining tool in the impending war with Eden, but that Zimmer was John Rourke's only chance to force the infamous Nazi doctor, Deitrich Zimmer, to perform restorative surgery on John Rourke's wife, Sarah.

Without John Rourke's taking him to Admiral Hayes and helping him to present the Diversion Theory, Thorn Rolvaag knew that precious hours, perhaps days, would have been lost in reaching the right ears.

If Martin Zimmer were somewhere beyond the height of the volcano's shield, Thorn Rolvaag could not just calmly go ahead with his measurements and escape to safety. He would have to confirm that Zimmer was or was not here on the volcano and if Zimmer were there, return the favor to John Rourke by communicating that data.

Rolvaag turned to Bremen "Look Carl, you can do these measurements as well as I can. We both know that. I'll stay in radio contact with you, answer any questions you might have, but I'm going up to take a look on the other side of the shield. You've got a gun. Keep it handy."

Thorn Rolvaag slung the SP-89 forward on its sling, drawing the bolt rearward and upward then slapping the bolt handle down out of its notch, letting the bolt fly forward to strip the top round from the magazine. A second magazine was clipped beside and parallel to the first. He had sixty rounds of ammunition. To save on weight, he had left his conventional-sized handgun aboard the aircraft.

He looked at Bremen, "All right, I'm going. Be alert. You know as well as I do that one of these cracks could turn into a full lava flow at any second."

And then, Thorn Rolvaag changed direction and started toward the summit of the shield. He started asking himself questions, the principal of which as he moved through the purpling darkness was, just what would he do if he did see Martin Zimmer and a squad of Nazi commandos? He forced the thoughts from his mind as he quickened his pace.

42

The fighter banked gently, evenly, but rapidly to port under her hands as she climbed it in preparation of another ascending sweep over her assigned section of the grid. Even with the best night vision equipment available, all Emma Shaw could see was the blackness of the ocean.

And she still wasn't one hundred percent firm in her mind as to what action she would take should she see the Admiral's helicopter. She listened attentively as the revised orders had come in over the new frequency she'd been instructed to tune to, these instructions relayed to her in person from the crew chief on the flight line just as she was prepared to close her canopy.

It was hoped that the faked radio messages that would be sent out over the usual frequencies would delude the men aboard the stolen helicopter, but there was no reason to assume that they wouldn't be scanning a wide range of frequencies and pick up the *en clair* transmissions despite the precautions. The new orders were based on a theory of John's, and the idea did make sense. If she had stolen the Admiral's helicopter, she would have done what John supposed the Nazis were doing. And, because of her agreement with the new orders, she was doubly frustrated searching empty ocean.

But, orders were orders, and she usually obeyed them.

She attained level flight and almost immediately contacted her wingmen. "This is Lookout Five to Lookout Five Alpha and Bravo. I'm at altitude and about to begin next search sequence. Signal that you copy, Over."

Lookout Five Alpha and Lookout Five Bravo responded in turn.

She queried them as to their positions. Alpha was finishing a search pattern, had picked up a blip of something on the horizon and gone to investigate, but the blip turned out to be only a Russian freighter steaming toward the Orient. Bravo was nearly at altitude and would be commencing his next search pattern approximately a minute after Commander Emma Shaw began hers.

She started into a dive, the chest holster which carried her Lancer 2570A2-C 9mm Caseless pressed hard against her left breast by the G-Force. Emma Shaw hoped that John Rourke was right, that instead of out here somewhere over the vast expanse of the Pacific, the Nazi commando team and their prize, Martin Zimmer, were someplace safe — where they could be found by John Rourke . . .

There were seven men, two of them in Navy dress whites, all the others in work uniforms, one of these — he was tall, slender — Rolvaag observed through the binoculars to be in manacles of some sort. The men in dress whites were changing clothes while the chained man spoke to them. The man in chains — as Rolvaag watched, the handcuffs were removed and so was the belly chain — looked to be black, all the others white.

But, once the chains were removed, the black man appeared to be peeling away his skin.

Thorn Rolvaag took his eyes from the tubes of his vision intensification binoculars, squinted, closed his eyes, opened them again. There was a fumarole less than fifty yards from where Rolvaag lay in hiding just inside the cone, the noxious, sulphurous smell of volcanic gas discharge giving him a headache. The interior of the crater was upwind of the fumarole and the seven men seemed unaffected. Soon, Rolvaag knew, it would be necessary for him to don his breathing unit, either that or pass out.

He wished that he could hear what was being said . . .

Croenberg smiled as he sat on the end of a flat rock in order to tie his track shoes. A good officer learned to realize when it was wisest to discard even the best thought-out plan in the face of enor-

213

mous opportunity. Such was now the case. He had planned to leave young Martin shackled, then order the men to execute him. But this idea was even better.

"And, so you see, Gruppenführer, this place is most unacceptable. We could all die here, because this volcano might erupt," Martin Zimmer went on, prattling as always about his safety, his comfort.

"Martin, would your old friend let you be endangered? Of course not!"

"The Gruppenführer is right, Herr Zimmer," Rauph said in Croenberg's defense, slipping a web harness across his shoulders as he spoke. "All of us, Herr Zimmer, are devoted to your safety even at the cost of our own lives."

"Indeed," Croenberg agreed. One shoe tied, now the other.

The shoulder harness Rauph donned was fitted with a knife on either side, one beneath each armpit. Rauph seemed never to be without it. "The Gruppenfürer could not have known about the volcano, Herr Zimmer. Is this not so, Herr Gruppenführer."

"Indeed, Rauph. But, it is a happy circumstance, bringing confusion to our enemies and enabling us to hide here better while we await transportation. I am certain it is nothing to worry about." And the volcanic activity was proving fortunate in another way that Croenberg could never have imagined but in which Croenberg now saw considerable advantage. This would cost him the lives of five loyal comrades, of course, but to have had these men survive with the guilty knowledge they would have possessed might have been too dangerous to suffer at any event. So, they would have had to be killed at a future date. It was better to let them die now.

He was reminded of the Pharaonic method for keeping a secret. The ancient Egyptians would have slaves bury their treasure or their kings — the present occasion would be more similar to the burial of a king — and these slaves guarded by trusted priests. The priests would kill the slaves, then the tongues of the priests would be cut out to keep the secret forever.

Croenberg would especially miss Rauph, and Croenberg toyed with the idea of sparing the young officer's life. But to take the field commander away might have looked suspicious to the other four men. Croenberg looked at Rauph as he said, "I think, my

214

friend, that it is best for me to establish that the safe house to which we intend repairing is, indeed, safe. We cannot risk our Martin's being recaptured. I had not anticipated the enormity of the search force arrayed against us. Would you agree, that I should go on alone and send the plane back?" Croenberg had, wisely, ordered that all frequencies be scanned, and as a result knew that Doctor Rourke had second-guessed their basic plan. But Croenberg followed through with it anyway based on information he had heard while setting the scanning monitor. That information was in the form of radio communications between the control tower at Pearl Harbor and the massive cargo planes which filled the skies above the base and flew from Oahu toward the island of Hawaii. There was an evacuation in progress because Kilauea was erupting.

Because of the way Croenberg phrased the question, Rauph could not contradict him without appearing insubordinate or, at the least, distrustful. "Yes, Herr Gruppenführer. That does sound best, that the safe house should be investigated. But, I would volunteer, Herr Gruppenführer, to undertake this mission personally."

Was Rauph smarter than he supposed? Croenberg dismissed that idea. "Good man, but I shall go it alone, I think." And Croenberg clapped young Rauph on the shoulder. He genuinely liked the boy for his ruthlessness, his obedience, his loyalty, his courage.

"Gruppenführer?"

Croenberg turned to look at young Martin, worked to disguise the disgust he felt for this young man. Nearly all of the theatrical makeup was off and Martin's own face was once again his own. "Yes, Martin?"

"Is it safe to wait here? The volcano, I mean, the eruption?"

"These volcanoes in Hawaii are always doing this, Martin! You should read more, my young friend. You will be perfectly safe." In fact, as the snippets of radio traffic had indicated, this volcanic cone was quite possibly the least safe place on the face of the earth, now.

Croenberg glanced at his watch beneath the beam of the small flashlight from his pocket. In two minutes, if the pilot were prompt, he would board the vertical takeoff jet and be gone.

And the death of young Martin and of Rauph and all the others would be a great tragedy rather than a murder which would need to be hidden beneath more murders . . .

As Rolvaag donned the oxygen breather, he heard the thunder of jet engines from above. And, as he looked, he saw a V-stol cargo craft swooping in from the west out of the purple night.

He spoke into his radio set as soon as the air flow was adjusted to his comfort. "This is Rolvaag calling Navy 189 Charlie 18. This is Rolvaag calling Navy 189 Charlie 18. Come in Navy." He forgot to say "Over," so he added that lamely.

The pilot's voice came back to him. "This is Navy Helicopter 189 Charlie 18, Doctor Rolvaag. Reading you loud and clear. Over."

"Patch me in—" That was the correct term, he thought. "Patch me in at once to Doctor Rourke. I have what he's looking for." Rolvaag watched as the V-stol landed near the center of the crater. But only one man walked toward the aircraft. And it wasn't the one who looked like a somewhat weaker version of John Rourke himself.

43

John Rourke stripped away the radio headphones. He stayed in the chair beside the console, staring at its buttons and dials and diodes as he told Paul Rubenstein, "Rolvaag has spotted them. One of them left by jump jet, but the others—six men, one of them Martin—stayed behind."

"Where?"

Now Rourke stood up and looked at his friend. "The volcano."

Paul literally took a step back. "The one—ohh shit."

John Rourke smiled at his friend, then looked at the communications officer who stood near the door. "Ensign?"

"Yes, sir?"

Ensign Clyde was a pretty young woman in her very early twenties, light chocolate brown skin and the darkest brown eyes Rourke could remember combining to give her a look of wonderful innocence. "Ensign, I need your help."

"Whatever the General would require, sir—"

"It's a favor. This radio message. I know you have it on tape and it's logged automatically on the computer. I want you to hold back on notifying base headquarters of the contents of this message for fifteen minutes."

"But, sir, I—"

"Ensign. This will be an easy favor." And John Rourke reached under his jacket and drew one of the twin stainless Detonics .45s, not actually pointing the gun at her, but letting her see it. "Now you can say I forced you to cooperate." And Rourke looked at Paul. "I'm taking a helicopter and going in. You keep an eye on the Ensign until fifteen minutes have passed."

217

"Another way, John. You're not going alone."

"He's my son—I can't ask you—"

"I'm your friend," Paul reminded him. "You can't stop me, even with one of those." And Paul nodded toward the pistol. "But Michael's arm's still bothering him a little. And I don't think Annie or Natalia should come along."

John Rourke felt the corners of his mouth raising slightly in a smile. It would be like the old days, the two of them, friends in life and friends to the death. "All right. But Rolvaag says the eruption is already starting. It could be hours or minutes before the top of that mountain blows, and he thinks that's only a prelude to an even larger eruption."

"Then we'd better get started. And the Ensign can accompany us to the airfield. Then she can walk back. That'll give us fifteen minutes or more."

John Rourke looked at Ensign Clyde and smiled. "Sorry, Ensign."

44

Thorn Rolvaag could hardly see. The fumarole near where he had hidden to observe the men in the cone now spewed gas at such a furious pace that great clouds of the vile sulphurous mixture enveloped the mountaintop. But the interior of the cone, when he'd moved out, was still free of the gas, instead the winds still blowing the gas out toward the sea.

Although he considered his work done—he'd reported to Doctor Rourke, returned the favor done to him—he would have been forced to evacuate the position at any event, no choice left to him unless he wished to be killed.

The vents which lined the shield like great glowing veins had begun to spill forth magma. It was pahoehoe, fluid and fast moving. And, even as he moved along the shield now, it was necessary at times to change from his intended path, as geysers of magma would spout before him, brightly flaming liquid rock soaring skyward, raining down and scorching the ground, flowing before him as if the mountainside itself were his enemy, trying to trap him in its killing ground.

The oxygen mask was a blessing, because without it he would have been dead.

A lava flow was moving downward along the shield roughly from right to left in relation to Rolvaag's line of travel. He jumped it, only about eighteen inches wide here, running now before he was truly cut off. He spoke into his radio again. "Navy, come in and get us. Come in and get us."

"I'm already on my way, Doc. Keep your radio open so I can home in on you. If you shoot off a flare, I'll never see it. Be

219

ready, 'cause I'm not anxious to wait. Out."

Rolvaag kept moving, panting into the radio, "Carl? Do you have the pressure measurements?"

There was no response.

"Carl? Answer me, damnit."

But there was no response. Rolvaag, his breath coming so fast he was afraid that he would hyperventilate on the oxygen mixture, scanned the shield below him, for some sight of Carl Bremen. If the young man had gotten into trouble, gotten hurt, Rolvaag knew he would never forgive himself.

The ground only a few yards ahead of Rolvaag split and the mountainside trembled. Rolvaag fell. Magma rolled up with more force than Rolvaag would have imagined possible, spouting into the purple smoke already engulfing the mountainside and flowing like white water over rapids across the slabs of volcanic rock it dislodged, pushing them along with tremendous force, tearing loose every rock and boulder in its path.

"Carl. I need you to answer me. The helicopter is coming in to get us. But I need you to answer me."

There was still no answer.

As Rolvaag moved, he realized suddenly that he was lost, that the entire landscape had so violently and suddenly altered that there were no landmarks. And fear, cold and sickening and overpowering seized him, and his breathing was so rapid now that he was becoming light headed. "Carl!"

There was still no answer.

Thorn Rolvaag stopped dead in his tracks. He forced his breathing to slow, spoke as calmly as he could into the radio microphone before his lips. "Navy, can you hear me?"

"Reading you Loud and Clear, Doc. If you hold to your current position, I'll find you. Keep talking me in. Then we can find Mr. Bremen together. Over."

"That seems like a good idea."

"Glad you see it my way Doc. Keep talking. What's your favorite baseball team? Over."

"The Oahu Eagles."

"Terrific pitcher, Oakton. If he could hit as well as he throws

220

he'd be the top man in the league. Whatchya think about Staddler? Over."

"Staddler's okay. My kids like Staddler because he's so young. Needs seasoning."

"I'm right over you, Doc. Look up and you should see me. Over."

Rolvaag could hear no ambient sound except the explosions of rock surrounding him. It was a battlefield, and nature was the enemy. But, as he looked up, he thought he saw the clouds of gas swirling in a regular pattern. Then there was a beam of light, bright but indirect, like something seen through a dirty window. "Do you have a searchlight on?"

"That's us, Doc. We'll let down a ladder. Don't try climbing out, just secure yourself to it with your extraction harness and we'll get you out of here, get you down safe, then get you aboard and we go after Bremen, okay? Over."

"Okay. Yes. But hurry. Bremen must be in trouble."

"Affirmative that, Doc. But we'll find him. Hang in there. Over."

Rolvaag had no choice . . .

The helicopter John Rourke stole, a gunship specially fitted for combat land/sea rescue, was equipped with diving gear, not only the hemosponges and suits with which Rourke had become familiar since his first encounter with the civilization of Mid-Wake, but also conventional tanks. Rourke knew the purpose of these; small, about the length of a Twentieth-Century policeman's nightstick and only roughly twice the diameter, they were for emergency air supplies when there was no time to don full gear, or for giving an emergency air supply to someone in the water. While Paul, who had turned into an excellent pilot, considering his brave but rather inauspicious beginning, flew the craft toward the island of Hawaii, John Rourke checked the air tanks to make certain they were fully pressurized. In conjunction with gas masks, he could jury-rig breathing apparatus for them. Because the eruption would foul the air where they were going . . .

Thorn Rolvaag leaned against the wall—it was called a bulk-head, he remembered—and watched hell unfold beneath him as a frighteningly vivid panorama of fire and ash and sulphurous fumes and molten rock reached up into the night toward them. And, somewhere down there, Bremen was in trouble if not already dead. Rolvaag, still sweating from fear and exhaustion, spoke into the radio. "Carl, find some way of signaling to us, please. You can hear me. I feel it. I know you can hear me. Find some way of making a signal."

But, what could Carl Bremen do? A flare would go unseen, even the brightest flare.

Rolvaag shouted forward to the crew of the Navy helicopter. "There must be some way!"

"This Mr. Bremen, Doc, he pretty sharp with electronics?" It was the pilot who called back to him. And Rolvaag got to his feet, unsteady, unsteadier still because of the turbulence surrounding the helicopter. But he started forward. The pilot, a black man named Butler, began again to speak. "Assume he can hear us but we can't hear him, right? Otherwise, we're really outa luck findin' him. But what if we can talk him through changing his radio around so he can't receive, but he can send. Then he can talk us in. He'll feel cut off, but we can find him. He's probably scared shitless by now, so you'll have to prep him for it, but if you figure he trusts you enough, maybe this'll work."

Then Butler turned to his copilot. "Jim, get up and give the man a chair."

The copilot vacated his seat and Rolvaag sank into it. "But I don't know if I could change a radio around. Maybe I could, but I don't know if I could talk him through it."

"I can. You start talking to him on your radio, then when you figure it's time, turn him over to me, Doc. It's his only chance."

Rolvaag nodded. He controlled his breathing as best he could, then switched his radio on. "Carl, this is Thorn Rolvaag. I want

222

you to listen to me very carefully. And I'm praying that you can listen to me."

Beside Rolvaag, Butler sat bolt upright in his seat. "We're losing oil pressure in the main rotor. Strap in, Doc! We're goin' down. Jim! Get a Mayday out with our position!"

45

Great plumes of smoke and ash, alive with particles of molten rock, flared thousands of feet upward into the night, illuminating the volcano's shield and almost the entire southern portion of the Island of Hawaii. Below Rourke and Rubenstein now the wreckage of the Navy helicopter whose transmissions they had heard — a Mayday signal — was lit by the spewing volcanic vents surrounding it.

It was a question of immediacy.

Paul landed the helicopter as near to the crash site as possible in the event there were serious injuries, but it was necessary as well to keep two other considerations in mind: First, that the landing site was safe for the moment from the effects of the eruption and second that the actual landing could not be observed from within the cone, where Thorn Rolvaag had indicated that Martin and the others were located.

There was nothing to guarantee, of course, that they were still there. Indeed, remaining was folly. But, Rourke had to check, could not run the risk of losing Martin. But, to have allowed Ensign Clyde to alert the base to the fact that Martin had been located would have precipitated even greater difficulties. If the Navy located Martin and the commando unit, there was always the possibility that Martin would be killed. And, if the base were alerted, there would be no preventing Michael, Natalia and Annie from coming to the scene.

By now, of course, Ensign Clyde would have reported the message and what subsequently happened. The base would have scrambled helicopters to come after them and, doubtless Michael, Natalia and Annie would be along.

Rourke made it that they had their fifteen-minute headstart and nothing more, and the few minutes' time they had been on the ground was cancelled out by the amount of time it would have taken Pearl Harbor to scramble choppers to go after them.

The HK-91 slung from his shoulder, its pistol grip tight in his right hand, the ScoreMasters thrust into the waistband of his trousers, John Rourke kept to the right side of the rocky defile they paralleled. Paul Rubenstein, his German MP-40 submachinegun in his right fist, walked on the left. Their weapons, aside from Rourke's twin stainless Detonics CombatMasters, worn in the old double Alessi rig under his battered brown leather bomberjacket, and the little A.G. Russell Sting IA Black Chrome (Rourke always carried the two Detonics Mini guns and Sting IA) and Paul's Browning High Power, had been stowed in the trunk of the FOUO car Rourke had driven. Rourke's full-sized ScoreMasters, Rourke's two-inch barreled Smith & Wesson Centennial and his Crain Life Support System X knife and Paul's second High Power and the old Gerber MkII fighting knife, weapons that had helped Rourke and his friend survive as long as they had them coupled with the intelligence to use them properly, were too much to carry in this new, "civilized" world.

Here, on the face of Kilauea, there was no civilization, only the struggle to survive. When the Mayday signal had come from the crashing helicopter carrying Rolvaag, neither Rourke nor Rubenstein had questioned the necessity of what had to be done first. There was the immediate risk of lives at stake. Martin would have to wait.

Using a portable direction-finder from the rescue helicopter's equipment stores, set to the open frequency signal of the downed chopper, John Rourke guided them ahead, homing in. And, just ahead, in the flare from a rupturing vent, Rourke saw the machine.

The pilot was good at his work, John Rourke reflected. Through the radio built into the gas mask John Rourke wore, he said to Paul Rubenstein, "Over there, about two hundred yards,

225

almost obscured by that rock uplift. See it?" It was closer to Rubenstein than it was to Rourke.

"I see it. It looks like the cabin area is intact, but what I can see of the rest of it looks like the tail section's sheared away and the—look, down there."

Rourke followed with his eyes in the direction where his friend gestured. Two of the enormous blades from the helicopter's main rotor had furrowed themselves into the rock, almost forming the shape of a cross, molten rock surging up around them. "Let's see if they're alive," Rourke said, starting to change direction.

Veins in the face of the rock were opening with alarming rapidity, sections of the shield higher up along the cone starting to float away on the magma beneath, huge slabs of the blackened rock periodically slipping downward, stalling, lava building up behind them. So far, none had dislodged completely. When one did, any person in its way would be dead. The rock itself might weigh tons and the lava behind it would turn flesh to ash.

Traversing the shield now, it was necessary as they moved toward the downed helicopter to constantly alter their course because of freshly opening veins of magma. The gas rising from fumaroles higher up the face of the mountain was becoming thicker, and volcanic ash covered their clothing, anything exposed. The gas masks they wore were of the type incorporating integral hoods, and Rourke was for once grateful for the design which he usually found a nuisance. His coat protected his weapons, except for the LS-X knife and the HK-91. The knife would not be affected by the falling ash and the HK was as rugged a firearm as ever made, either in its semi-automatic sporter form as Rourke carried it, or as a selective fire battle rifle.

The side of the mountain trembled so violently that Rourke nearly fell. But he kept his footing, swaying with the motion. There were belches of flame from some of the wider veins in the rock, spouts of lava shooting upward. The volume of ash increased to the consistency of a sudden downpour, and there was a terrific roar which apprehended Rourke's attention, making him turn to face the summit. Ash spewed from very near to the cone now and lava was flowing in a river of molten rock several yards

226

wide perhaps a hundred yards back, huge slabs of rock floating in it, battering out a channel.

Rourke and Rubenstein, side by side, clambered over a dislodged slab of volcanic rock. Beyond it lay the partially destroyed Navy helicopter.

There were emergency lights lit within and Rourke said to Paul Rubenstein, "Maybe we're not too late." But, they might already be too late to survive. More than fifteen minutes had passed and, with the pace of the eruption moving at such a frenetic rate they might not make it off the mountain alive, let alone get Martin.

They kept going . . .

Michael Rourke looked at Natalia, then at Annie, then across the desk at Admiral Hayes. "You're telling me, Admiral, that you can't let any aircraft approach the volcano. What the hell are my father and my brother-in-law supposed to do, then, wait? They'll be flying out. All I'm saying is we can get a few helicopters in there and give them some assistance. We don't even need a crew. Give us one chopper. Natalia and I can fly it. She's a terrific helicopter pilot."

Admiral Hayes smiled at them with soft, blue eyes, as if she understood something they did not and somehow felt sorry for them all because she did. "I even ordered the planes involved with the evacuation effort anywhere within five miles of the south face to go into a holding pattern. Visibility any closer than that is near zero and the ash that's spewing into the air is clogging air filters on some of the helicopters, causing their engines to stall out. If I let you take a helicopter, I'd be sending you to your deaths. That's why I had the Shore Patrol bring all of you here under guard. I hold the deepest respect for your family, and your dedication to one another.

"I think that all we can do now," Admiral Hayes said, "is pray that Doctor Rourke and Mr. Rubenstein are somehow able to make it out alive. The helicopter carrying Professor Rolvaag is down. We can't even risk getting an aircraft in there to look for them. Our hands are tied, so I suggest we clasp them together."

Michael Rourke was weighing the possibilities concerning how best he could steal a helicopter, and when he looked at his mistress and his sister, he could see that Natalia and Annie were doing the same. He could pray while they flew.

46

Where was Gruppenführer Croenberg? Martin Zimmer, his hands shaking and the pit of his stomach freezing cold, grabbed Rauph by the shoulder and spun him around. "We will all be killed here, Rauph! You have to do something! Now!"

"The Gruppenführer may be having a difficult time getting in because of the eruption, Herr Zimmer. But I am certain—"

"Fool! You must do something now. I will be killed here. The volcano is erupting, man! Are you blind? Get me to safety!"

"Herr Zimmer, we are all stranded here until the Herr Gruppenführer returns. Where can we go?"

Lava was spewing out of spreading ruptures in the living rock, pouring down and away from them, but the rock beneath Martin Zimmer's feet seemed to shake more violently by the second. How soon before the interior of the volcanic cone would crack, and lava would consume them all in flame?

"What if the Gruppenführer isn't coming back?"

Rauph looked at him as if he were insane. "Not come back? Herr Zimmer! What you say! The Gruppenführer would not abandon us, his men, nor certainly you, the son of Deitrich Zimmer, the leader. Never! He has been delayed. That is all, I am certain. At any moment the aircraft will return and we will be taken from this hell. Do not be afraid."

"Afraid! You dare say that I, that I am afraid!" Martin Zimmer turned away, walked off, trying to control his breathing, trying to control the trembling of his entire body. If Croenberg had left them here to die, there was nothing that they could do.

And Martin Zimmer not only did not want to die, but the world could not be denied his leadership . . .

John's hands had worked furiously over the pilot, closing up the sucking chest wound over the man's left lung. A small blade from the tail rotor had sheared away, cut through the gap where the tail section had been, penetrated the pilot from back to front and buried itself in the control panel. The other crewman was dead, his neck broken.

Paul Rubenstein worked over Thorn Rolvaag, who was unconscious when he and John found the downed helicopter. He was now just coming around. "Bremen. Gotta find Carl."

"Carl?"

"Bremen."

"Take it easy," Paul told him.

"He's out there somewhere, down."

Paul Rubenstein's mind raced. Assuming that Rolvaag knew what he was talking about, this Carl Bremen, perhaps the graduate student who had accompanied Rolvaag in the taking of his pressure measurements, would have to be below where they had landed their helicopter. Otherwise, he and John would have seen the man. "Look. I think I can find him. Lie still, all right."

"Butler?"

That was the name on the pilots uniform. "John's helping him. The other man's dead."

"Jesus!"

"Whatever," Paul nodded. As often as he heard it, he would never accustom himself to the way non-Jews used the name of the one whom they considered the Son of God. Annie rarely took the name of the Lord in vain, or that of the one she believed was his Son. "You just take it easy. If you feel it will help, pray for your friend. I think we can find him."

John had cursorily examined Rolvaag after putting a hasty compression bandage to the pilot's wound, pronounced Rolvaag seemingly okay. There was no way to tell about any possible concussion.

As Paul Rubenstein looked around in order to confer with John, John was not looking at him. John's face in the yellow light of the emergency overhead lamp seemed more a mask of determination than anything human, as he said, "I heard what you said. You and Rolvaag should be able to get the pilot here down to our aircraft. Then leave them there and look for this man Bremen. Give yourself a time limit. Then, one way or the other, get airborne. If you can do it safely, come over the cone and look for me and for Martin."

"John—"

"Let me finish. We're out of time. You know that as well as I do. The whole side of the mountain could blow away at any second. We don't have more than twenty minutes or so of oxygen left. Once we go to breathing regular air, we've got maybe a few more minutes before the gas puts us under. The only thing we can do is this—you take care of these men, and I'll go after Martin."

"But—"

"It's not just for Sarah, Paul; Martin's still my son."

Paul Rubenstein didn't try to argue; he would have done the same himself had Martin been his and Annie's son . . .

Any professional military person, perhaps only after one too many drinks, would admit that there were times when orders had to be ignored; but, Emma Shaw had never so obviously gone against orders in all her life.

But there wasn't any choice.

The radio traffic told the story, and it was a story she could not accept.

John and his friend, Paul Rubenstein, were trapped on Kilauea and the helicopter they had stolen was their only out. A helicopter would have as much chance of making it through the storm of lava, ash and gas as a snowball in Hell. And it was Hell where John and Paul Rubenstein were.

But if she could reach the volcano in time—unless the whole thing were blown sky high by then, which according to the radio traffic could take place at any second — she could get her V-stol fighter bomber in there. It would be a tough jump if she had a lot of people to pack in the bomb bay, but she'd taken off out of tight spots with a full load of blockbuster bombs and they weighed more.

She could do it.

In her mind's eye, she was picturing how the people would have to pack in along the fuselage in order not only just to fit but to keep from being thrown about against the bulkheads once the aircraft accelerated out of the vertical mode.

There might be some bumps and bruises, but she could make it, in and out.

Or try, at least.

Emma Shaw signaled her wingpersons, "I'm gone, to Kilauea. Return to base. Shaw Out." And she banked the tip of her portside wing and broke formation . . .

Natalia Anastasia Tiemerovna — would her last name someday soon be Rourke, as Michael's wife? she wondered, hoped — dropped her purse.

The Shore Patrolmen paused and she bent over. As she raised up, the Bali-Song was in her right hand and she used it like a Yarawa stick, hammering it in an uppercut to the nearest man's testicles. Michael's left crossed the jaw of the third man as Natalia's man doubled over and Natalia simultaneously grabbed for the muzzle of his rifle and chopped him into unconsciousness with a blow to the side of his neck.

Annie had the third Shore Patrolman against the wall of the corridor, the muzzle of the little pistol John had given her — it was an Interams Firestar 9mm Parabellum — touching the tip of the man's nose. "Get his gun, Michael," Annie ordered.

Natalia swung the borrowed assault rifle onto the two inert men while Michael disarmed the man on whom Annie had the drop. "I'll fly it; I am better at it," Natalia said matter-of-factly.

Michael was clapping the third Shore Patrolman in his own cuffs, and said, "Agreed. But first we have to steal one."

Michael made stating the obvious so charming sometimes. Annie moved to the corridor door, looking out. "We're clear. Take their car, get to the field and do what we have to."

Natalia looked at the Rolex on her left wrist. It would take them longer to reach the island of Hawaii than there was time remaining before the eruption — according to the estimates of Doctor Betty Gilder, Rolvaag's colleague — would be at full force.

That meant that John and Paul had no chance at all.

But Natalia knew them better than to accept that; they would not. "Let's hurry," she said, running for the door, still holding the Shore Patrolman's assault rifle.

47

Thirteen minutes of air remaining according to the diode counter, two twenty-round magazines for the HK-91 clipped together, whole sections of the mountainside floating off on rivers of lava, John Thomas Rourke reached the crest of the summit, and from the top of the shield looked down into the crater.

He was reminded, oddly, of an ice flow. Except for the difference in materials, the plain at the interior of the cone was like that, whole sections of it broken off, riding on the lake of magma beneath, the volcanic veins, brilliantly illumined in flame, like the veins of the human body, but distended and discolored and ready to burst.

Paul should be back at the helicopter by now, or nearly so. Hopefully Paul would listen to him, give only a reasonable amount of time to find this fellow Bremen, then give it up and get airborne. Hopefully, but not likely. Paul would no more leave a man out here to die than John Rourke would.

So, if Paul could not find the man, Paul was as likely doomed as Rourke himself felt. Logic dictated that once he set foot into the cone, aside from Martin and the other five men there, all heavily armed Nazi commandos, the magma would, at the least, trap him, at worst explode around him.

There was no choice.

John Rourke began to climb over onto the interior of the cone, picking his way to avoid the luminous coals and the growing fissures. The plain within the cone was like a valley, broad from end to end, narrow from side to side, like another valley often spoken of, the valley of death . . .

* * *

He left Rolvaag, the scientist a little fuzzy-headed from his in-juries, it seemed, but eager to do whatever could be done, with the injured pilot safe inside the helicopter—as safe as one could be on the slope of an erupting volcano. And Paul Rubenstein told himself that somehow, if he were unable to find this man Carl Bremen, or unable for some other reason to return, that Rolvaag and the pilot—seriously but not mortally wounded, still able to talk, to hear—would in one way or another get the helicopter airborne.

John had known the real way of it when he'd said what he said. John wouldn't have left this Bremen, the graduate student, here on the mountain, and neither would Paul Rubenstein. And Paul Rubenstein had often wondered if women lied to each other as often as men did? John knew. Paul knew.

Paul went on his way, searching on the slope below for the hapless graduate student Carl Bremen. John would be at the cone by now, perhaps already moving onto it.

The mountain shook so violently that Paul Rubenstein could hardly keep his footing. John knew that the eruption would be complete in a matter of minutes, perhaps, and then they would all die.

Paul Rubenstein knew it, too.

Before they had parted, after John had helped get the pilot out of the crippled helicopter, Paul took the extra few seconds to clasp John Rourke's hand, to say perhaps for the last time, "My friend."

Without knowing John Rourke, one could not understand the true meaning of those words.

48

Perhaps the entire earth trembled. It felt as if that were true as the first shockwave came. John Rourke fell to his knees, making the third leg of a tripod with the butt of the Heckler & Koch rifle, keeping himself from falling prone by strength and force of will as the mountain heaved and the very floor of the plain here within the cone rose, sank, then split with an ear-shattering crack. Lava flowed from the enormous wound in the living rock like suppurating pus, lava geysering skyward with such intensity that, in the next instant, the very darkness rained fire.

The six men—Martin one of them—who had taken refuge within a natural rock fortress at the very center of the cone had not yet seen him. Rourke imagined them rather preoccupied with their own survival at the moment; the sea of magma rolled beneath them and waves of the liquid rock upthrust and crashed and lashed out in fiery fury, the very rock on which the fortress was set floating like a raft on the tempest-tossed fire.

There was still a bridge leading out to the fortress and John Rourke, as he descended the volcanic shield, started toward it. They had not seen him, but if he were spotted he would be without shelter from their fire. He thought of Paul, praying that his friend would get the helicopter up and out of the ever-expanding inferno.

Fumaroles were everywhere, great spouts of noxious gas and acrid charcoal-colored smoke belching skyward on all sides of him, an enormous cloud hanging low over the interior of the cone, its greyness alleviated only by the falling pieces of yellow hot rock. The interior of the cloud glowed orange and purple.

Ash rained everywhere, forcing Rourke to smudge it away from his mask's protective eye-covering every few seconds just so that he could see. The action of the HK-91 was covered with it.

Rourke, running as best he could, still keeping his balance, neared the bridge leading out to the island of rock on which the fortress floated.

As John Rourke stepped onto the bridge, the mountain roared its anger again and the bridge twisted, angled to Rourke's left. But Rourke kept his balance. The bridge was narrowed now, the volume of magma suddenly increased. The fiery liquid rock splashed within inches of his combat-booted feet. Should a wave of the lava lap over his feet, what little protection the leather afforded would be vaporized in a microsecond and so would his flesh beneath.

Rourke kept moving.

In the same instant that he smudged away more of the ash from the lenses of his mask, gunfire tore into the rock beside Rourke's feet, energy bursts crackling through the air near his head. Rourke brought the HK-91 to his shoulder, the rifle's safety already thumbed off. Rourke fired, not knowing whether the volume of ash would have been too much for the firearm. But the HK worked, the first shot, then a second and third hammering into the rock fortress, great chips of the rock flying upward, a man in seaman's clothes falling through a niche in the rock. The man's energy weapon fired as his body vanished into the sea of boiling lava.

John Rourke quickened his pace, his only hope now to get into the fortress and fight it out at close range. Stranded here, he would not only be visible and easy to pick off, but was also prey to the rapidly diminishing width of the bridge of rock along which he trod.

Rourke ran forward, across the bridge.

Another energy weapon was fired toward him, blue-white bolts of plasma flickering through the maelstrom of molten rock and burning ash. Another energy bolt, then another. The bolts intercepted the rain of debris, making the bits of rock explode like shrapnel around him. Rourke's body was pummeled with the rock, bits of it clinging to the old leather jacket he wore, burning like phosphorous. Rourke swatted at a piece with his gloved left hand and the leather of the glove smoked.

Rourke kept running.

He was near the island of rock now, the mountain shaking so violently that most of his concentration was consumed with keeping his balance.

One of the Nazis rose up from behind the fortress wall some ten feet above and fired almost point-blank. John Rourke was already moving, throwing himself forward, flush against the rocky surface of the fortress wall. As Rourke's hands caught to the wall, the mountain shuddered again, only more violently than before. The island of rock twisted, lurched and the bridge fell away. Rourke clung there, his rifle swinging wildly at his side on its sling.

The Nazi who had fired at him was above him now, bringing his energy weapon to bear in line with John Rourke's head. Rourke released his grip to the rock with his right hand, hanging above the molten sea beneath him only by the fingers of his left hand as his right hand groped for the pistol grip of the HK.

The Nazi was shouting something at Rourke, but Rourke could not hear it—the thunderous cacophony of the eruption filled his ears with nothing but the sounds of the mountain's destruction. Rourke's gloved right hand closed around the pistol grip of the HK-91. Rourke punched the rifle upward, firing, then again and again, the rifle's recoil force tearing at Rourke's right wrist, torquing in his hand.

The head of the Nazi who stood over him exploded and the body fell back and away, out of sight.

John Rourke let go of his rifle, grasping instead for additional purchase on the rock as the fingers of his left hand began to slip.

Rourke swung there.

Two of the men with Martin were gone. That left three more, and Martin Zimmer himself.

Bremen seemed more dead than alive as Paul Rubenstein at last slung the young man over his right shoulder in a fireman's carry. But there was breathing, a pulse and heartbeat. A slab of rock—

massive-seeming from the swatch it had cut in the rocks around it—had evidently dislodged and crashed down near Rolvaag's graduate student, breaking up, huge chunks of it surrounding Carl Bremen. There was a wound to Bremen's head, bleeding heavily. But Paul Rubenstein remembered John's often stating that head wounds were deceptive, and frequently showed a great deal of blood in disparate proportion to their size.

Paul had cleared away some of the rocks after applying a make-shift bandage to the head wound. Then, after determining as best he could that neither Bremen's neck nor back seemed broken, he moved the man, hauled him awkwardly into a standing position, then bent into him for the carry.

As Paul trudged back along the slope, changing direction every few steps to avoid trickles and larger flows of magma, he realized that the helicopter might well be gone; if Rolvaag had any sense and could get the pilot's help, it would be.

But as Paul Rubenstein reached the summit of a rock upthrust, he saw it below. His heart sank. Rolvaag and the pilot were out-side, some fifty feet back from it, the starboard side of the heli-copter had half-vanished into an open crack in the surface of the slope, magma spewing up from the crack, the machine itself on fire.

There was no escape from the mountain's eruption now, but he would try. They were doomed . . .

John Rourke edged along the fortress wall, at any moment ex-pecting the waves of boiling magma to crash upward and cover him, or expecting another of the three remaining Nazis, or per-haps even Martin himself, to fire down at him.

Rourke reached a split in the wall. He looked up. The fortress rose some fifteen feet here, the rock slick and grey, but the crack—a foot or so at best—perhaps wide enough that he could use his hands to pull and his feet like wedges. The HK rifle slam-ming against his side, Rourke started up.

* * *

Emma Shaw would have shut off her radio, except that there might be an incoming transmission from the helicopter John Rourke and Paul Rubenstein had taken. But she shut off her awareness of the transmissions ordering her to return to base, threatening her with court martial for disobeying direct orders.

Ahead and miles below, the southern portion of the island of Hawaii looked like an inferno. And she began programming her onboard navigation computer for the dead center of the eruption, Kilauea's cone . . .

The Navy helicopter pilot, Butler, could walk with a little help from Thorn Rolvaag. There was nothing to do with Carl Bremen but carry him. Since Paul already had the man, he told Rolvaag he would keep him across his shoulder as long as he could, then give Rolvaag a turn.

Oxygen in their breathing units was at varying levels, Rolvaag's—not a jury-rigged thing like the one Paul Rubenstein wore—having almost thirty minutes remaining. Paul gauged his own supply at five. Both the injured Bremen and the Navy pilot, Butler, wore units like the one worn by Rolvaag.

Paul, as he walked in a long-strided commando walk down the face of the slope, was already working out what he would tell Rolvaag. And, although Paul Rubenstein detested the very idea of a lie, under the circumstances it would be best. "I have a second oxygen tank back up the slope. You three go on. I'll look for the tank." Or, could he fake a sprained or broken ankle?

No matter what, he would use the last of his oxygen going back for John. He couldn't just leave him. And, if he—Rubenstein— was going to die, as seemed now inevitable, he would rather die with his friend.

"Rolvaag. Listen. Your turn on Bremen. Then take him and you and Butler go on. I'm going back for another oxygen tank. Otherwise, I'm already dead. Just keep going. I'll catch up." And Paul Rubenstein shifted Bremen down, helped Rolvaag in getting the man onto his shoulder.

Then Paul Rubenstein started back up the slope, toward the fire-brimming cone of the volcano to find John Rourke. He kept to a metered pace, because if he moved too rapidly, the oxygen would burn up all the faster . . .

John Rourke lay wedged within the crack in the rock fortress walls, catching his breath. That was becoming progressively more difficult, the supply in his air tank down almost to empty. He could survive a while longer at reduced efficiency once the tank was fully depleted, and he imagined the burning lungs and aching heads of the men within the fortress, his enemies, all mere human beings.

Perhaps—but the helicopter should be gone. Paul would see his obligation to Rolvaag and Butler and this fellow Bremen, if Paul was able to find him—see his obligation to get them to safety.

No win.

John Rourke pushed himself up out of the wedge.

Waves of magma lapped at the fortress walls, the island on which the fortress floated lurching madly as Rourke clambered to the top of the fortress wall.

Inside, in the flaring of the erupting lava, Rourke could see two of the men prone, inert, lifeless-seeming. Another crawled across the surface of the rock floor. The last clutched an energy rifle.

This last man looked up, shouted in English, "The legendary Herr Doctor at last! Now I can die well!"

The man started to raise his weapon. But the effect of the air quality slowed him, Rourke realized.

Rourke jumped.

John Rourke's body impacted man and rifle simultaneously, driving the rifle skittering away over the rocks, driving the man down.

It was adrenalin-rush taking over, because the man wriggled from beneath him as Rourke caught his wind. The oxygen bottle was empty. Rourke struggled to his feet. The man braced him, a knife in each hand.

Rourke stripped away the mask.

"Die with honor if you dare!"

John Rourke lurched back, coughing as he drew his first un-aided breath, light-headedness, nausea, sweeping over him. But his right hand went to the hilt of the Crain LS-X knife. Martin lay off to the side, staring at them. They would all die here, Rourke realized, but perhaps he could teach this son stolen from him at birth that there was honor. And that would, at least, mean something.

"All right," Rourke rasped through clenched teeth.

And John Rourke drew the Crain knife, holding it like a short sword as the Nazi with a knife in each hand threw himself into battle. The knives moved in the man's hands as if they possessed their own life, were capable of action independent of the man holding them. Where the man's body was slowed by the effects of the bad air and exhaustion, the knives seemed unaffected, whirring in short arcs and downsweeps inches from Rourke's body.

Rourke's head ached. Nausea consumed him.

At last, the man with two knives was close enough and Rourke's blade locked against one of the two knives, Rourke sidestepping, attempting a kick to the man's right knee.

"Rauph! Look out for the bastard!"

It was Martin who shouted the words. John Rourke reeled from them as the man with two knives—Rauph, Martin had called him—spun away. Tears welled up in John Rourke's eyes, from the burning irritation of the gas, he told himself. But also, perhaps, because of Martin.

This was his son, his enemy.

Rauph dove forward, feinting with the knife in his right hand, the knife in his left poised to piston forward. It was a professional knife fighter's move. But John Rourke had seen it before.

Rourke dodged right, sidestepping the knife in Rauph's right hand while Rourke's own blade hacked outward to intercept Rauph's left arm.

Steel met flesh and Rauph screamed, the knife falling from Rauph's suddenly limp fingers. Rourke's knife had sliced to the bone of the forearm, laying the flap of flesh and the clothing above it back. Blood spurted from everywhere along Rauph's lower arm as Rauph spun inward toward Rourke. The knife in Rauph's right hand was in a saber hold.

Rourke wheeled left, angling his blade downward, catching Rauph's blade. Rourke's right elbow smashed upward, impacting Rauph's mouth. Rourke disengaged from Rauph's blade in the same instant, Rourke stepping back.

Rauph's head snapped away, blood spurting through Rauph's teeth. Rauph slashed outward with his knife. Rourke held the Crain LS-X in a saber hold as well, thrusting it forward into Rauph's throat just below the Adam's apple, recovering, withdrawing his blade as Rauph's blade backswept.

Rauph started to collapse.

Rourke turned to his left, the blood-dripping knife still in Rourke's right hand. And Rourke saw Martin, his son. Martin held an energy rifle. "You mother fucker!" Martin shouted, firing. John Rourke dove right, an energy bolt crackling through the air inches from Rourke's head.

And Martin sprayed the weapon now, Rourke rolling into the rocks near him, up to his feet, lurching forward as he ran just barely outdistancing Martin's gunfire. He would not kill Martin, not now, perhaps he never could.

Martin's energy weapon fire struck first one, then the second of the two surviving Nazis who lay unconscious near the fortress wall as Martin kept firing, indiscriminately, firing as rapidly as the trigger could be pulled it seemed. Energy bolts gouged deep into the rock wall on all sides as Rourke ducked and jumped to cover.

Martin kept firing, trying to lead Rourke now.

John Rourke dodged, turned back, jumped toward the center of the rock enclosure, reaching for Rauph's lost energy rifle. Rourke grabbed it at the muzzle and hurled it toward Martin.

The weapon struck Martin at the neck and right shoulder.

Martin collapsed to his knees. Rourke was already up, the butt of his HK-91 slamming against Martin's right forearm, knocking the energy rifle aside. Martin shrieked up at him. "Look!"

John Rourke didn't turn his eyes. Rourke gagged for an instant, coughed, nearly vomited. His eyes streamed tears from the gas and ash.

"Look! We're saved!"

Above him, there was a roar distinct from the roaring of the volcano, and John Rourke grabbed Martin Zimmer Rourke by the front of his shirt, dragged him to a standing position as Rourke cast his eyes upward.

Coming down out of the clouds of gas and ash and fire was a V-stol fighter bomber.

The craft descended on twin pillars of fire, like the *deus ex machina* of Greek tragedy, a machine of the gods as the means of divine intervention to save them.

But the rock fortress surrounded by lava was too small an area for any craft to land in.

As if the pilot, whoever he was, had read Rourke's thoughts, as the aircraft stabilized some sixty or so feet above them, a cable snaked downward, coils of it falling fewer than ten yards from them.

"We can get out! We can save ourselves!"

Rourke looked at his son, Martin. "Watch out for the prop washes. They could be deadly." Rourke coughed. "Go on. Hook the cable around you. The pilot can winch it up."

Rourke shoved Martin ahead, warning him again, "Look out for the prop wash! It's straight vertical." Where the jets struck, fragments of rock were beaten up into cyclonic funnels. Rourke lurched after his son for a few feet, stopped. He turned, ran back to where the two unconscious Nazis lay. By rights they were dead after Martin had fired so indiscriminately as he sprayed the interior of the rock fortress; but, if they were not, Nazis or no, Rourke could not leave men to die here.

His rifle safed and pushed away behind his back, Rourke, coughing, gagging in the ash and dust and gas, his eyes streaming tears, found the first of the two. The man was dead. The second man, his face shot away.

Rourke peered upward, the V-stol still above. And, as Rourke threaded his way between the propwashes of the downwardly firing jets, the cable snaked downward again. Rourke caught up its end, falling to his knees as he did so. There was a hook on the end of the cable. Rourke wound a length of the cable round his

244

body beneath his buttocks, hooking on. He jerked at the cable, but there was no way to tell if the pilot or winch operator (if there was a two-man crew aboard) could see him.

But the cable began slowly to move.

Rourke dragged himself to his feet, feeding out cable through his still-gloved hands.

The cable was nearly taut. There was an instant of weightlessness, his feet off the ground, a sickening pendulum motion carrying him dangerously near the propwash from the portside engine. And then he was rising. The ash was thicker here and Rourke held his breath against it as he passed through a denser portion of the cloud. The V-stol pilot had to be insane coming here, fouling his engines. At any second, one or both could cut out, and at this altitude in the vertical mode either scenario would bring the aircraft crashing downward.

Rourke could see the opening above him. When he looked below, lava was just starting to overflow into the fort.

And there was Martin, reaching down to him. Perhaps there was a spark of feeling in the boy. "I'm all right, son," Rourke shouted up, his throat catching from the dust. Rourke coughed, light-headedness gripping him.

Martin's hand reached out to him. John Rourke took it.

Martin was pulling him up, over the lip of the fuselage door, to safety.

John Rourke looked up. "Son—"

But then he looked past Martin's face. Emma Shaw stood beside Martin, a .45 automatic in her right hand, the pistol aimed at Martin's head.

"Son—I—"

"Fuck you," Martin hissed, letting go of Rourke's hand, dropping to his haunches in the tail section of the fuselage.

Emma holstered the pistol at her right thigh. There was a second pistol in a chest holster over her left breast. "We gotta get outa here, John. Watch him. We're on computer." Emma Shaw ran past him.

Rourke just knelt there. The door started to close and the sudden rush of clean air from the aircraft's environment system made

245

him at once shiver and feel faint. He looked at his son. "You all right?"

"They're going to kill me. Kill that bitch and fly out of here and I'll give you anything you want. Anything! You like her? I'll give you a dozen better than her and when you're—"

"I want Deitrich Zimmer to operate to save your mother, Martin, to get the bullet out, to restore her to us."

"Fine. Fine. Anything. Now kill the—"

Rourke coughed, shook his head. "Paul might still be down there. And Doctor Rolvaag and the others. And I won't kill Emma Shaw. But if you get Deitrich Zimmer to save your mother's life, there's your chance. You're my son. I thought I'd have to kill you, someday. But I can't. I won't let anyone hurt you, God help me. You're your mother's and my flesh and blood, son."

Martin Zimmer, panting, breathing heavily, just stared at him beneath the yellow overhead lights.

John Rourke leaned back against the bulkhead. The aircraft was already in motion, rising. "Emma! Paul's down there. Some others. We've gotta—"

"I'll sweep for them until we find them, one way or the other, John. Come forward if you can," she shouted.

Rourke dragged himself to his feet. Without bombs, stripped of most of what consumed space, the fighter bomber's aft section was roomy enough so that Paul and the others would fit in. And the aircraft had ample power, Rourke knew.

He lurched forward, holding onto the copilot's seat, unslinging his rifle, slumping into the seat beside her.

"You all right, John?" Emma Shaw asked him, not looking at him.

"You're a brave woman. Thank you for saving my son." Below them, the entire interior of the cone was almost consumed.

Emma Shaw wore no helmet, no mask. He watched now as her tongue darted out, licked her lips. "John, if I hadn't kept a gun at his head, he would never have helped you."

"He's still my son. Nothing can change that. I finally realized that." Rourke peered through the canopy glass, his eyes scanning the slope. The V-stol flew perhaps a hundred feet over the sur-

246

face, terrain following. And, lying prone beside a lava fissure, John Rourke thought he saw something. "Can you land there? Or maybe like you did over the cone?"

"I can't land, but you can rope down on the cable if you're up to it. Or just keep an eye on the computer controls and Martin and I'll—"

"No. I'll do it."

Rourke dragged himself out of the seat. Emma tugged at his sleeve, offering him an oxygen mask. "Here, but slow."

Rourke nodded, pressed the mask over his face, inhaled shallowly, still coughed, almost choked. He took another breath, then another, pushing the mask away. Too much and he'd run the risk of passing out. He started aft.

Rourke's hands held to the grab straps as he stood there, the aircraft descending.

"What the hell are we doing?"

"My friend is down there. Other people, too."

"We could get killed! I'll give you—"

"Shut up, Martin!" Rourke shouted, coughed, leaned heavily against the bulkhead. The vertical motion stopped. The door opened upward and inward.

Rourke looked to the winched cable above him and near the door. The controls seemed simple enough. "Okay, Martin. You let this down, help Commander Shaw. Then we'll all get out of here." Martin didn't move. "Do it!" Rourke snapped.

Martin came to his feet. Rourke let out some of the cable, and as he looked below he could see movement. It was Paul, had to be Paul, waving up at him. Rourke closed the cable around him, fed out more of it. Emma joined them. "I've got it, John. Hurry, but be careful. My air intakes are nearly thirty percent clogged. Once we're over forty-one percent, we could lose an engine at any second."

"I'm on my way." And Rourke jumped into open space.

Rourke descended toward the slope, trying to control his breathing to minimize intake of the dust and ash. New vents were opening along the slope everywhere he looked, broad rivers of lava streaming downward across the slope and toward the sea far beyond, ribbons of flaming light in the darkness.

As Rourke neared the ground, he could see Paul with greater clarity, his friend's right trouser leg cut away up the seam, the submachinegun Paul had always called a Schmiesser lashed to the outside of Paul's leg, probably with its sling.

Rourke's feet touched the ground and he unhooked, released the cable, moved as rapidly as he could across the broken ground toward his friend, dropping to one knee beside Paul. Paul clasped his hand. "Martin?

"Alive."

"Lost my balance during one of the quakes and my foot caught in a crack. Think I broke my knee, or pulled it badly," Paul shouted to him over the roar of the eruption and the noise of the jets. "I was just getting started again. You all right? What about Martin's pals?"

"He's all right, they're dead, two by his hand." As Rourke spoke, he coughed. "Where are the others?"

"You don't have them yet? They were on their way down the slope."

"We'll get them next. Can you walk if I help?"

"Yeah," Paul nodded, coughing. "My lungs may never be the same, though."

John Rourke got Paul up, pulled Paul's right arm across his shoulders, started back with him toward the cable. "You're getting heavy," Rourke observed, joking.

"No, just old," Paul grinned.

They reached the cable, Rourke helping his friend to get the cable around him, hook it. Then Paul gave the cable a jerk and it started up, Rourke slumping down to his knees, waiting. And he looked toward the summit, but the cone was no longer there. A vast column of ash and dust obscured it, and the glow from within it was the lava, belching upward, destroying the old cone and building a fresh one.

Rourke looked back to the V-stol; the cable was winding down toward him again. Rourke reached for it, encircled himself with it, gave a tug as he hooked on.

Immediately, he was starting upward. He concentrated his gaze toward the downslope, searching for any sign of Rolvaag and the others. Nothing.

When he reached the height of the V-stol, Paul had a gun on Martin, Emma reaching out for Rourke. Rourke took her hand and arm and swung inward. "I'm all right."

"Paul's going to ride up front. He'll know where to look."

"Good idea." Rourke unhooked from the cable. Emma helping him, Paul started forward. "What happened to the helicopter?"

"While I was out looking for Rolvaag's graduate student, Bremen, a vent opened up under it and the chopper slipped forward into the lava."

"And you came back for me," Rourke said, saying nothing else. The fuselage door closed. Rourke stared at Martin. The aircraft began to ascend. "You see what I mean, son? Like when you said I should just save you and me and kill Emma and leave the others. People don't do that to one another."

"Where the hell have you been? People fuck each other every day, dad—shit. You go live on your damn mountaintop with the gods and do all this noble crap. We don't need anachronistic fools like you anymore."

"You don't understand," Rourke tried to explain. "Honorable people keep their promises, can rely on one another; friendship is a bond, just like love, joining people in a way that circumstances can't pull apart. A friend, a child, a wife, that's forever, Martin. Can't you see that? You can learn to. It's not your fault."

"You want me to be the same damn good guy you always were? For what? Where's your wealth? Where's your power? You're into all this emotional shit. Where's your happiness!? Faithful to some bitch lying in a damn coma and—"

John Rourke slapped Martin across the face. "She's your mother, boy! Don't talk that way, don't you ever—"

"Might makes right! There we agree—"

John Rourke turned away.

From the cockpit, he heard Paul shouting, "I see them, John!"

"I can land there," Emma called aft. "There's a flat enough spot. I can make a vertical."

John Rourke murmured, "Thank God."

"God? You actually believe in God? You are a fool!" Martin taunted. "Think God's so all powerful? Then why didn't He stop my real father who raised me from shooting your wife, huh? Why didn't He keep this friggin' volcano from erupting, huh?"

"I don't know the answers to questions like, that, Martin. No man does. All we can do is try, try to do the best that we can."

"Why? For points with God when you die? Be real!"

"No! Not for points with God," John Rourke shouted, coughing, shaking his head. "No. You do what's right because it is what's right. Everything doesn't have to profit you something, Martin. God or not—and I believe in God—but even if there wasn't God or a heaven or a hell, what would that do to change how a man or woman should be? What's right is right and nothing changes that. We do what's right and honorable because that's what it means to be a human being."

Martin looked away.

Rourke felt sick to his stomach.

The aircraft was landing vertically.

"Touchdown!" Emma shouted.

John Rourke liked a person who preferred the intimacy of human speech—even shouted—over a radio transmission. The fuselage door opened. In the second after, there was the shudder of contact. Paul called back, "I'll watch Martin!"

"Right."

Emma was already walking aft, jumped down from the opening in the fuselage, Rourke behind her. Rolvaag, the pilot and the third man, who had to be Bremen, were coming toward them, the pilot leaning on Rolvaag, the third man walking, falling, getting up.

"You help Doctor Rolvaag with the pilot," Rourke ordered, running past Emma Shaw, toward Bremen.

Lava flows were moving inexorably down the slope, the flows blending into one another as new vents opened, rivers of enormous width flowing downward. The gas here was less thick, and comparatively little ash fell. Rourke reached Bremen, letting the man collapse into his arms.

Rourke slung Bremen over his shoulder. Rourke looked back toward the V-stol. Emma was helping Rolvaag get the pilot aboard.

Rourke walked as rapidly as he could. With the added weight of Bremen on his shoulder, running was out of the question, given the state of his lungs and the air quality.

The ground shook. As Rourke looked back, another fissure had opened, wide, blowing lava in an enormous upjetting plume into the purple and orange blackness above.

Rourke reached the V-stol, Emma Shaw and Rolvaag reaching out to take Bremen.

Rourke handed Bremen up, then clambered in after him.

There was a localized control for the fuselage door and Rourke activated it, the door gliding to. Emma started forward. "I'm getting us out of here."

"Right," Rourke nodded. Already, Rourke was to his knees, beside Bremen.

"This could be a rough takeoff. We've got a lava flow bearing down on us," Emma Shaw called back.

Rourke could hear the engines revving. "Everybody brace yourselves. Martin, get me the oxygen out of the survival kit on the bulkhead there," and Rourke gestured toward the kit. As Rourke looked back at Bremen—the head injury didn't appear too severe and Bremen was breathing—he suddenly realized what he'd done.

Rourke started to his feet.

But Martin already had the survival kit open. There was an energy pistol in it.

"Fire that in here and—"

Martin leveled the energy pistol toward John Rourke's head. Rourke dove toward his son, shoving Rolvaag and the injured pilot Butler out of the way. The aircraft was into vertical takeoff mode. There was no stopping now without crashing.

Rourke's left hand closed over the pistol. Martin's right knee smashed upward into John Rourke's testicles.

John Rourke flew back against the bulkhead beside the fuselage door. Martin Zimmer Rourke's left hand punched outward, not to Rourke's face, but toward the localized door control.

The V-stol went into horizontal flight and Rourke was thrown back. Martin was on top of him, beating at his head with

251

the energy pistol. Rourke's left elbow smashed upward into Martin's chest. Rolvaag jumped onto Martin's back.

Martin twisted round, the energy pistol firing, blasting a hole twice the size of a basketball, in the fuselage opposite the door. The V-stol shuddered, Emma Shaw shouting, "Stop him!"

The dual slipstream though the open fuselage door and the hole opposite it tore at Rourke's exposed flesh.

Martin was up, leveling the pistol toward the cockpit. "If I'm going to die, you're all going to die, damn you!"

John Rourke reached up from his knees. Martin kicked at him. Rourke grabbed for Martin's foot, caught it, twisted.

Martin sprawled back against the bulkhead, swinging the muzzle of the pistol once again toward the cockpit as Rourke, to his feet now, reached for his son. "And damn you, father!"

The aircraft lurched.

Martin fired.

The energy pistol blew a hole in the overhead.

John Rourke's left fist snaked upward toward Martin's jaw, catching Martin at the jaw's tip. Rourke reached for Martin with his right hand, trying to close his hand over Martin's wrist.

The aircraft shuddered, twisted violently in midair, started into a dive.

Martin's head snapped back.

Rourke's hand closed over Martin's wrist.

Martin slipped backward.

"Son!" John Rourke screamed the word over the howl of the wind.

Martin's wrist slipped through John Rourke's fingers.

Their eyes met.

Hatred.

Martin's body fell away, sucked out into the slipstream.

John Rourke lurched after him.

The plane was into a dive now.

John Rourke's hands reached out into the slipstream after his son. The ground, crisscrossed in veins of golden light from the lava, was reaching up to take them.

Hands were on Rourke's shoulders, dragging him back inside.

Rourke sprawled against the starboard fuselage bulkhead, Rolvaag and Butler, the Navy pilot, grabbing at him, holding him. "You'll be killed!" Rolvaag shouted.

"I have it under control!" Emma Shaw shouted, the aircraft leveling off, as Rourke and the two men flanking him slammed hard against the bulkhead.

"John! Are you all right?" Paul's voice.

John Rourke stared out into the purple darkness, where his son had gone.

John Rourke never said to Martin, "I love you."

Now, he never could.

On one level of consciousness, he could hear Rolvaag saying, "It wasn't your fault."

He could hear Emma Shaw saying, "I've got radio contact with a helicopter that'll follow us back to Pearl in case we have to ditch. Major Tiemerovna's flying it. Your son and daughter are aboard, too, John. It'll be all right now."

Son.

John Rourke's eyes filled with tears. He made the Sign of the Cross. "God forgive me, I killed my own son," John Rourke whispered, prayed.

THE SEVENTH CARRIER SERIES
By PETER ALBANO

THE SEVENTH CARRIER   (2056, $3.95/$5.50)
The original novel of this exciting, best-selling series. Imprisoned in a cave of
ice since 1941, the great carrier *Yonaga* finally breaks free in 1983, her mad-
dened crew of samurai determined to carry out their orders to destroy Pearl
Harbor.

THE SECOND VOYAGE OF THE SEVENTH CARRIER   (2104, $3.95/$4.95)
The Red Chinese have launched a particle beam satellite system into space,
knocking out every modern weapons system on earth. Not a jet or rocket can fly.
Now the old carrier *Yonaga* is desperately needed because the Third World
nations—with their armed forces made of old World War II ships and planes—
have suddenly become superpowers. Terrorism runs rampant. Only the *Yonaga*
can save America and the Free World.

RETURN OF THE SEVENTH CARRIER   (2093, $3.95/$4.95)
With the war technology of the former superpowers still crippled by Red China's
orbital defense system, a terrorist beast runs rampant across the planet. Out-
armed and outnumbered, the target of crack saboteurs and fanatical assassins,
only the *Yonaga* and its brave samurai crew stand between a Libyan madman and
his fiendish goal of global domination.

QUEST OF THE SEVENTH CARRIER   (2599, $3.95/$4.95)
Power bases have shifted drastically. Now a Libyan madman has the upper hand,
planning to crush his western enemies with an army of millions of Arab fanatics.
Only *Yonaga* and her indomitable samurai crew can save the besieged free world
from the devastating iron fist of the terrorist maniac. Bravely, the behemoth leads
a rag tag armada of rusty World War II warships against impossible odds on a
fiery sea of blood and death!

ATTACK OF THE SEVENTH CARRIER   (2842, $3.95/$4.95)
The Libyan madman has seized bases in the Marianas and Western Caroline Islands. The free world seems doomed. Desperately, *Yonaga's* air groups fight
bloody air battles over Saipan and Tinian. An old World War II submarine, *USS
Blackfin,* is added to *Yonaga's* ancient fleet and the enemy's impregnable bases
are attacked with suicidal fury.

TRIAL OF THE SEVENTH CARRIER   (3213, $3.95/$4.95)
The enemies of freedom are on the verge of dominating the world with oil blackmail and the threat of poison gas attack. *Yonaga's* officers lay desperate plans to
strike back. Leading a ragtag fleet of revamped destroyers and a single antique
World War II submarine, the great carrier must charge into a sea of blood and
death in what becomes the greatest trial of the Seventh Carrier.